T0159061

Behind the Mask

Behind the Mask

A novel by
Sonica Jackson

iUniverse, Inc.
New York   Bloomington

iUniverse books may be ordered through booksellers or by contacting:

iUniverse
1663 Liberty Drive
Bloomington, IN 47403
www.iuniverse.com
1-800-Authors (1-800-288-4677)

ISBN: 978-1-4401-8503-8 (sc)
ISBN: 978-1-4401-8504-5 (ebook)

Printed in the United States of America

iUniverse rev. date:11/5/09

In Jesus' name, I thank God for allowing me to do this again. You are truly a wonderful God and I am so thankful to have You in my life. Thank You for helping me to grow everyday in my Christian walk and being patient with me, throughout my shortcomings.

I give plenty of thanks to my mom for believing in my dream and I definitely want to give a special thanks to my dad and Aunt Pat for recognizing how serious I am about my career by showing their support.

I want to give a very special thanks to my Pastor Jesse Curney III at New Mercies Christian Church for helping me to understand more about what it means to have a true relationship with God and that being a Christian doesn't mean that you won't have issues to overcome. And I must give a big thanks to Pastor Phillip Mosby and Gwynnis Mosby for much love and support.

I definitely want to thank my friends Laquiesha, Leah and Jennifer for just being you and supporting my dream. I cherish every moment we spend together because in this crazy world, it's good to have people around you that can make you laugh…even when you're going thru some things. I can't forget my homegirls Fatima and Nikki, who have been ridin' with me for years. NOBODY can take y'all place. I love y'all like crazy!

Ursula, you know that I can't leave you out. You are wonderful and you are gonna take this world by storm as soon as you tap into the power that God has given you. Ivy, you are an amazing person. I wish you much success. Robert, Chanelle, and Samantha (Ms. Barbie Doll), I thank you all for your support.

To Ms. Jolly, Latanya, Falessia and Sonia, you guys already know that I thank you for supporting me because every time I've came out with a book, you guys bought it hot off the press. Elliott and Gayle, I'm so glad that I have brothers like you two. You guys are wonderful.

Roderick Tate, sorry that things didn't work out the way that I wanted them to but I do thank you for thinking of me. Believe me, that goes a long way.

Dana, continue to stay focus. It will pay off. Shundra, thank you sooo much for the support and the sisterly love. William Talford, you know that I can't forget about you; thanks for your support and keeping me updated on what's going on in the "writer's world". It's been very helpful.

Tina, Tamara and Patsy, thanks for all the love, support and laughter. Nalesha, it was a great pleasure meeting you and I hope that you really enjoy reading this book as much as I enjoyed writing it. To my wonderful sisters Corina, Stephanie, Tariqca, Toya and Brianna, this book is dedicated to you all.

*To all my readers, thanks for everything!

Let me just say for the record that this book was intended to be entertaining… and that's it. Now of course, we live in a crazy world and there are people out there who like to run their mouths and start a lot of mess. But before anyone gets the rumor mill started, please note that I didn't write this book about ANYBODY. All the characters are fictional. However, if starting rumors is how you get a bang out of life and if the rumors will increase my book sales to the point where I'm able to buy a big house in Alpharetta Georgia and a black Cadillac XLR with black leather interior seats and an amazing stereo system in it that sounds awesome when I bump my Musiq Soulchild CD, then so be it.

Smooches!

Not everyone who goes to church is saved. Some call them, *church folks*. And every church has them. They come in both genders and they are totally different from Christians. Some people say that *church folks* are the biggest devils in the church. Well, maybe that's true. For those of you who never encountered *church folks* or don't know what it is that they do, here are some examples:

- They only come to church to show off their outfits.
- They come to church to try to find them a man.
- They come to church to try to find them a hoochie so that they can get them some booty.
- They try to sleep with the pastor.
- They get extremely upset if someone sits in their seat. Then, they tell the person, "How dare you sit my seat! I've been sitting in that same seat for ten years!"
- They sit in the church and gossip about everyone that walks thru the door.
- They steal from the church.
- They don't give anything to the church.
- They cause chaos in the church.
- They have to have their say in *everything*. This means that they just don't know when to sit down and shut the hell up.
- They think that they run the church and that everyone should listen to them and do what *they* say. This means that they're so selfish that they never want to take other people's ideas into consideration.
- They smile, hug and claim to love you but talk about you like a dog behind your back.
- They think that if they pray a long time and impress God with long words, they think that their prayers will get answered quicker.
- They pretend to catch the Holy Ghost, just to be seen by others.
- They think that speaking in tongues makes them holier-than thou.
- They think that if they get involved in the Welcome Committee, the Usher Board the choir or any other kind of ministry, they can continue to live a corrupt life without having to worry about the consequences.
- They ask God to forgive them of their sins but NEVER make an attempt to change.
- They hate to see other people get blessed.
- If they are in a position to help someone, they don't. Instead, they say, "I'll pray for you."
- They don't care if they do wrong and justify it by saying, "God knows my heart."

If you are laughing at this point, then that means that you have encountered one of the *church folks* and you understand what I'm saying. However, if the hairs on the back of your neck are standing up and your body temperature has risen because you're mad as hell because of what I've stated, then that means that I have just described YOU!!!

Bible-Wavers

A POEM

Here she comes
Ms. Holier-than-thou
Churchy white dress
Churchy white shoes
Churchy white hat
Churchy attitude
But wait a minute
Pump the brakes
Pause the tape
Saturday night was your night
Wasn't that you in your red party dress
Red party shoes
Red party lipstick
And party attitude
That was you
Backing that thang up for Tyrone
Making your booty clap for Ronald
And *dropping-it-like-it's-hot* for Charles
Forgive me for feeling confused
I just didn't know
That a Saturday-ho can sing a Sunday solo
With your Bible under your arm
Telling everybody what they're doing wrong
Justifying your actions
Getting involved in every ministry
From the trying-to-be-God ministry
To the *let's-take-the-people's-money-and-*
buy-the-pastor-a-cadillac-on-twenty-two's-ministry
But wait a minute
Pump the brakes
Pause the tape
Forgive me
I don't mean to be
A wart on your ass
But I think I'll pass

When you advise me
To have the preacher lay his sinful hands on my forehead
Because you think that I have the devil in me
It amazes me
How the preacher turns his nose up at me
And he wants to be worshipped like he's God
But wait a minute
Pump the brakes
Pause the tape
Mr. Preacher, do you mind if I ask you a few questions?
Such as
Is it Christ-like
To lay your pipe
All in the pulpit
Laying your churchy hands in places they don't belong
Laying your churchy dollars in the g-strings of women
Conduct churchy gossip
Abuse your wife
Doing doggy-style with the treasurer
And getting laid by the secretary
Having gay relations with the choir director
Smoking weed with the deacons
You're such a clown
Sunday morning comes around
You put on your robe
And it's show time
Taking over the minds of your members
Being something that you're not
Melissa needs food for her kids
But you show her the door
Claiming you have no more
So then you dedicate your sermon to me
Because I'm not wearing white
I'm not with the "in" crowd
Such as Ms. Holier-Than-Thou
It's funny
You wear all that white
But your heart is so black
God's not having that
He will tell you to step back

Do you hear what I'm saying?
Things that are traditional are not necessarily biblical
This is why people stray
Because you teach that God is far
But yet He is so near
And He will accept you as you are
Just open your heart.

-Sonica

Rita

Lord, have mercy. If one more tone-deaf skank joins the choir, I'm gonna lose my mind, I thought to myself. On Thursday nights, I come to watch the choir rehearse the songs that they choose to sing for the following Sunday.

Every Thursday night, it's the same thing; big-butt Brenda tries to out-sing everybody, Tameka's cell phone goes off every five minutes and Stephanie constantly complains about the selection of songs. Now, a new member by the name of Janet has decided to join this mess and the funny part is that she really thinks that she can sing.

While on our way to choir rehearsal, I said to my husband Shawn, "I thought you said that you wasn't gonna allow anyone else to join the choir because it's already full."

"I *did* say that," he replied.

"So why did you let Janet join? She hasn't even finished the New Members class yet."

He smiled and said, "Well honey, I saw her potential when I first met her and I didn't want it to go to waste. So that's why I allowed her to join."

Humph. He wasn't foolin' me. He let her behind join because this Janet person is Brenda's cousin and since Brenda is one of the biggest tithers in the church, she probably threatened to take her "business" elsewhere if Shawn didn't allow her cousin to join the choir.

See, Brenda is the type of person that likes to intimidate Shawn, simply because she has a lot of money. She's the one that gets upset if she's not singing a solo damn near every Sunday as if she's giving a concert. She is also the one that is always coming to the church financial meetings, getting on everyone's nerves and urging Shawn to handle the church money the way *she* thinks that it should be handled.

While at choir rehearsal, Shawn was in his study, working on yet another boring sermon. Sometimes, I wish that I've never married a pastor because being a "first lady" is not all that it's cracked up to be.

First of all, you have to deal with a tremendous amount of pressure of trying to be this wonderful, God-fearing, happy, soft-spoken, dainty lil' wife with no voice of your own. It's nothing but a show. I know that first ladies had to act like that, back in the day. But this is 2001. We shouldn't have to be phony anymore.

What angers me the most is the pool of women that crowd around my husband with their damn skimpy outfits on, saying things to him like, "Pastor Owens, your sermon really moved me" and "Pastor Owens, you are such a man of God." One dizzy broad had the nerve to ask Shawn if he could lay his hands on her pelvic area to heal her from menstrual cramps.

Humph. I knew that their agenda was to sleep with my man. But I try to stay calm throughout all of that because it doesn't look good for a thirty-six year old woman to be smacking the hell outta some hoochies.

The most surprising thing to me is the amount of women that are envious of me because I'm married to a pastor. Of course, they don't say it to my face but I can tell by their actions or certain comments that they make, that they wish that they could be in my shoes. Little do they know that I would trade places with them in an instant because Lord knows that I'm getting sick of dealing with the people in the church.

Not a day goes by that our phone doesn't ring from either a deacon, deaconess, usher, an Elder, somebody in the Welcome Committee or Ella needing prayer for the one-hundredth time. I'm sick of it. They treat us as if my husband and I don't have a life.

When I talk to Shawn about it, all he says is, "Rita, God has called me to be a teacher of the Word and to be there for my flock. So if they need me, it's my duty to be there."

"But you can't be everywhere. You're only one man. If the leaders of the church can't figure out things on their own, then why are they leaders? I'm sick of our quality time always being cut short because somebody needs something. And why can't Ella pray, herself?! She acts as if your prayers are lined in gold and will get to the Lord faster than her own."

"Look, you knew that when I got called to pastor, that a lot of people were gonna take up a lot of my time."

"So are you sayin' that they're more important than me?"

"No, but remember what it says in our church mission statement: *Sweet Harmony Springstone Baptist Church is dedicated to helping others to become dedicated servants unto the Lord.* So lighten up, Rita. Everything's gonna be alright."

Due to those types of arguments, there have been plenty of days when I have packed my bags with every intent of leaving his behind. But every time I wanna leave, he convinces me to stay by saying that he doesn't want me to give up on him and that he will make things better for us. But after a few days, things go back to the way they were and I remain frustrated with him.

Our marriage wasn't always like this. When Shawn and I first met, he was a club promoter down in The Flats, which is an area in downtown Cleveland where a lot of clubs are located. Every weekend, The Flats stayed packed full of people. You could see tons of people walking into clubs, coming out of clubs, throwing up in the streets from too much alcohol, police harassing folks, taxi cabs everywhere and loud music playing from one club to the next.

It was a Saturday night when I met Shawn. I was with a group of friends and we walked into this one particular club and Shawn was standing in the doorway while we were getting our purses checked. He was light-skinned with a pencil-thin mustache and tall with a solid build. I tried not to stare at him but the minute his dark-brown eyes met mine, I knew that this night was gonna change my life, forever.

All night long, he bought me drinks and at the end of the night, he offered to take me home. I said to him, "Uh…I'm not so sure that I want you to know where I live. Besides, I came with my friends and I expect to leave with them, only."

He smiled and said, "I'm sorry. I don't mean to be aggressive like that. It's just that I'm enjoying your time so much, that I don't want the night to end. But I respect your wish to only leave with your friends. Do you think that I can call you sometime?"

"Sure. I don't mind that." After I gave him my number, my friends and I hung out a lil' while longer before deciding to end the night at around four a.m.

The next morning, I didn't give Shawn a second thought. Usually when a person goes to the club and they get someone's number, you either never call them or you were so drunk on the night that you met them, that you don't even remember them the next day.

But at around nine a.m the next morning, Shawn called me and said, "Good morning, beautiful."

"Who is this?" I asked.

"You don't remember me?"

I thought for a minute and said, "Are you the guy that I met at the club?"

He laughed and said, "Yes, this is Shawn. I was calling to ask you if you would like to meet me for breakfast. That is, if you're not too tired."

"Okay," I heard myself say. I really didn't wanna be bothered but since he was paying for breakfast and I didn't have to cook, I decided to go.

We had breakfast at Bob Evans by Northfield Road and we talked about a lot of things. To my surprise, he had a lot of interesting things to say that kept my attention. I told him that I was a police officer for Cuyahoga County and he seemed very shocked when I told him that.

"A police officer? You're so beautiful, I would've never thought that you were an officer of the law," he said.

"Are you sayin' that a beautiful woman can't be a cop?" I asked.

"Oh, no. It's just that I see you as a model or something like that. What made you wanna get into law?"

"No reason in particular. I guess that I just like having authority."

"Oh, I see. So how long have you been a police officer?"

"Ten years. I joined the academy when I turned twenty-three, after having a line of dead-end jobs. So what about you? What made you wanna be a club promoter?"

"Actually, this is just a quick hustle for me to pay the bills. I'm actually getting myself ready to become a pastor."

"A what?"

He smiled and said, "A pastor, Rita. Yep, I said it."

"But why?"

"It's my calling. It's been my calling since I was eighteen-years old. Now that I'm thirty-four, I've experienced some things in life and it's time for me to live my life for God." This wasn't the first time that I met a man who said that God called him to be a pastor. But I could tell that Shawn was serious about this.

Ever since that breakfast date, Shawn and I were inseparable. Everywhere he went, I was with him and he treated me like a lady. I felt special. He had a good head on his shoulders and he knew what he wanted to do with his life.

The first time I heard him preach a sermon was on Thanksgiving Day of '98, the same year that we met. The moment he spoke, I got goose bumps. He was so serious and powerful. I was deeply moved and I wanted to be a part of his life forever because he made me feel secure. A year later, we got married and have been married for two years and they have been the most difficult two years of my life.

First of all, Shawn has a nineteen-year old daughter named Joy from a previous relationship. I have no idea why the girl is named Joy because she's definitely not a *joy* to have around. If anything, she's the ultimate witch of the earth.

Fortunately, she doesn't live with Shawn and I but when she comes around, she's hell to deal with. She's one of those high-yellow hepha's that walk around, thinking that her doo-doo don't stink. She has long, dark-brown hair, green eyes, Coke-bottle figure with a stank attitude to match.

It's a shame for someone that beautiful to have the ugliest attitude. She thinks that I'm not good enough for her father and the girl had the nerve to tell me that, straight to my face. That was the day when she almost got her behind kicked. It took Shawn and his brother Sheldon to stop me from snatching her bald.

Since that day, when she comes around, the hepha don't even acknowledge my presence in my own damn house. When I say something to Shawn about it, he brushes it off by saying, "Don't worry about it, Rita. She'll grow on you."

Yeah, like a boil, I thought to myself. With all the mess that goes on in our marriage on a regular basis, I'm surprised that I stayed in my marriage for even this long. But nowadays, things haven't been too bad since Taurus and I have been getting "well acquainted."

Taurus is Brenda's husband and for the past six months, we've been discretely "enjoying each other's company." He is Shawn's best friend and is an Elder in the church. He's everything that Shawn *used* to be: attentive, good listener, affectionate, fun and a great pleaser in bed.

The minute I laid my eyes on him, I knew that I was in trouble. He was tall with smooth, dark-brown skin, broad shoulders and a killer smile that made me weak all over. When I met him, I thought to myself, *How in the world did someone like Brenda end up with a man like that?* He had the presence of a king.

I tried my best to stay away from him but each time that I felt his shiny, dark-brown eyes graze my body, I knew that it was only a matter of time when Taurus and I would be victims of temptation. We made sure to never be seen together so that no one could make any accusations about us. But when we did get together on certain days, it was magic.

Taurus was sprung on me because I treated him the way a man likes to be treated. See, Brenda talks down to him and calls the shots in their marriage, as if he doesn't have a spine. But when he's with me, I make him feel like a real man. And it's not just about sex. I am the woman that he felt comfortable talking to about anything and he was a great listener when I needed to vent about all the things that I'm going thru with Shawn.

After choir rehearsal, I walked into my husband's study to see if he was ready to go. "I'm almost finished, baby. Give me about five more minutes," he pleaded.

"Okay," I answered, "I meant to ask you if there was anything in particular that you wanted to eat for dinner."

"I can't think of anything specific at the moment."

"Well, I thought that maybe we could go to Hot Sauce Williams and get some chicken wings," I answered.

"That's fine with me. Anyway, how did the choir sound to you?"

Like crap, I thought to myself. "They were very nice," I lied.

Shawn

RITA, RITA, RITA. I love her so much but I just wish that I'd taken in a lil' more thought before marrying her because she isn't too thrilled with the idea of being a first lady. And it's so obvious. All I knew was that I wanted to marry her because she was an intelligent and beautiful woman with sexy long legs, curly brown hair, the most beautiful golden skin I've ever seen and a bright smile.

I mean, I love my wife but sometimes I wonder if she loves *me*. I try to do the right thing but it seems like what I do is never good enough. Just two nights ago, we ate dinner at home and neither one of us said a word to each other. When we went to bed, the only word we uttered was 'goodnight'. We went to sleep with our backs turned and we stayed that way, all night.

Humph. Here I am, a Pastor, giving marriage counseling and my *own* marriage is falling apart before my very eyes. I have to admit that some of the problems do stem from outside sources; my mother, for instance. She thinks that Rita is not good enough to be my wife and she's felt that way from the beginning.

"Rita don't love you," she once said, "She just wants to get married because she wants the show. She's not the type of woman that will take marriage seriously."

"Mama, that's not true. I believe that she loves me and wants the same things in life that I want."

"You may think so but I know her type, Shawn. Will you listen to your mama, for once?"

"I love you, mama. But when it comes to Rita, I'm gonna listen to my heart."

"Okay…but you'll be sorry."

Truth be told, I don't regret marrying Rita because I do believe that God put certain people in your life for a reason but I do question her loyalty to me. Sometimes, she act like she loves me and sometimes she don't. If she's not happy with this marriage, she can best believe that the feeling is mutual. Something has got to change.

Even though my marriage is not the way I would like for it to be, I definitely wouldn't cheat on her. For starters, I'm a pastor and I know better than that. Even though I have run into many pastors who cheat on their wives like it's nothing, I don't play with God like that. Although I do have my issues, I never had the interest of getting involved with another woman behind my wife's back.

One of my friends named Chris, is a pastor in Shaker Heights and when I told him of the problems that I was having in my marriage, this fool actually thought that I should have me another woman on the side.

I said to him, "Chris, are you crazy? Are you trying to get me to experience God's wrath? I'm a pastor, Chris. And so are you. You should know better than to even say something like that."

"We're pastors but we're still human."

"But we are in a position of leadership in Christ. Our job is to teach people who are lost and help them to build a relationship with God. How in the world can we teach the lost of we're lost, ourselves? What I'm gonna do is pray about my marriage and ask God to fix whatever is wrong with it. I'm not gonna cheat. That just makes the problem worse."

"Well, that's *your* choice. I've done it, I like it, I desire it and I will continue to keep the other woman around. In fact, my wife knows about her."

I looked at him like he was crazy. "Are you serious, Chris? You mean to tell me, that Lisa knows about your infidelity?"

"Yep. She was upset, but hey, what can she do?"

"How did she find out? Did you catch you in the act?"

"No. Trina called Lisa and told her some things."

"Trina? Isn't she your church secretary?"

He grinned and said, "Yep. She's the other woman."

"You're messin' around with the church secretary?! Have you lost your mind?!"

"Nope. I'm just as sane as you are. But anyway, let me get back to what I was saying; Trina and I had got into an argument and out of spite she called Lisa and told her that we've been messin' around for the past two years. And although that's true, she still didn't have any right to tell her. Man, she told Lisa everything."

"When you say that she told your wife everything, are you saying that she told her *everything*?"

"Yep. When I got home, Lisa and I got into a heated argument over it and then she lit our king-size bed on fire."

"What?!"

"You heard me, man. She lit the bed up. I put the fire out and set the bed outside. Then she put me outta the house that night and I stayed over Trina's house."

I was blown away by what Chris was telling me. "How long ago was this?" I asked.

"About a month ago. After that happened, Lisa and I have been trying to get pass it but our marriage isn't the same at all. It's just existing."

"Chris, I can't believe you are doing this to your wife."

"Well, that's life. About a month ago, Trina came to my house while my wife was there and they were outside yelling and cussing each other out."

"Where were you when all of this was going on?"

"I was in the house, eating breakfast. All of a sudden, I heard all of this shouting and cussing. So I ran outside and I saw Trina up in Lisa's face. Before I had a chance to break them up, Trina slapped Lisa. So I grabbed Trina and pushed her in the bushes. The neighbors called the police on all three of us. It was total chaos."

Although Chris and I are friends, I did lose a tremendous amount of respect for him after he told me all of this, not because he cheated on his wife but because he was still doing it and didn't care. No *real* man of God would ever put his wife thru this kind of mental anguish and act like it's okay to treat her this way.

My wife may not be the best wife that she can be but I can't stoop so low as to cheat on her. And I don't care what Chris say; his behavior is extremely inappropriate. Lisa is a woman who is highly respected in the community. Everyone loves her. She's a great wife and a great mother to her kids. Chris' infidelity is not something that she deserves.

Joy

I KNOW A tramp when I see one. It's not a hard thing to figure out. I mean, I'm not a judgmental person but I know that when my dad married Rita, I knew that he was gonna be dealing with a handful because Rita ain't nothin' but an ultimate skank.

The first time I met her, she had the nerve to say to me, "*Hmmm.* You don't look like Shawn, at all."

I said to her, "What do you mean? I'm light-skinned just like him."

She grinned and said, "Not all light-skinned people look alike, sweetie."

"I didn't say that. But I do know that most people would disagree with you when you say that I don't look like my dad."

"Well, I'm not most people."

Boy I hate her. I haven't had much quality time with my father since she's been in his life. I mean, my dad still comes around but not as much as he used to. And oh, how wonderful it was for him to show up to my nineteenth birthday with that woman on his arm.

I held my party at my mama's house and when Rita walked thru the door, the hairs on the back of my neck stood up. She waved hello to my mom and I and helped herself to a plate of food as if she *supposed* to be there. My mom, being the cordial person that she is, smiled and welcomed her into her home with no strife. That's my mama. She's always been the type of person that didn't get involve in conflict and I usually admire that. But it was moments like those when I really wanted mama to snatch Rita up.

I pulled my dad to the side and asked, "Why is she here?"

"What do you mean, Joy?" he asked, with a confused look on his face.

"I don't want her here, dad. This is *my* party and I only want my family and my friends here. She's not my friend and she is most certainly not family."

He looked at me with anger in his eyes and said, "You listen to me; whether you want to accept her or not, she *is* a part of this family because she's my wife. That's the woman I love. You don't have to like her but I would at least want you to respect her."

"Dad, she don't even respect *herself*, coming up in here dressed like a two-dollar whore."

"You watch your mouth, Joy."

"I just call them as I see them. She's no good."

"Well, let me be the judge of that, okay? Don't you know that you hurt me when you disrespect her?"

"Well, I don't mean to hurt you. I just don't want nobody to do you wrong."

He smiled, put his arms around me and said, "I know you mean well. But trust me, your dad is okay."

I smiled at him, letting him know that I was gonna be cool about it and I went ahead and enjoyed the rest of my party. Everything was cool and after the party was over, I went home and that's when things got even better because my man showed up at my apartment; my man, Taurus. He came to bring me my birthday gift, which was a beautiful set of diamond earrings.

Taurus is the ultimate love of my life. He's an Elder at my father's church and when I met him for the first time, I thought that he was the most beautiful man that I've ever laid eyes on. And apparently, he must've felt that I was irresistible too because we started dating and have fallen in love. So far, we've been together for about seven months.

Even though he's married to some big-bone chick at church named Brenda, I know that I'm the only one he loves. Besides, I look a lot better than Brenda. A couple of weeks ago, he was telling me that he was gonna divorce Brenda and marry me as soon as I finish college.

"Why wait until then?" I asked him.

"Because the timing will be right. I want you to focus on getting your degree. If we try to get married now, you would have to focus on getting your degree as well as planning a wedding. I don't want you to be under that much pressure."

"*Hmmm.* Well, I guess that makes sense. Besides, not only would we be planning a wedding but let's not forget the time we will need for honeymooning," I said with a smile.

He laughed and said, "Baby, I can't wait to marry you. Brenda is…"

"Oh, please. Don't talk to me about her. She is such a pest. She tries to run dad's church as if it's her very own. I'm so sick of her. I wish that you and I could just leave Cleveland and go far away and never come back."

"Don't worry. One day, we will be able to do just that."

My best friend Monica and I were at the church, trying to brainstorm and figure out what type of Easter program that we needed to put together. Since the Easter program was such a success last year, dad decided to leave Monica and I in charge of that, from now on. But Easter was about a month away and we didn't have anything together.

"So did you tell your mom?" I asked her, in regards to her pregnancy.

"Oh no. I don't think I will ever tell her," she explained, while we hangin' out at Randall Mall.

"Well, soon you won't have much of a choice. You can't hide a baby forever."

"I won't have to. I'm getting an abortion."

"What?! Monica, you can't kill your baby. Your mama didn't kill *you*."

"Joy, I was planned. My parents were married and financially stable when they decided to have children. They went by the book. As for me, I'm still in college and I work part-time at the church. There's no way that I can take care of a baby. Besides, Josh and I have broken up and he is definitely not someone that I can see helping me take care of a baby. No way. So I'm gonna get the abortion. And considering the fact that I work in your *daddy's* church, I don't need people staring and judging me because I had a child out of wedlock. You know how people in your daddy's church like to be in everyone's business. And remember, you had an abortion too."

"Yeah, you're right. But don't make the same mistake I did. I wish that I had kept my baby. And you don't need to worry about the people in the church. They have to answer to God for their *own* problems. I really don't want you to abort the baby but it's your decision."

She smiled and then said, "So how are things with you and your dad? I imagine things are fine between you two since he did show up at your birth-day party."

"Well, we're kinda getting along better. I'm trying to accept the fact that he's happy being married to a skank. And did you see that get-up that she had on at my party?"

She laughed and said, "Oh, yes. She looked like a hooker."

"Girl, yes. Wearing an outfit that looked like it came off the bargain rack."

We both laughed and then she asked, "Why wasn't Taurus there?"

I looked at her like she was outta her mind. "Girl, you know that my relationship with Taurus is a secret. If word got out that we were seeing each other, things would get crazy."

"How so?"

"Because he's still married, Monica."

"But didn't you tell me that he's divorced?"

"He's not divorced, yet. He's still getting things in order."

"Oh, I see. Well, are you sure that you wanna be dealing with him, Joy?"

"Of course. He tells me all the time how much he loves me and that I'm the only woman for him." Monica was silent and looked like she was in deep thought. So I asked, "What's wrong?"

"Um…nothing," she replied, "I just want you to be careful because married men are known for not leaving their wives. I tried to tell my cousin Crystal the same thing but she wouldn't listen."

"Oh please. Your cousin Crystal is a totally different story."

She sipped her Sprite and said, "Her story is not that different from yours, Joy."

I was starting to get irritated. "Monica, what are you talking about? Crystal was chasing Anthony. I didn't chase Taurus. He pursued *me*."

She shook her head and said, "It doesn't matter who pursued whom. The story remains the same. Crystal's situation was just like yours. She was soooo in love with Anthony and he promised to leave his wife. He wooed her, bought her things and took her places. But the minute that his wife got wind of his "extracurricular activities" and threatened him with divorce papers, Crystal started to see a different side of him. Not only did he *not* leave his wife but he left Crystal with an STD, a bunch of bills and jacked-up credit to the point where my mom had to co-sign for her apartment. She never got to spend any holidays with him and she soon found out that she wasn't the only woman that he was seeing on the side. Now what if that happens to you?"

"It won't."

"And how do you know this?"

"Because I'm his *everything*. He told me so."

"*Humph.* I'm pretty sure that at one time, he told his wife the same thing."

Taurus

SOMETIMES, I CRACK myself up. I get away with so much and my life just keeps on getting better and better. For me to juggle two women plus a wife and nobody knows anything, that's a talent. Instead of writing novels, I should write a manual on how to attract stupid women. It amazes me how stupid, women can be. They lose more and more common sense as the years go on.

I mean, let's be serious; outside of the good money that I make as a writer, my wife Brenda is a well-known hairstylist all over Cleveland and she has a prestigious list of clients from singers to actors that pay her big money to keep them looking good. For a big woman, she looks better than most petite women out there and has style and class of her own. We have two beautiful kids together; a son named Dillon whom is eight-years old and a daughter named Kiera, whom is five.

We live in Beachwood, which is one of the most high-class suburban areas in Ohio, in a beautiful home that many can only dream of living in. Eating steak and lobster is like an everyday-thing to us and most of our clothes are either custom-made or are bought from places like Saks 5th Avenue. And as far as transportation is concerned, people turn their heads and almost trip and fall when they see us riding in either our Range Rover, Mercedes or Jaguar.

In other words, I have invested way too much time and money into my marriage to just walk away. And I'm definitely not gonna walk away from her to be with two broke ho's. If I were to leave my wife, I would at least have the sense to be with someone who either has the same status as Brenda or better. Rita and Joy are not even close.

First of all, Rita can't figure out what she wants to do with her life. After Shawn convinced her to leave the police academy, she wanted to start an organization for battered women but she didn't follow thru on it. Then she wanted to start an organization for teens that deal with peer pressure. After two weeks, it became too much work and so she let that fall thru the cracks as well. She's never finished anything that she started.

Each time she quit something, I ask her, "Why did you quit?"

And she would give me the same, stupid response, "It just wasn't working out."

"What do you mean it wasn't working out?" I asked.

"Well, it was starting to become a bit too much. So I quit."

With her jumping from one idea to the next, it showed me that she was unstable. And then again, maybe she felt that she didn't have to do anything, simply because she was married to a big-time pastor. But little did she know that Shawn was not much of a big-time *anything* like she thought.

If she only knew how much debt he has created within the church, Rita would die. Shawn owes a lot of money to a lot of people. Don't get me wrong, though; he provides a good living for himself and his wife but he ain't got it goin' on like some of the wealthy pastors that people see on TV. Not by a long shot.

Now as far as Joy, she's just a young thang that I have great sex with. I knew that I had to have her by any means necessary. She reminded me of my first love; tall, beautiful butter-colored shapely legs that led up to a small waist, which led up to the perkiest set of breasts in the world. She was so mesmerizing. We became attracted to each other and it was so obvious, that it almost made me feel uncomfortable.

To my surprise, she's smarter than Rita. See, Joy talks to me about politics and things that are going on in other countries. Sometimes when we talk, I feel like I'm talking to someone fifty-years old. But she's a young woman and she has a lot to learn about life. I'm just a married man that just wants to have some fun.

But she allows me to get in her head and feed her all types of lies about me leaving my wife. Sometimes, I do think that maybe I should leave her alone and let her live her life but it's obvious that she doesn't want to let me go. She's clingy. If I let her go, it would completely break her heart into a million pieces.

She helps with putting activities together for the singles ministry at the church but she almost thought that she would have to go into hiding, once she found out that she was pregnant.

She called me on the phone and said, "Taurus, I'm pregnant and I'm scared," she said, with her voice trembling.

"What do you mean you're pregnant? You told me that you were on birth control."

"Well, it didn't control *this* birth. I don't know what to do. Taurus, there are too many people at the church who look up to me. I can't come around them with my belly stuck out and unmarried. What kind of example is that to set for the church, me being knocked-up by a married man? *And* I'm the daughter of a pastor. Do you know what the church would say about this?"

"Don't worry. I have the money for the abortion. We can get that done as soon as possible."

And we did. I went with Joy to the clinic and she was in there for a couple of hours. When she was released, she looked like she was in a tremendous amount of pain. That's when I knew that our "dealings" was getting way outta hand. I though to myself, *This young woman has her whole life ahead of her. Leave her alone and let her go on with her life before you end up ruining it. Enough is enough.*

But the more I tried, the harder it was to let her go. We continued to have sex with each other and I started visiting her more and more. I couldn't help it. I know that eventually, I will have to let her go. It may hurt her for a while but she'll get over it. Once she meets a guy at college that she really likes, she'll probably forget all about me.

And that's good because she really don't need to take me seriously. Neither does Rita. Besides, if I don't put an end to things, something tells me that someone is gonna find out about me messing around with Rita and Joy and then my wife Brenda and Shawn are gonna find out about it.

On the other hand, even if Shawn does find out, what can he do? If he said or did anything, he would be a fool to do so because he knows that I know some things about him that Rita, Joy and the church don't know…and I'm sure that he wouldn't want me to let the cat out of the bag.

For starters, Joy is not his only child; he has another daughter by a woman he met in Cincinnati. Joy's mother doesn't even know about it. The other daughter's name is Summer and she was born around the same time as Joy. Nobody knows about her except me and his brother, Sheldon. That's because Shawn usually confides in us about everything.

Shawn and I became friends years ago when he used to be a club promoter and I used to be a taxicab driver, down in The Flats. The last time he saw Summer, she was turning ten-years old and when he went to Cincinnati for her birthday, he got into a heated argument with her mother and hasn't been back since. That was almost ten years ago.

Also, what people don't know is that he used to buy and smoke weed, while he was still studying to be a pastor. And I definitely know about that because I used to smoke it with him. *Humph!* He is such a hypocrite. It amazes me how he can get up in the pulpit and preach to people about the life *they* should live and he ain't nothin' but a snake in the grass.

I guess one can say that he's a good actor. Sometimes, it amazes he how he can put on this act as if he doesn't have any issues, like he got it all together. And sometimes, I just stand back and watch people come up to him and hug him and shake his hand like he's Jesus Christ himself.

If I didn't know him, I would probably be fooled as well. But I know better. Outside of church, nobody would think that he's a man of God. When he hangs out with me, he plays cards for money and he likes to drink. Brenda also knows about his bad habits, which may be the reason why he lets her do what she wants to do in the church, scared that she might run her mouth.

Today was the first Sunday of the month so of course, Shawn held church longer than usual. I kept looking at Rita as she was sitting in the front row, looking like a queen. All the way across the room, Joy was sitting in the back, looking at me with a smile on her face. I turned around to look at my wife Brenda and could see her looking at Joy with enough heat in her face to boil water. Brenda doesn't like Joy, at all.

Once church was over, Brenda didn't greet anyone like she usually does. She was very quiet until we got in the car. That's when she started interrogating me. But I played it cool because I didn't want to set off any alarms.

We were riding down Kinsman Road to get something to eat and she said, "Um...Joy seemed to be all smiles today."

I said," Yeah, she seemed to be in a happy mood."

"I guess so. I wonder what she's so happy about."

"I don't know."

"Are you sure about that? The whole time that the benediction was going on, she was smiling at you."

"Well, you know how young women are," I said, trying to sound uninterested in the subject.

"*Humph.* Yeah, I sure do know how young women are...especially young women like Joy. She's fast. Always have been. But if she wants to be that way, that's her business. What I have a problem with is being disrespected right before my very eyes...and in the church no less. I'm not gonna have that. So next Sunday, her eyes betta be fixed on something else or I'm gonna fix her eyes myself."

"Brenda, listen to yourself. You're almost thirty-seven years old and you're talking like a high school teenager."

"No, I'm talking like a wife who don't like a woman flirting with her husband."

"She's young, Brenda. That's how young women are."

She looked at me real hard and said, "Why are you taking up for her?"

"I'm not. I'm just saying that maybe you should just calm down and lighten up. She hasn't approach me or anything so therefore, you don't have anything to worry about."

"Taurus, I never said that I was worried about anything. *Humph.* That lil' hepha can't compete with me."

I looked at her and smile. *She's jealous and she knows it*, I thought to myself. I've never seen this side of my wife before. She usually thinks that no woman can compare to her and thinks that every woman is beneath her. To see her acting like this was a laughable experience.

But seriously, I'm gonna have to have a talk with Joy and let her know that that type of behavior in front of my wife is very disrespectful. Maybe if I tell her that, she won't act like that again because if she do, I know that Brenda will blow her top and have parts of Joy's body scattered all over the church.

One

————◆•◆•◆————

(Rita)

MOST PEOPLE LIKE to wake up to the smell of breakfast cooking, coffee brewing, the pitter-pat of little children's feet or sunlight peeking thru their bedroom window. I don't think anyone likes to wake up to the cackling sound of his or her mother-in-law. Especially if their mother-in-law is anything like my mother-in-law, Grace.

That woman came straight from the pits of hell. She's a vanilla-colored woman, short, kinda heavy and wears her stringy peppered-colored hair in a very long braid down her back. Her eyes are as black as coal and without her saying much, you can almost find out what she's thinking when she's looking at you.

When I came downstairs in the kitchen, she was sitting at the table eating bacon and eggs with Shawn. When she saw me, she rolled her eyes and continued eating. Shawn greeted me but his stank mama didn't say a word.

That woman has been pure hell since the day we met. She has made it very known that she doesn't think that I'm good enough for her son. She has once said to me, "I don't think that you're fit to be a first lady." The nerve of her. I wanted to kick that wheelchair from up under her and beat her with it.

While Shawn was eating breakfast, I gave him a look as if to say, 'What the hell is she doing here?' He got up from the kitchen table, pulled me to the side and said, "Mama is gonna be staying with us for about three weeks."

Boy, was I pissed. "Why?" I asked.

"Because her kitchen got flooded last night, due to a pipe busting. So it will take about three weeks for it to be remodeled."

"And? That doesn't mean that she has to come over here. Doesn't she have other relatives that she can bother?"

"C'mon, baby. Be a lil' more sensitive. I know that you two don't really get along but y'all will only have to deal with each other for three weeks."

"Those three weeks are gonna feel like three years."

"Rita…"

"Alright, alright. I guess I can be civilized while she's here."

He smiled and said, "That's all I'm asking. Listen, I have to go somewhere but I'll be back in a few hours. Can you watch mama for me?"

"Is that some kind of sick joke?"

"Rita, *please*. Do this for me. Maybe this will be your chance to really get to know her and for her to get to know you."

"First of all, I don't need for her to get to know me. And secondly, I already know what I need to know about her and frankly, I don't like what I know."

"Rita, I will be back later, okay?" he said as he grabbed his jacket and headed for the door. When he left, I walked back in the kitchen and saw Grace, still sitting at the kitchen table.

She looked at me and said, "Well, good morning."

"Good morning, Grace," I quickly answered.

After I ate breakfast, I grabbed the vacuum cleaner and started to vacuum my living room floor, like I usually do on Mondays. Over the loud noise, I heard Grace call my name. "Yes?" I answered.

She looked at me and said, "You might wanna do that some other time. I'm about to go take a nap and I don't want that noise to disturb me."

I turned off the vacuum cleaner, looked at her like she was crazy and said, "Grace, you might wanna take your nap at some other time because right now, I'm gonna clean my house. Besides, it's ten o'clock in the morning. It seems too early to be taking a nap."

She wheeled herself over to me and said, "First of all, this is not your house. This is my son's house. And secondly, I can take a nap whenever I want to."

"Grace, let's not get started, okay? Whether this is your son's house or not, I am his wife. So whatever belongs to him, also belongs to me."

"That's what *you* think."

"That's what I know. At anytime, if I feel like kicking you outta here, I can. So don't think for one minute that I don't have any say-so. If I want you gone, I can have you gone."

She laughed and said, "You think you know everything, don't you? Shawn will never let that happen. He loves me more than you. Can't you tell? You were obviously against the idea of me staying here for a few weeks but as you can see, I'm here. And why? Because what *you* want, doesn't matter. I will always come first as far as Shawn is concerned and there's nothing you can do about it."

"Wrong again, Grace," I stated as I pushed the vacuum cleaner to the side. I was so angry that I grabbed Grace in a headlock, yanked her out of the wheelchair, dragged her all the way outside and onto the front lawn. She was trying to fight me off of her but of course, I was much stronger. Then I took her wheelchair, folded it up, got into my SUV and drove over it several times.

The whole time that I was doing this, she was cursing me out while she was sitting on the front lawn. If I wasn't too pretty to go to jail, I would've ran over *her*. Once I got all of my anger out, I got out of my SUV, grabbed her wheelchair and tossed it to the curb for the trash man to pick up.

"You're gonna pay for this! Wait until I tell Shawn!" she yelled, but I ignored her.

Once I pulled my SUV back into the garage, I walked back over to Grace, whom was looking at me with extreme rage in her face. I said to her, "Now, I'm gonna go back inside and leave you to your thoughts. When I'm done cleaning and I have had a stiff drink, then I will let you back inside but only if you will shut your mouth. For the meantime, you have this whole front lawn to sleep on, since you insist on taking a damn nap. And you may wanna crawl under our tree, since it looks like it's about to rain."

"Girl, you didn't," my sister Marilyn said when I told her what I did to Grace. I went over to Marilyn's house later that day, to eat and hang out.

I smirked and said, "Yes I did. After I was finished doing what I needed to do in the house, I went ahead and helped her in the house and made her sit on the couch. I turned on the TV for her and left the house to come over here."

She was in total shock. "What do you think Shawn is gonna say about that?"

"I really don't care. I'm sure that when he gets home, she's gonna give him an earful but I don't regret what I did. She had that comin' and I don't have a problem doing it again. She pushed me too far."

"Well, I guess you needed to do what you had to do. Anyway, you won't believe what I did yesterday."

"What? Give me the scoop."

She laid back in her chair and said, "I slept with my therapist. His name is Kyle and the tripped-out part is that I found out that he's married to the principal at my son's school."

I almost choked on my sandwich. "You did what? Marilyn, how could you do something like that?"

"You got a lot of nerve. Aren't you the first lady of your church and you're sleeping with Shawn's right-hand man?"

Damn. She's right, I thought to myself. I said, "Okay, I know I'm doing wrong. I'll be the first to admit that. But you don't need to be doing wrong just because *I* am."

She laughed and said, "Honey, believe me, I wasn't thinking about you when I slept with Kyle."

"Marilyn, how in the world did this come about?"

She sighed and said, "Well, I went to him, seeking advice about what I needed to do about Paul. I know that Paul and I have been separated for three years but I've been hoping that one day he would finally come to his senses and come home. Kyle has been there when I needed a shoulder to cry on, he's prayed with me and he's even offered to sit with both Paul and I and have us talk things out, together. So a few days ago, I called Paul and asked him if we could sit down and talk things out. Do you know what that bastard said to me?"

"What? Something stupid?"

"He said to me, 'I don't have time for that. I'm busy working on a project at my job.' I said to him, 'Paul, this is important. Don't you wanna save our marriage?' He then says to me, 'Marilyn, right now is not a good time.' And then he hangs up in my face."

"Wow. He truly *is* a bastard. But how did that come to you sleeping with your therapist? Wasn't he the one who offered to sit down with the both of you, together?"

"Yeah. Well, I went over to Kyle's office and explained to him what happened. I was so upset and crying and he held me close until I calmed down. Then, all of a sudden, we looked into each other's eyes and kissed each other. Then we…well…you know."

"This is unbelievable. How long are you gonna keep this up?"

"Actually, it only happened one time. We realized that we made a mistake and decided not to deal with each other anymore. But I have to say that it's kinda awkward when I pick Jesse up from school and I see Kyle's wife there."

"I bet it is," I said.

All of this really took me for a loop. But I must say that it kinda doesn't surprise me. Marilyn has always been the type of woman that was able to have any man that she wanted. Men have always flocked to her. When she was in high school, she was the one that constantly stayed in fights with the other high school girls because all the boys liked her. Dating was never an issue for her.

The football players in high school used to drool over her and when she became a lawyer and started working around a lot of men, she used to always get red roses just for the heck of it or someone was asking her out to dinner. But honestly, I can see why men fall for her; she's absolutely beautiful.

She has shiny, black, naturally wavy, long hair with fair-colored skin that's as smooth-looking as a baby's bottom. She's tall like me and always keeps her body in tip-top shape. When she walks, she makes sure that everyone notices her curvaceous hips since she walks with a serious switch as if her body is saying, "Look at me! I'm sexy!" It's funny to see her now, especially since she was a pudgy lil' thang when she was a little girl. But I guess we all grow up.

When I walked in the door of my house, Shawn was standing at the entrance with a look that could kill anyone. All of a sudden, he grabbed me by my arm and pushed me up against the wall. It *really* caught me off guard. I never saw Shawn so angry. I pulled away and looked at him like he was crazy.

"My mother told me everything, Rita. I want you to pack up your things and leave. What if my mother had caught pneumonia and died because you left her outside in the rain?"

At least she wouldn't be in this house, I thought to myself. "Well, I did bring your mother back in the house," I explained to him.

"You had no right to put her outside!"

"You had no right to leave her here with me! She's *your* mother, not mine. I'm sick and tired of you not having a damn spine when it comes to her!"

"Watch your mouth!"

"No! All she do is disrespect me and constantly reminds me about how much her *boy loves his mama*."

"So what! What's wrong with me loving my mother!?"

"You love her more than me! You're a pastor but yet you don't practice what you preach. I thought that the spouse is supposed to come first. Isn't that what it says in the good book? Well, if that's true, how come I don't come first in *your* life? Why does everything come before me, including you ol' mama?! And then you have the nerve to get mad at me because I threw her lil' old behind outside in the rain. Oh, please. Do you think I give a damn? If I could do it over, I would've placed her in front of a bus."

He stared at me so hard, it was almost scary. Then he said, "You know what your problem is? You have a lot of hate in you. And I can't keep dealing with this. You need to get your things and get out."

I looked him dead in the eyes and said, "With pleasure. Have a great life...with your mom."

Two

(Shawn)

"Why are you surprised? You know how Rita is," Chris stated, as we were having breakfast at a diner. I told him what happened between my mom and Rita.

I explained, "Well, I didn't know that she would act like that with my mama."

"Why would you think that? You know them two can't stand each other."

"But I never thought that it would go this far. I don't know what to do."

"Kick Rita's ass."

"Chris! Man, you're a pastor. Don't speak like that."

"*Humph.* Let's get real; pastor simply means paycheck."

I couldn't believe my ears. "Are you listening to what you're saying? You used to be the one that talked about God and how wonderful He is and how you couldn't do anything without Him. I mean, *you* were the one that helped me get to know Christ better and told me that I would make a good pastor. Now, to hear you talking like this, I simply can't understand it."

"Shawn, I'm being real. Being a pastor doesn't equal *perfect*. That's what people tend to forget. We have needs, we get upset and we get horny, just like everyone else. For me, being a pastor of a church is mainly about the almighty dollar. I don't know about you but I got bills to pay. The mortgage isn't gonna get paid on its own. I can sit and quote scriptures all day but that's not gonna stop the bills from coming in. Don't get me wrong; I love God but this is a business and whether you want to admit it or not, you're a part of this business, too. I look at it like this: The more people shout and dance all over my church, the more people will join my church and the more money I will make. And honestly, most of the money comes from the women at my church. That's why I stay looking good and smelling good because I know I am what they came to see. Man, you should see how they act when service is over; women run up to me like I'm a superstar, talking about how much they enjoyed the service. What they are really saying is that they enjoyed *me*. And having your share of women is so, so easy to obtain because most of the women that go to church are some of the most loneliest, horniest, desperate women that I've ever met. If a man ever wants to get a woman in bed, he can always find that woman in the church."

I wanted to disagree with Chris so badly but what he said about the women in his church, was pretty much true. There have been a couple of times when I visited his church and I saw how the women reacted towards him after service; gazing into his eyes, smiling from ear to ear and touching his hand.

"Chris, don't you think that you sound full of yourself?"

He took a sip of his coffee and said, "I'm just telling it like it is."

"That's not how it is. That's how you made it to be, for yourself. But as far as I'm concerned, that's not my reality. When I got called to preach, I took this walk very seriously. And I still do. Yes, there are plenty of temptations out there but I choose to walk a straight path because at the end of the day, I have to answer to God for any wrong-doing that I may have gotten myself into and in no way, do I want to upset the man upstairs. I'm human but I'm still a man of the cloth and so are you, which means that God will hold us much more accountable for our sins than the average person. So yes, you are right about us being human but we have a responsibility to Jesus Christ to bring the lost to him. So if you have any respect for God, you would step down and accept the fact that this is definitely not your calling."

He leaned back in his chair and looked at me as if he couldn't believe what I just said to him. "Man, who do you think you're talking to?" he asked.

"Apparently, a brotha who has no idea who God is."

"Oh, really? So I guess you have all the answers, huh? Who are you to tell me to step down? I got in this game before *you* did."

"That's my whole point, Chris. This is nothing but a game to you. Just in case you didn't know it, hell is real and if you continue to play with God, that's exactly where you are gonna end up. Can you honestly say that God is pleased with the way that you are living your life?"

"The more money I make at this, the more I am convinced that God is definitely pleased with my life."

"Wow. Obviously, nothing that I'm saying is getting thru to you so I'm just gonna leave the matter alone. But Chris, I pray that you finally understand what it means to have a true relationship with God."

"And I pray that you get your head out of the clouds, Shawn."

"Marcus, in order for me to find out the problem, you're gonna have to be honest. If you want your marriage to get better, don't hold back the truth," I stated to him. Marcus was in my office for a one-on-one counseling session.

Him and Stacy have been having problems in their marriage for a year and a half. It doesn't really surprise me because they were both only twenty-years old when they got married. So they really don't know what love is and what it takes to keep a marriage together. But it's beyond me as to why they waited so long to get counseling but apparently, it must be worse than I thought because they won't even have counseling, *together.* Today was Marcus' first day of counseling with me.

"Well, Pastor I'm afraid that if I tell you my problem that you will tear me down about it."

"Marcus, *nobody* is gonna beat you down about anything. I'm just trying to help you and Stacy get your marriage back on track. I'm not here to judge or criticize you and whatever you tell me, is strictly confidential."

He leaned back in his chair, took a deep breath and said, "For a while, I've been having sexual thoughts about men. It's getting to the point where the thoughts are so overpowering, that I don't even get sexually turned on by my wife anymore. There are certain guys at my job that I am attracted to and have thought about having sex with but I know that if I was to do that, there's no turning back. Pastor Owens, I've tried to block these thoughts from my mind but it doesn't help. I don't wanna hurt Stacy but I have to be honest with her and with myself."

"So I take it that you haven't told her about this?" I asked.

"No I haven't. She would be absolutely devastated."

"But you know that you're gonna have to tell her because each day that you go without telling her, it's just gonna eat away at you, more and more. She probably will be hurt when you tell her but she will be *more* hurt if you don't. That kind of topic is definitely something that you need to discuss with her, immediately. And the reason why I say that is because if you are already having strong urges to have sex with men, there's a major possibility that you *will* have sex with men. And if that becomes the case, I'm pretty sure that Stacy wouldn't want to be in the midst of that. If you love her, you need to tell her."

He moved one of his dreadlocks away from his face and said, "What if I tell her and she leaves me?"

"I'm not gonna lie to you, Marcus; there is a possibility that she might. But would you rather her stay and then you cheat on her? With a man? You don't wanna hurt her, right?"

"No, I don't."

"That's good. And before we end this counseling session, you and I are gonna pray about this matter. I know that it took a lot of courage for you to be honest with me. Use that same courage to be honest with your wife. And no matter what anyone tells you, God can deliver you."

With a puzzled look on his face, he asked, "Delivered? What do you mean?"

"Well, do you *wanna* have these sexual urges toward men?"

"No."

"Do you love your wife?"

"Yes, I do."

"Do you wanna stay married to her?"

"Yes."

"Well, there's nothing in God's word that says that you can't be delivered from what it is that you want to be delivered from. But you have to want it for yourself. If you want to be delivered from these types of feelings, you can. You've made your confession and confession is the beginning of deliverance, Marcus. If you do not want to feel this way towards men, ask God to deliver you from it because if you love your wife like you say you do and you wanna stay married to her, do what's necessary to *keep* your marriage. But the choice is yours. However, I have to tell you that it works on both ends; there's a possibility that she's not gonna want to work it out, once you tell her this. But if she does decide to leave you, I will help you get thru it. My door is always open and you know that."

"Thanks, Pastor. I really appreciate your help. And I'm gonna tell her. It's gonna take a lot of courage but I can do this. I hope that Stacy and I can work this out."

After our session was over, I prayed with him just like I said I would. Then I said, "Well, I'll be meeting with your wife tomorrow for counseling. I won't be telling her anything about our meetings and I'm gonna show her that same courtesy. Hopefully, after talking to her, I'll be able to counsel the both of you together, without you guys trying to kill each other. Take care of yourself, Marcus. Call me if you need anything."

"Thanks. I will." When Marcus walked out of my office, something in my spirit told me that he wasn't gonna tell his wife *anything*.

And obviously, I must've been right because when Stacy came into my office the next morning, I got the notion that she wasn't aware of anything that Marcus and I spoke about. When she walked into my office, she came in with such a sweet spirit that I felt bad that she was with a man who is having a hard time desiring her.

Stacy is a very short and petite lady who looked like she couldn't harm a fly. When she sat down in my office, she smiled and then all of a sudden her face turned into a frown and then tears started to roll down her face. She quickly removed them with her hand and hung her head, low.

"I'm sorry, Pastor. I don't mean to be crying like this," she said in a soft whisper.

"You don't have anything to be sorry about. If you need to cry, you have that right," I explained.

"Pastor, I don't know what it is that I'm doing wrong. All I know is that something is not right in my marriage with Marcus. And I'm scared that we are not gonna make it."

"What makes you think that you're doing something wrong?"

"Because he's not happy with me."

"Did he tell you that?"

"Not exactly. But he's not affectionate like he used to, every time I ask for some quality time, he always act like he has something else to do. I hate to think that he's cheating on me but what else am I supposed to think when you have a husband that's not even having sex with you? Did you get a chance to speak with him yesterday?"

"Yes, we did talk. Did you guys speak after he left my office?"

"No. He came home, ate a sandwich, took a shower and went back out the door."

I had to almost bite my lip, just to keep from telling Marcus' secret. "So he left the house without saying a word?"

"Yes, he did. I've tried to talk to my mom, just to get some motherly advice and the whole time that I was trying to talk to her, she was constantly over-talking me and saying things like, 'I told you not to marry him.' Who wants to listen to that? Pastor, I love my husband and I want to spend the rest of my life with him. When I met him and saw those dreamy, dark-brown eyes and that gorgeous smile, it was like love at first sight. I was used to dating those high-yellow brothas with the good hair but Marcus was like a Nubian god with that deep, dark skin and he was so tall and moved with such confidence, like he ruled the world. But of course, it wasn't just those things that attracted me to him. It was also about how interested he was with my life. He supported my goals and helped me to achieve some of them. And from what I can recall, he's never even raised his voice at me. He's always been the calm person throughout most of many situations. But lately, he's been in rare form and I don't know why. It's like he don't care about anything, anymore."

I leaned back in my chair and said, "Well Stacy, I do believe that he does care because if he didn't, he wouldn't have made any attempt to see me yesterday."

"Yeah, I guess you're right."

"If you two will agree on having a counseling session *together*, I'm sure that we will be able to get to the root of the problem. As long as God is God, there's absolutely nothing that can't be fixed. But it's up to the both of you if y'all want to work it out. See, I can sit here and talk to the both of you separately but honestly, that's not fixing the problem. You guys are communicating with *me* but y'all are not communicating with each other. You have to get to a point where y'all are able to look each other in the face and talk like civilized adults about what it is that's bothering you and be willing to admit where it is that you both are falling short in the marriage."

"You're right, Pastor. When I get home, I'll go and talk to Marcus and see if he will agree to have a counseling session, together. Maybe that will open the door for healing."

I smiled and said, "Well, it can."

Three

——◆•◀◀◆▶▶•◆——

(Joy)

TODAY IS THE first day of spring and also the day of my cousin's wedding. I'm one of her bridesmaids and I'm rushing to pack my dress and shoes so that I can get dressed at the church. My cousin's name is Carmella and we have been as thick as thieves since we were five-years old.

Her mom and my mom are sisters and since my parents didn't stay together long enough to make me a brother or a sister, my relationship with Carmella has been the closest thing to a sibling. We used to go to school together but we didn't attend the same classes, simply because she was a year older than me.

Carmella is the only girl out of three brothers; Simon, Stanley and Saul. And considering that she's the youngest, of course she's always had everything laid at her feet. But she's not the stuck-up type at all. *Everybody* loves her and she's always been able to make friends, very easily. However, a lot of skinny girls in high school couldn't stand her because although she was a heavy-set girl, she was very popular with the fellas.

The guys used to go crazy when she walked by. I think it's because she was such a confident person. She never let her weight become a problem for her. Besides, she carried her weight so well. Her nickname in high school was 'Red Bone' because of her light complexion and her long, reddish-colored hair, which was always kept together.

She was definitely a hot commodity with the fellas but the lucky man that she ended up with, was Mark Barnes. He was one of the football players in high school that all the girls wanted because he was the pretty boy type; light-skinned with good looks and good hair.

He's cheated on her several times in the past with stupid women but he never left her and she never left him. So of course, I found it to be of no surprise when she called me and told me that she was engaged to Mark.

It was ten a.m when Carmella called me on her wedding day and said, "Girl, I'm scared."

"Scared of what? What are you talking about?" I asked.

"I don't think I can do this. I mean, what if I end up not being the wife he wants? What if time goes by and he decides that he doesn't want to be with me anymore?"

"Carmella, you're trippin'. First of all, you and Mark have been together for a while and have been thru a lot, together. *A lot.* But yet, you guys still stayed together and obviously you're the only woman he wants in his life, otherwise, why would he go thru all the trouble of buying a ring and helping you put the wedding plans together? He must be serious, Carmella. You're just nervous, that's all."

"Yeah, you're right. I guess I am acting a 'lil crazy. It's just that this is such a major step."

"Of course it is. But you will be okay. Do you love him?"

"Absolutely! You know that."

"Do you love him more than anything?"

"Of course."

"Do you want to marry him?"

"Yes, I do."

"Then let's get the party started. I'll be at the church in a few minutes."

"Ok. Joy, thank you so much for talking to me. You really calmed me down."

"Girl, no problem. I'm sure that I'll be acting the same way on my wedding day."

"Speaking of which, I have a surprise for you when you come to the church."

"Oooh. What is it? Tell me now."

"Nope. You'll have to wait until you get here."

"Well, answer me this: Will I be happy when I see it?"

"Trust me, Joy. You'll be smiling from ear to ear."

Contrary to popular belief, big girls are the most beautiful women in the world. I truly became a believer of that when I saw Carmella walk down the aisle in her wedding dress. She was so graceful and every piece of her, was flawless from top to bottom.

I felt a tear fall down my face as she and Mark exchanged vows. *I wish it was me*, I thought to myself. I knew that they made a great decision to get married. And after Carmella got over that nervous feeling, I could tell that she knew that she made a great decision, too.

During the reception, Carmella grabbed me by my hand and took me over to a very handsome guy that looked very familiar but I couldn't remember his name. She obviously told him some things about me because when he saw me, he was grinning from ear to ear.

"Hi, Joy. Do you remember me?" he asked.

I smiled and said, "Uh...well...you look very familiar but..."

"Oh, girl please. You know who this is. This is the surprise I was telling you about. This is Clay. Remember him now?"

My eyes grew to the size of marbles. I haven't seen Clay in years. He used to be our childhood friend from kindergarten to fourth grade. Back then, he was chubby and wore thick glasses and a lot of kids used to pick on him. The only friends that he had at the time, was Carmella and I. But when his parents moved to another city, he had to switch schools and so we lost touch with him.

"It's so good to see you," he said as he gave me a hug. *He smell like heaven*, I thought to myself.

Carmella smiled and said, "I'm gonna let you two catch up and I'm gonna get back to my hubby."

"It's been years since I've seen you, Clay. You look great," I smiled.

"Thanks. So do you. We have a lot of catching up to do," he said with a smile.

"I agree. How did you know that Carmella was getting married?"

"Well, it was by accident. I was shopping in Beachwood Mall and I ran into her. She told me that she was getting married and she asked me if I could come. So of course, I said yes. I told her that I was in college studying journalism and that I should be done in about a year."

"Really? What school do you go to?"

"The University of Akron."

"That's a nice school, Clay. I've heard nothing but nice things about that school. I go to Kent State University."

"What's your major?"

"Business management. I figured that with a degree like that, I can get a job almost anywhere."

"You're right." Then he smiled and said, "I'm so glad that we had a chance to see each other again. It's been so long."

Too long, I thought to myself. "So did you come by yourself?" I asked, trying not to sound like I was eager to find out if he had a girlfriend or not.

He smiled and said, "Yep. I'm here by myself. And you?"

"Same here. Just me, myself and I."

"Well, would you like to dance?"

"Sure. That would be nice."

He gently took my hand and led me to the dance floor where we slow-danced to a song by Mariah Carey. As he put his strong arms around my waist and I relaxed my arms around his neck, I heard myself say, "I'm so glad I ran into you."

He whispered, "I feel the same way."

Four

(Taurus)

SHAWN AND I decided to go get our suits custom-made for Easter and while we were out, Shawn ran into an old friend of his, named Candace. When he saw her, his whole face lit up like a Christmas tree. But I can see why; Candace is absolutely beautiful.

She has high cheek bones like an Indian, flawless mocha-colored skin, a body like a dancer, the most beautiful smile that I've ever seen and long soft-looking brown hair that swept her shoulders when she walked. She looked like a painting.

When she saw Shawn, she said, "Oh, my God! Shawn, I haven't seen you in such a long time!"

Shawn hugged her and said, "Wow! You look great! It's nice to see you."

"Same here."

Shawn then looked at me and said, "Taurus, this is Candace. She's an old buddy of mine. She used to be a bartender, down in The Flats."

"It's a pleasure to meet you," she said, as she shook my hand.

"My pleasure," I answered. Then I found me a seat away from them but I could still hear their conversation.

"So, how have you been? What have you been up to?" Shawn asked Candace, while grinning ear to ear.

She smiled and said, "Well, I've started my own catering business and I just moved back to Cleveland, a few months ago."

"Hmm. What made you move back to Cleveland?"

"A divorce. I didn't have any family in California so when I got divorced, I decided to move back to Cleveland around my family and friends."

"Divorced? I didn't even know you had got married."

She smiled and said, "Yeah, I was married. It only lasted four years. One day, we were sitting down at the kitchen table and he said that he was in love with someone else and said that he wanted a divorce. The next thing I knew, he reached in his back pocket and pulled out the divorce papers for me to sign. I never even saw it coming."

"Wow. I'm sorry to hear that."

"Don't be sorry. Sometimes, things don't work out the way that you would want them to. That's life."

"*Humph*. I guess so."

She smiled and asked, "So Shawn, what have you been up to, lately?"

"Well, I've been living my life, trying to keep my church together."

"What do you mean?"

"Well, I'm a pastor of a church."

Candace's eyes got big and she said, "Are you serious?! You? A pastor?"

He laughed and said, "Yep. I have a nice-size congregation."

"Wow, Shawn! How long have you been a pastor?"

"Just a few years...not very long at all. You should come and visit my church when you get the chance. I'm sure you'll like it."

"I'll definitely keep that in mind. What's the name of it?"

"Sweet Harmony Springtone Baptist Church."

"Oh, wow! I drove by that church a couple of times. I didn't know that was your church."

"Yep, it is. Well anyway, I gotta go but I hope to see you there, one of these Sundays."

She grinned and said, "I'll be sure to visit. Take care of yourself."

"You do the same, Candace."

When she walked away, Shawn watched her with a smile on his face. I wondered if she noticed the wedding ring on Shawn's finger...better yet, did *he* notice it on his finger, while he was talking to her. But who am I to say anything? He ain't doing nothing but admiring God's beauty. There's nothing wrong with that.

Something's not right. I mean, I know that Joy doesn't mean anything to me but I still don't like to be ignored. Several times this week, I've called her and left tons of messages just to see how she's doing and haven't got one call back. It's starting to aggravate the hell outta me.

A couple of days ago, I went to her apartment to see if she was home. I knocked on the door for a long time and there was no answer. So I got back in my car and waited for at least three hours for her to show up. But she never did. I don't know why she's acting like this but I'm gonna get to the bottom of it.

Humph. Imagine the anger that was raging inside of me when I saw Joy show up in church with some brotha tagging along. I've never seen him before and I couldn't help but to think that he was the reason why I haven't heard from her. He had his arm around her the whole time that service was going on… and I didn't like it.

When church was over, I almost broke my neck trying to catch up to her and find out who the hell was this guy that came with her. But I knew that I needed to be smart about my approach because I didn't want to bring attention to myself and have anyone wonder if something was going on between Joy and I. And I most certainly didn't want to alarm my wife. So I remained cool when I approached Joy.

"Hi, Joy. I've been trying to reach you. Did you get any of my messages?" I asked.

"Yes I did, Elder Nate. But I will get back to you at my earliest convenience."

Earliest convenience? Why is she being so formal? I thought to myself. "Hello, there. What's your name?" I asked her male "friend", since Joy didn't bother to introduce us.

He shook my hand and said, "I'm Clay. Nice to meet you."

Then Joy looked at me and said, "Well, I gotta go. Clay and I are going to get something to eat."

"Well, don't you wanna introduce him to your father? I'm sure that he would like to meet Clay," I stated, trying to find out if Clay has already met her father.

Clay answered, "Oh, I already met her father at dinner, last weekend. We hit it off great. He's a great Pastor."

"They had a lot of fun together when they met," Joy added, "Anyway, we gotta go. Have a nice Sunday afternoon."

"Nice meeting you," Clay said to me.

Go to hell, I thought to myself. When they both walked away, I noticed that Clay was holding her hand. *Who does he think he is?* I thought to myself. I don't know if this Clay person is supposed to be her boyfriend or not but he could *never* be me.

Five

(Rita)

It's been about two weeks that I've been back home with Shawn. However, we really haven't talked things out since I've been back. It was *my* decision to show back up at the house and since he didn't change the locks on the door, I politely walked in with my bags. When I walked in, Shawn was sitting on the couch, going over what looked to be his sermon.

When he saw me, he took his glasses off and asked, "Why are you here?"

I answered, "Because I live here. I am your wife and I belong here."

With that, I carried my bags upstairs and didn't hear another peep out of Shawn. So I thought that I won the battle. However, for the past few days, he's been walking around the house barely speaking to me and we've been eating dinner in total silence. Sometimes, he doesn't even give me eye contact. But, oh well. If he's waiting on me to apologize, he might as well stop waiting.

One night, we laid in the bed side by side, steadily looking up at the ceiling. Then Shawn took a deep breath and said, "This isn't right."

"*What* isn't right?" I asked in a soft tone.

"This marriage. We haven't seen eye to eye in a long time and if we don't get it together, we're not gonna make it."

"Well, what do you think we should do about it?"

"I don't know. Maybe we need to learn how to listen to each other. It seems that the both of us try so hard to get our point across, that neither one of us take the time to listen."

"I agree. So how do we get to that point?"

He turned on his side to face me and he said, "Tell me what it is that's bothering you and how we can make it better. Make it plain."

"Shawn, don't you have things on your mind as well, that's bothering you?"

"Yes but I want to listen to you, first. I want to save our marriage, Rita. So tell me what it is that I may be doing that's making you unhappy."

I sat up and asked, "But how many times have we had talks and have tried to work out our issues? How do I know that things are gonna work out this time?"

"Because I'm not willing to give up. I love you, Rita. I love you enough to work it out. So tell me what it is that you have issues with so that we can work on them, together."

I let out a deep sigh and I said," Shawn, you are a wonderful man and I love you so much. But you're weak."

"I'm weak? How?"

"When it comes to certain people such as your mother, you turn into a little boy who can't say no. I understand that she's your mother but when she's around, you treat me as if I'm *not* around. You know that she doesn't like me at all and because she doesn't, she disrespects me all the time, which really makes me angry. But what makes me even angrier is that you don't do anything about it. I'm your wife. You're supposed to stand up for me but you don't, so therefore, that puts me in a position where I have to stand up for *myself*, even if that means throwing her out of my house. You stand in the pulpit and preach this and preach that but half of what you preach about, you don't even follow. If you did, we would have a better marriage. Also, it would be nice if *you* would run the church instead of letting Brenda run it. Just because she brings in a lot of money into the church, doesn't give her the right to make you run it the way she see fit."

"Rita, the only reason why I take Brenda's opinion into consideration is because she gets angry very easily and I really don't wanna deal with that. Not only that, she always threaten to leave and go to another church when her opinions are not considered when it comes to making decisions for the church. And if she leaves, you know that her husband Taurus is going with her. And I definitely need him in my corner when things start to become a bit much at the church."

"Then let her leave, Shawn. *You're* the Pastor. If you wanna run your church a certain way, then run it that way and tell Brenda to hit the bricks. You don't have to be under her mercy just because she gives the church a lot of money."

"But we need money to keep the church running."

"Shawn, I understand that. But if you continue to allow Brenda to take over, you will no longer have a church."

He looked at me with a puzzled look and said, "Why do you say that?"

"Because it is no secret that hardly anyone at the church likes Brenda and a lot of your members notice how she's trying to take over. If one person turns on you and leave, that may not cause a major effect. But if most of your church members turn on you and leave because of one person, you're gonna have a problem. Shawn, you have a lot of members who truly have a genuine love for your church and want to support you and your decisions. But you continue to make Brenda your decision-maker and all she's trying to do is be in the spotlight. She only gives, just to be seen. That's why she gave the church fifty thousand dollars, so that she can have her name on a stupid plague that can sit in the lobby for everyone to see. You're giving her way too much power."

"Okay. I understand what you're saying. Maybe it will be best if I sit down and have a meeting with her. I'm sure things can get worked out. Brenda can be understanding, sometimes."

"That's what *you* think."

"Rita, give me a chance to let me handle it, okay?"

"Okay. I'll let you handle it. But you haven't gave your input about how your mom disrespects me."

"But I've listened to every word. Things will change. I promise. As soon as I wake up in the morning, I'm gonna work on changing some things for the better. Goodnight, sweetheart," he stated as he rolled over to go to sleep.

"Wait a minute, Shawn. You never told me what's on *your* mind. I'm willing to listen to you as well."

He turned around to look at me and he said, "Rita, all I want is for you to be patient with me. Love me, regardless of my flaws. I know you may think that I don't care but I do care and things will get better. Some things may take time to fix but I will put forth the effort to fix them. I'm a man of God but I'm not a perfect man."

With that, I laid down with my arm around Shawn and slept very well.

Taurus has always been good in bed to the point where my whole body would shake in ecstasy. But this time, it seemed like his mind was elsewhere when he was on top of me.

"Taurus, what is your problem? Is it me?" I asked.

"What do you mean?" he asked, rolling off of me and putting back on his pants.

"Well normally, you'd be so into our lovemaking and then we would hold each other and talk. It just seems like you were trying to get it over with. What's wrong? Is Brenda getting on your nerves?"

"Rita, everything is fine. I'm just a 'lil stressed because I have a deadline to meet on this novel that I'm working on."

"Taurus, please. You've had deadlines in the past and you've never acted like this."

"Well Rita, I guess the pressure is kinda getting to me. Anyway, I was at church Sunday and I met Joy's friend, Clay. Have you met him before?"

"Yes. She's brought him to the house a few times and he's had dinner with Shawn and I. To be honest with you, I'm glad that she's been hanging with him."

"Why?"

"Because she's a 'lil better to deal with, now that she got someone special in her life."

"Special? What makes you think that he's special?"

"*Humph.* Well, he must be something because she always have a smile on her face when she's with him."

"How long has she known him?"

"According to her, they've known each other since childhood but they reunited at her cousin's wedding."

"So she couldn't do no better that that?"

I looked at Taurus like he was crazy. "What do you mean? The young man is an honor student in college, he's good-looking, has no kids and is quite fond of Joy. He's better than most men twice his age."

"Oh, please. He's just some young punk."

"Wow! Sounds like you're jealous, Taurus."

"Me? Jealous? Of a dumb dude?"

"First of all, why are you talking about him like that? You don't even know him. And what's with all the questions about this guy?"

At first, he didn't say anything. Then he mumbled, "No reason."

Six

---•◦•◦•---

(Shawn)

"HEAVENLY FATHER, I thank You for allowing me to see another morning. You are so merciful and I thank You for protecting me from all harm. As You know, Pastors such as myself, go thru a lot of things and sometimes it's hard to handle it all. But I thank you for providing me with the strength to make it thru the troubles that I face. I've made a lot of mistakes but I'm still here, living for You. In Your son Jesus' name, I thank You for being my protector and help me continue to stay strong in the Word. Amen."

After I finished my daily devotion, I went to the gym and started working out on the punching bags. I normally get on the treadmill and lift weights to stay in shape but when I have some things on my mind, I take it out on the punching bags.

Everything that Rita said about Brenda was correct but I'm trying to prevent the church from being separated. And sometimes, when you deal with people with money, they have the tendency to use the little power that they have to try to divide the church if their demands are not met. That's what I was trying to explain to Rita.

I had been so occupied with the punching bag that I didn't realize that two hours had passed, which meant that I was at least thirty minutes late for my counseling session with Marcus and Stacy. I called her to let her know that I was gonna be late and she told me some not-so-surprising news.

"Pastor, I'm leaving Marcus," she stated.

"Why?" I asked, as if I didn't know.

"Well, last night we sat down and had a talk and he said that he wanted to seek other interests. He then went on to say that his sexual preference has changed and that he has slept with a man."

I was shocked. I didn't think that it would go this far. "What did you say when he told you that?"

"I couldn't say anything. I cried my eyes out because I knew that my marriage over. There's no way that I can stay with him, after he told me what he did. This has been the most devastating news that I've ever received in my life but I'm not gonna lose my mind about it and get depressed."

I said, "Stacy, I'm really sorry that this happened to you. But God is on your side and He's gonna be there for you."

"I know. I'm so thankful that I found Jesus because if I hadn't, I probably would've lost my mind and try to kill Marcus. I'm really hurt but life goes on and I'm gonna continue to live my life and get thru this."

"That's a wonderful attitude to have and I'm gonna keep you in my prayers."

"Thank you, Pastor. And while you're at it, keep Marcus in your prayers as well because just like the Bible says, 'You reap what you sow.' He's put me in a position where I have to start all over from scratch."

"But do you know what's the good thing about starting over from scratch?"

"What?"

"Putting the past behind you. God is giving you this opportunity to start a new life because He obviously has something better in mind for you. Sometimes, we as humans start to think that what we have is a good thing and that nothing is better than what we have, already. Yes, we are supposed to always thank God for the life we are living and be thankful for the blessings that He has given us but we should never act like God can't bless us with more and that He can't bless us while we're in the midst of a storm. I know that this is a very hurtful thing for you to go thru but on the other side of this storm, there's a major blessing waiting for you. You already have the right attitude, Stacy. All you have to remember is that God is in your corner and He's not gonna let you down."

"Well, if God is allowing me to go thru this to prepare me for a major blessing, I wonder what the blessing is. Humph. Maybe it's a trillion dollars."

I laughed a 'lil and said, "Whatever the blessing is, I'm sure that you'll be happy with it. You take care of yourself and continue to pray and keep God first."

"I will. Thanks for everything, Pastor. I'll talk to you, later."

"Okay. Bye-bye."

I was very relieved that Stacy took the news well because she could've gone crazy and possibly killed him. But when God is with you, He can help you be in control of your emotions so that you can go thru your troubles without hurting yourself or someone else.

While on my way out of the gym, I got a call from mama. "Hi, mom. How are you doing?" I asked.

"I'm doing well," she answered, "I wanted to know if you can pick up my medicine up at the pharmacy and pick me up a pack of cigarettes."

"C'mon, mama. You know those cigarettes are the reason why you're taking that medicine."

"Just do what I ask, Shawn. I don't need you preachin' at me. If I want cigarettes, bring them. Okay?"

I took a deep sigh and said, "Okay, mama. But your health is failing because you continue to do the wrong things."

"Well, if you continue to stay married to that demon that you got at home, *your* health is gonna be failing too."

I didn't even pay attention to that comment. "I'll be there in about an hour, okay?"

"Okay, sweetie. Bye-bye."

When I got over to mama's house, she was laying on the couch, watching reruns of *Good Times*. This is the highlight of her day, everyday. To her, if she doesn't have her daily dose of cigarettes, a can of Pepsi, bag of pork rinds and *Good Times*, life is not worth living. Sometimes it brings a tear to my eye, watching my mother slowly die, day by day. And what's worse is that she knows that she's dying and she doesn't even care.

"Hi, sweetheart," she said to me as I sat next to her on the couch.

"Hi, mom. Here's your medicine and cigarettes."

"Thank you, honey. You can go in the kitchen and fix you something to eat if you're hungry."

"Naw, I'm okay. Um...mama, I want to talk to you for a minute."

"About what?"

"About Rita."

"Wrong subject. Not interested."

"Mama, please. I know that you don't like my wife but I really would appreciate it if you could try to at least respect her when she's around. When you're in her house, treat her with respect."

"And why should I do that?"

"Because that's my wife and I love her. You are entitled to your own opinion about her but she's still the woman that I chose to be with. And honestly, *you're* the one that pick fights with *her*. I will admit that she didn't handle the situation right when you and her got into an argument, a few weeks ago. She should have never thrown you out of the house like that. But *you* are the one that always provoke her, every chance you get. It hurts me to say this but if you can't respect my wife, especially in her own house, then you're not gonna see much of me. I'm not asking you to be her friend. I'm just asking you to respect my decision as to whom it is that I love. See, I'm trying to keep peace between my wife and I and as long as you and her are constantly getting into it, she's gonna be upset with me because she thinks that I'm not stepping in and doing something about it."

"Okay. I'll try to tolerate her so that you can be happy. But you're gonna find out about Rita and when you do, you're gonna wish you had listened to me when I tried to warn you about her. She's up to no good and it wouldn't surprise me if she's cheating on you."

"Oh, mama please. Rita is not cheating on me."

"Boy, you are such a fool. I have lived a long time and I know a cheat when I see a cheat. She's foolin' around on you, Shawn. Mama wouldn't lie to you."

"I don't believe that Rita would do something like that to me. She's not that type of person. But if she is doing something like that, let me handle it. Okay?"

"Do what you wanna do, Shawn. But be on your guard."

At church, it wasn't as pack as it usually is. I guess it's because it was raining outside. People don't really like to come out in the rain. But Candace didn't seem to mind. I forgot that I invited her to my church so when I saw her, my heart almost dropped in my stomach. Although nothing went on between Candace and me, a feeling of fright came over me when I introduced her to my wife. From the look on Rita's face, I could tell that Rita didn't like her.

"It's nice to meet you," Candace said, when I introduced her to Rita.

"*Humph.* Same here," Rita remarked as she quickly shook Candace's hand.

To break the tension, I asked Candace, "So did you enjoy service?"

"Yes, I did," she replied with a smile. "It was wonderful, Shawn. You are an awesome Pastor. I'm proud of you."

"Thank you. Feel free to come back anytime."

I felt the heat come off of Rita and slap me in the face. *Oh Lord, I hope my wife didn't think anything by what I just said to Candace*, I thought to myself.

"Excuse me Candace, but me and my husband have to go. Thanks for stopping by," Rita stated as she tugged on my arm.

"Sure, no problem," Candace said with a puzzled look on her face. I could tell that she knew that Rita wasn't too happy with the idea of Candace being there.

While Rita and I was walking to our car, Rita said, "Um…were you ever gonna tell me about *that?*"

"About what?"

"About that! Her! Miss Thang!"

"Rita, there's absolutely nothing to tell. She's just an old friend. A couple of days ago, I ran into her at Randall Mall when I was with Taurus and I invited her to my church. There's nothing going on."

"Shawn, don't play with me. I saw how she was looking at you."

"I didn't see her looking at me in any certain way. Don't jump to conclusions."

"I'm not gonna jump to conclusions. But if she tries to slither her way onto what's mine, I will jump on her and bash her head in."

Seven

❖•❖•❖

(Joy)

CLAY IS THE man. These two months with him have been the best two months that I've ever had. I wake up every morning, thinking about him. He has spent so much time with me and has made me feel like a queen. We talk on the phone for hours and he always have something positive to say about me.

He hasn't said anything about having a relationship with me but I'm sure that we're getting to that point. Besides, when I introduced him to one of my friends as my boyfriend, he didn't seem to mind it at all.

Taurus, on the other hand, has been calling my cell phone and leaving millions of messages as if he has lost his damn mind. Each message is as dumb as the last one. Most of them sound like this: *"Joy, this is Taurus. Where have you been? I'm worried about you. I've been calling you and calling you and you haven't returned any of my calls. Why are you not calling me back?"*

Or I would get messages like this: *"Joy, I think you're being extremely childish! I don't appreciate you ignoring me like this!"* With each message, I laughed my tail off. As far as I'm concerned, I don't want Taurus anymore. My time with him was great but I'm moving on. I'm a young woman and I don't wanna spend my young years with a man who can't fully commit to me because he has other "obligations."

Not only that, but I got sick and tired of being someone's lil' secret. And I guess it took me being with Clay for me to realize that. *Humph.* How foolish I was to think that I could have a future with a married man. My friend Monica was right.

The first time I told her about me being with Taurus, she said, "Joy, I'm not trying to condone what you're doing with this man. And you don't need me to tell you how wrong it is for you to be getting involved with him. But if you're gonna do wrong, at least do it right."

"What do you mean?" I asked.

"If you're gonna mess with a married man, at least have the common sense to know that it is what it is. Know the rules."

"What are you talking about? What do you mean by 'the rules'?"

"Joy, there are four rules when it comes to messing around with a married man that every woman should know, if they want to do something as disgraceful as that. The first rule that you must know is that he is not gonna leave his wife for you. That's the bottom line. If you think that he is, please put that thought outta your head because it ain't gonna happen. And even if he *does* leave his wife for you, he will do the same thing to you. So please don't bother to pick up a notebook and a pen and start planning y'all future together because it's not going down like that. The second rule to messing around with a married man is that the ball is in his court, meaning that he is entitled to deal with you however he wants. If he decides to not call you or visit you for a few days or a few weeks, you don't have the right to question him about it. He's not your man. He doesn't have to spend the holidays with you if he doesn't want to and more than likely, he probably won't. He can kick you to the curb if he feels like it and you don't have the right to get upset about it. The third rule is that it's all about the sex, sex, sex."

"Oh, please. It's not all about that, Monica. He takes me out, buy me things like shoes, clothes, jewelry…"

"And he's doing all of that, just so that he can get the sex, sex, sex. Duh! When he buys you things and takes you out, he's making an investment in you. That's all. When someone makes an investment, they want to make sure that they are making an investment into something that they can make good on. Nobody wants to invest their time and money into something and don't have anything to show for it. So therefore, if he's gonna buy you this and buy you that and you ain't even his wife, you can best believe he's gonna expect something in return. And what he's gonna want in return is some of your goodies. Now, if you wanna give up the booty just to get some cute shoes, that's your business. But he is not gonna invest money into you, just so that you two can cuddle. And the fourth rule is that your emotions are not an option."

"What do you mean?"

"Don't get emotionally attached. That's just a complete waste of your time because he is not gonna get emotionally attached to *you*. If he wants to deal with emotions, he has a wife at home."

When I thought about it, all of what she was saying was true but I was so dumb, that I didn't care. But now that I'm spending time with Clay, I now realize that I want my *own* man. There's no way that I would ever want Taurus back. His fat wife can have him all she wants. Besides, he's thirty-five years old. He's way too old for me.

For it to be a Friday night, it didn't seem to be very busy, downtown. Clay and I decided to double date with Monica and her new boyfriend, Todd. So I picked a restaurant that all four of us could meet at and just have a good time.

But the minute that Monica and Todd walked into the restaurant, I knew something wasn't right. Neither one of them was smiling and Monica's eyes were red as if she'd been crying.

"Hey girl! What's up?" I said, trying to lighten the mood.

"Nothing much," Monica answered, softly. Monica's boyfriend didn't say a word. He just grabbed the menu and started looking at it as if nothing was wrong.

To break the tension, Clay said to Todd, "So...uh...I heard that you got a new job in Maple Heights, doing work on a construction site. How do you like it so far?"

"I don't work there anymore," Todd stated, without even looking up from his menu.

"So where do you work?" I asked.

"I don't work anywhere."

Monica intervened and said, "He's actually looking to do something else that he's more comfortable doing."

"Oh. What is it that you're comfortable doing?" Clay asked.

Todd answered, "I wanna be a rapper. I'm working on my CD and I'm trying to get it played in the clubs."

I asked, "Are you serious?"

"Hell yeah. Why wouldn't I be?"

"Well, the entertainment business is a very hard business to break into. It may take a long time for you to finally make money off of it. How long have you wanted to do this?"

"Not long at all. One day, I was watching TV and I saw a music video by DMX and I decided right then and there that I wanted to do what he's doing."

"Right then and there, huh?" Clay asked.

"He's been at home, practicing his rhymes in the mirror and he seems to be really good," Monica stated, trying to show him support.

Clay gave me a funny look and then he said, "Well...uh...Todd, can you show off your skills for us right now?" I kicked Clay's leg under the table because I really didn't wanna hear any of Todd's rhymes but Todd went ahead and granted Clay's wish. Todd went into this God-awful rap that was worse than a migraine headache. It went like this:

"Pockets full of cash. That's what I need.
I got lots of ho's and a lot of weed.
I have a tight ride and my pockets are phat.
So don't hate on me 'cause I'm all that.
I gotta big house with a lake in the back.
I know you wanna be me, but you're too wack.
Me and my girl eat steak and shrimp.
And all the ho's want me 'cause they know I'ma pimp."

Unbelievable. That was the worse rap that I've ever heard. I couldn't believe that he actually considered putting that mess on a CD. And after he said his rap, he had the nerve to lean back in his chair as if what he just did, moved the earth. I looked over at Monica and she looked as if she was so embarrassed. I guess I would be too if I was dating an idiot.

"Well, I guess we need to go ahead and order something to eat," Clay said, as he picked up his menu.

"Mmmm. The pecan-crusted tilapia sounds good," Monica said as she was looking at her menu, "I think I'll try that."

"No. You need to have a salad," Todd said to her.

"But that's not what I want."

"But that's what I'm paying for and as long as I'm paying for it, you will eat whatever I tell you to eat."

Then I said," Monica, can you come with me to the bathroom for a second? I have something to show you."

"Sure. Okay," she answered.

When we walked into the bathroom, I leaned up against the wall and asked her, "Monica, why are you dealing with someone like this?"

"What do you mean?"

"First of all, his so-called rap skills are absolutely terrible and he doesn't even respect you enough to let you order your own meal. Is he always like this?"

"Oh girl, you trippin'. He just wants me to lose a few pounds. That's all. He said that I'm gaining weight."

"Who cares! Truth be told, you *need* to gain some weight. You're already a size four. It's *your* body. Not his. He doesn't have the right to tell you to lose weight. Instead of him worrying about your weight, he needs to worry about his weak rhymes."

"Leave him alone. Joy. He's gonna be somebody. You'll see."

"See what? Monica, he was sitting at the table, rapping about stuff that he don't even have. What he rapped about was a fantasy."

"Don't they all rap like that?"

"No. Mos Def doesn't rap about that mess and neither does Common. They made a name for themselves by just *being* themselves. Todd was rappin' about ho's and his so-called big house. *What* big house? According to you, he lives in the projects with his mama and his uncle."

"So what, Joy! At least he has a dream that he's trying to pursue! He isn't a preppy college boy, like Clay."

I crossed my arms and looked at her in total disgust. Then I said, "At least Clay wants to educate himself and he doesn't have the maturity of a fifth-grader."

"Are you sayin' that Todd is stupid?"

"Hell yeah! Not only that, he's lazy. He quit a good-paying job to do something that he's not even good at. Then, he has the nerve to treat you as if you're under his feet. Shouldn't that bother you? At least Clay can stand on his own two feet. If it wasn't for you helping Todd put together his resume and teaching him what the word 'resume' meant, he would not have had a job in the first place."

"That's enough, Joy. You have crossed the line. He may not be the man of my dreams but he's still *my* man and I don't appreciate you talking about him like that." Then she stormed outta the bathroom and I followed behind her, still trying to talk some sense into her.

When we reached our table, she grabbed her sweater and said to Todd, "Baby, let's eat at home. I'll cook you a big steak."

"Cool. I didn't wanna come to this stupid restaurant, anyway," Todd said as he was getting up outta his chair, "Fix me a bake potato with my steak too. And make sure that it's right."

"Of course, sweetheart." Then they started walking outta the restaurant, hand in hand. Monica looked back at me and rolled her eyes. I took a deep sigh and sat down at the table.

"What just happened?" Clay asked me.

I looked at my menu and said, "Let's just order something to eat."

I forgot that I was in charge of the decorations for a play that the church was putting together for the month of May so when I showed up late, a lot of the work was already done. So after about an hour of putting the finishing touches on certain things, I said good-bye to everyone and headed for the door.

As I was walking to the parking lot, I saw Taurus leaning up against his car as if he was waiting for someone. How stupid I was to think that I could simply walk to my car in peace and Taurus wouldn't bother me.

I heard him walking right behind me so I turned around and asked, "Taurus, what do you want?"

He said, "Well, well, well. I'm surprised that you even remember my name. Why haven't you called me back? I've been leaving you several messages."

"Taurus, I'm busy and I most certainly don't have time to *waste* time with you."

"Humph. I guess now that you're hangin' around that uppity negro, I'm a waste of your time, all of a sudden. You wasn't sayin' all of that when we was sleeping together."

"That was then. Things have changed. Taurus, there was no future with us so I have decided to move on."

"Humph. It's kinda hard to move on when everyone knows your business."

I looked at him like he was crazy. "Taurus, what in the world are you talking about?"

"If I went and told everybody what went down between us, it will put you in a bad light and make you look like trash."

"Ha! Brotha, you can do whatever you like. I will not stop you. Just in case you didn't know, if you tell everyone my business you will also be telling *yours*. Not only that, Brenda would have your head on a platter and my dad will swiftly kick you outta the church and you will have the reputation of being a cheater. I may catch a lil' backlash but that will only be if I admit to anything. It's my word against yours and considering that nobody has ever seen me hanging with you and everyone has seen me with Clay, nobody is gonna believe a word you say."

"Oh, really? Did you forget that I have your number? I can show people that and they will know that we've been involved with each other."

I laughed and said, "Are you really that stupid? Almost *everyone* in this church has my number. You're not proving anything by telling everyone that you have my number. Taurus, just accept the fact that I'm with someone that I really want to be with. So I really would appreciate it if you would leave me alone."

"Well, I…"

"Taurus, do yourself a favor and get a life. Stop wasting your time trying to come up with some way to drag me thru the mud. You'll only be hurting yourself." After that, I politely walked to my car, leaving Taurus standing there looking like a big fool.

Eight

————◆•••◆————

(Taurus)

THIS IS NOT how it was supposed to be. Joy 1was on *my* turf so therefore, she was supposed to play by *my* rules. I don't know who this Clay person think he is but he's not gonna take over. Joy is mine. No man is supposed to step on another man's territory and as far as I'm concerned, Joy is not leaving me unless *I* say so. *I'm* the one that's in charge of this situation. Not her. And certainly, not Clay. This ain't over and I guarantee it.

I was at home, writing a couple of chapters for my next novel when I received a phone call from Brenda, saying, "I'm gonna need you to pick up the kids from school, today."

"Why?" I asked.

"Because a heated argument almost became physical between two of my employees at my salon and I'm gonna have a meeting with the entire staff, today."

I sighed and said, "Okay but don't be too late. I have lots of work to do and I really don't need any interruptions."

"Interruptions? Your kids are not an interruption, Taurus. They are your responsibility just like they're my responsibility. *I* was the one that pushed their big-headed behinds outta my womb. The least you can do is pick them up from school without making a fuss about it."

"Can you please stop it with the whole speech? I told you okay."

"Okay. Just make sure that you get them."

When I arrived at my kids' school, Dillon and Kiera were waiting outside and when I pulled up, they ran to the car and jumped in. "Hi dad!" they both said.

"Hello, kids," I answered. "How was school?"

"Great. We made puppets. See?" Kiera said as she pulled a red cloth with plastic eyes, from her book bag.

"It's cute, sweetheart. Take care of it. Dillon, did you pass your spelling test?"

"Yep," he answered, "And the teacher said that she's proud of me."

I smiled and said, "Well, I'm proud of you, too. Keep up the good work."

Dillon and Kiera were steadily talking my ear off when all of a sudden, they got really quiet. Then I heard them whispering to each other and Kiera let out a giggle.

"What are you guys doing back there?" I asked.

Dillon said, "We found these under your seat. Does mama know that she left them in your car?"

When I turned around, Dillon was dangling a pair of pink, satin panties between his two fingers. I recognized them to be Joy's panties from when we had sex in my car, months ago. Here was my son, dangling the evidence of my discretion, in my face. I quickly snatched the panties from Dillon and placed them in my jean pocket.

How in the world was I gonna get myself out of this mess? Although my kids are innocent and don't know any better, they still have the tendency to open their mouths and say things that they shouldn't say and they might slip up and say something in front of Brenda, about what they found in my car.

So to prevent a disaster from happening and to get them to forget what they saw, I asked, "Would you both like some pizza for dinner?"

"Yeah!" they both shouted.

"Okay. I'll pick it up on our way home."

For the rest of the ride home, everything was okay. When we got home, the kids almost broke their necks, trying to get some pizza. "Wash your hands before you guys sit down to eat," I explained.

"Okay," they both said.

To be honest, spending this type of quality time with my kids was pretty nice. I've been so busy writing novels, going on book tours and having book signings that I haven't spent a lot of time with them. So I'm kinda glad that Brenda asked me to pick them up from school because I realized what I was missing out on.

After the kids washed their hands, they ran to the dinner table to sink their teeth into some pizza. I ate dinner with them and listened to their stories of what they've been up to at school and who they have a crush on. It was funny, listening to them. About an hour later, Brenda walked thru the door and saw the kids and me at the kitchen table.

"Hi, sweethearts," she said to the kids as she walked over to the dinner table and gave them both a hug. Then she leaned over and gave me a kiss and said, "Thanks for picking the kids up from school."

I smiled and said, "Sit down, baby. Have some dinner. I'm sure that you've had a long day."

"You can say that again," she said as she pulled her jacket off and sat down.

"So what happened at the salon with the two employees?"

"Well, one of the girls stole a customer from the other and of course, you're not supposed to do that."

"Oh, I see. So what did you do?"

"I penalized the girl who stole the customer by increasing her booth rent for a month."

"Ouch! Well, I guess that's the right thing to do."

"So what have you guys been up to?" Brenda asked the kids.

"Nothing," Kiera said.

"What about you, Dillon? How was school today?"

"It was fine, mommy," Dillon replied.

Then Kiera blurted, "Mama, you left your panties in daddy's car."

Brenda snapped a look at me. I knew that my life was over. Then she looked back at Kiera and asked, "What are you talking about?"

"Me and Dillon found your panties in daddy's car. But don't worry, mommy. We didn't lose them. We gave them to daddy."

I looked down at my plate and I didn't know what to say. Brenda's eyes were burning right thru me. My heart was beating so fast that I thought that I was gonna have a heart attack. *What am I supposed to do now?* I thought to myself.

Then Brenda looked back at the kids and said, "Go to your rooms."

"Awww, man. Do we have to?" Dillon whined.

"Yes, you have to! Go! Right now!"

After the kids scurried to their rooms, Brenda shot me a look that could've melted all the skin off of my face. "What are the kids talking about, Taurus? *What* panties?"

"It's nothing, Brenda. I have no idea where they came from. I was shocked to see them, myself. I was gonna ask you if they belonged to you," I lied.

"*Humph.* Oh, really? Where are these panties, Taurus?"

I pulled the panties out of my pocket and said, "See? These look like yours. I don't know how they got in my car."

She took the pink, silk panties from my hand and said, "Okay. Thank you, baby." Then she smiled and gave me a kiss before she headed upstairs to our bedroom.

Damn! That was easy, I thought to myself. I let out a deep sigh and put my head on the table, thanking God that things didn't get too drastic. I slept thru the night with Brenda's arm around me. That was a relief for me because then I knew that everything was okay and that I had dodged a bullet.

When morning came, I felt Brenda slither out of the bed but I didn't budge. A couple of hours went by and I was still resting, peacefully. That is, until I heard something click in my ear. I immediately opened my eyes and when I rolled over, Brenda was standing over me with a nine-millimeter gun, pointed at my face. I didn't even know she owned a gun. I was scared to death…and shocked.

I asked her, "Baby…uh…what are you doing?"

"I'm getting to the truth, by any means necessary. Bring your behind downstairs, right now," she demanded, with the gun still pointed at me.

I slowly got up outta bed, afraid that if I took my eyes off of her for one second, I would catch a bullet to my brain. As I was walking, she put the gun to my head and directed me to sit down at the kitchen table. When I did, the pink panties were sitting on the kitchen table.

She sat across from me with the gun still in her hand and she said, "I want you to take a look at these panties and then take a look at me."

I did what she told me to do and then I carefully asked, "What's the problem?"

"The problem is that these panties are for some skinny hepha. You know damn well that these are not my panties. You must think I'm stupid. First of all, I am way too thick to squeeze my behind in a pair of these. Secondly, I wouldn't be caught dead wearing something that ugly. Thirdly, we've never had sex in you car because as far as I'm concerned, you're too boring to be spontaneous. So who the hell does these panties belong to, Taurus? And you betta be honest if you wanna keep your head on your shoulders."

I sighed and said, "Baby, I don't know."

She shot her gun and when she did, a bullet grazed my ear which had me in a tremendous amount of pain. Then she yelled, "Do you think I'm playing with you!? I will blow your head off, Taurus!"

"Okay! I had sex with another woman. But she didn't mean anything to me. It only happened once."

"Who is she? When did this happen?"

"She was this woman that I met at a club. We had a one-night stand," I lied.

"A one-night stand?"

"Yes. We had sex in my car. But we never saw each other again after that."

"And when did this happen?"

"Months ago. Brenda, I didn't mean for this to happen. It only happened one time. I love you and there is no one else that I want to spend the rest of my life with."

She stared at me for a long time and walked away from the kitchen table with her gun still in her hand and took the panties with her. She stomped up the stairs to our bedroom and slammed the door behind her. And while she was upstairs, I didn't move a muscle from the kitchen table. After about several hours, she came down the stairs with three suitcases in her hand.

I ran to her and I said, "Brenda, I love you. Please don't go."

She let out a little giggle and said to me, "Brotha, I'm not going anywhere. *You* are. These are *your* things."

I let out a sigh and I said, "Baby, you don't wanna do this. We have a wonderful life together. Yes, I know that I messed up but I still love you. You are my everything."

"I don't wanna hear it, Taurus. Save all that talkin' and get the walkin'."

"But baby, where do I go?"

She swung the pink panties around her fingers and said, "Here's a tip: Whoever is the owner of these nasty panties, that's where you need to go."

Then she opened the front door and stood next to it, waiting for me to leave. *Maybe if I give her a few days to cool off, this will all blow over and things will go back to normal,* I thought to myself. "Well, can I at least put my clothes on before I leave?" I asked.

"No," she replied. "Go put them on in your car, since you like to do everything else in your car."

"C'mon, Brenda. I…"

"I'm not playing, Taurus! Get out! I don't wanna hear anything you have to say!"

I stared at her and saw the tears forming in her eyes and I knew that at this moment, nothing I could say or do would change anything. I slowly grabbed my bags and walked out of the door. She slammed the door behind me and I was left outside with three suitcases and a pair of boxers on my behind that I slept in.

I got in my car and drove for miles until I realized that I didn't have anywhere else to go. I stopped at a gas station's bathroom and put some clothes on my almost-naked behind. I couldn't believe that this was happening to me.

After I picked me up something to eat, I went and paid for a room at a lodge in Shaker Heights. I had my laptop with me to finish my novel but my thoughts were so cloudy, that I couldn't even concentrate. This was the worst day of my life.

Nine

(Rita)

My hair was looking a hot mess all this week so I made an appointment to see my hairstylist Yvette at her hair salon, Friday morning. When I went to my appointment, Yvette and I had our girl talk, as usual.

She's the main person that I talk to about a lot of things because she's not judgmental and half of the things that I've gone thru, she's went thru them as well. She even knows about my secret relationship with Taurus. For several years, she's been my best friend.

"Hey girl!" she greeted me, as I walked into her salon.

"Hi, Yvette! How has life been treating you? You look great!" I said, as I sat down in her booth.

"Thanks! I've been on this new diet where I don't eat nothing but fruits and vegetables for breakfast, lunch and dinner for ninety days. It has cleansed my system out and so far, I've lost at least fifteen pounds."

"Girl, that's wonderful. I'm proud of you."

Yvette was done with my hair in about two hours but I stayed longer, just to hang out. We ate lunch and since she didn't have any other appointments for the remainder of the day, we sat and chatted about things that had been going on in our lives.

"So how are things between you and Shawn? I remember that you said that you were having issues with his mama," Yvette stated as she took a sip of her tea.

I gave a half-smile and said, "Well, things are getting better. His mom was a major problem. I had to do something drastic in order for him to get the picture that he needed to do something about her."

"What drastic measure did you take?"

"I threw his mama outta the house."

She almost choked on her tea when I said that. "You did what?!" she asked.

"You heard me. One morning, she pushed my buttons really bad and I literally put her out of the house. I got sick and tired of taking all kinds of mess off of her."

"But doesn't she have her own house?"

"Yes, but she was staying with us for a few weeks because her kitchen was being remodeled."

"Oh, I see. What did Shawn say when you threw her out?"

"He was extremely upset with me and had the nerve to put me out of the house."

She looked at me as if I was crazy. "Are you serious? He threw *you* out?"

"Yep. But I showed back up at the house and made him take me back in. I told him that I wasn't going anywhere. I told him that I got tired of his mother disrespecting me and that he needed to do something about it."

"So did he?"

"I think so. I haven't seen her since I've been back. So I guess he had a talk with her and set her straight."

She took another sip of her tea and said, "Well, don't feel bad. I went thru the same thing with my husband, Charles."

"For real?"

"Girl, yes. His mama was staying with us and she was *supposed* to stay with us, permanently. But I couldn't deal with her. She was constantly telling me how to cook, how to clean, how to raise my kids and I has enough of it. And then one day, I was putting up some new drapes into the living room and she had the nerve to say, 'Who told you to put up those drapes? This is my son's house. You need to ask him, first."

"Girl, she said that to you?"

"Yes, she did. So I said to her, 'I don't have to ask his permission. This is my house also and I really would appreciate it if you would respect that.' Then she had the nerve to say, 'I don't have to respect you. If it wasn't for my son marrying your behind, you wouldn't even be here.' I wanted to snatch her by her face and throw her up against the wall."

"So did you?"

She laughed, flipped her red-tinted weave away from her face and said, "No, but I did bring it to Charles' attention. I told him that I was fed up with her and that I needed him to do something about it. And he did."

"What did he do?"

She took a sip of her tea and said, "Two days later, he put her old behind in a nursing home. What a relief. Our marriage has been so much better since he did that. Even our sex life has been better."

I laughed and said, "Well, I guess that's a good thing."

"You better believe it. So are you still messing around with Taurus?"

"Yeah but for the past week, I haven't been able to reach him. He didn't even come to church on Sunday. I hope he's okay."

"Girl, I'm sure it's nothing. You know how men are. He probably just needs some space."

"Well, I hope that's all it is."

My mother and I have never had a close relationship. We've always seemed to bump heads because we are so much alike. The way I am is because of her. For years, we've only spoken to each other on the holidays but for the most part, we've kept our distance from each other.

So it was very surprising when she called me early in the morning, saying, "Hi, baby. How are you doing?"

I was almost at a loss for words. "I'm fine," I replied.

"Well...uh...how is your day?"

"Mama, it's seven o'clock in the morning. My day hasn't even started yet."

She laughed a nervous laugh and said, "Rita, I know that we have our differences but I really need to talk to you. It's important. Can you come over?"

"Why can't you just tell me over the phone?"

"Because what I have to say to you, really needs to be said in person. Honey, I'm begging you. Let us sit down and talk. I really need to see you."

I let out a deep sigh and I said, "Okay but it will have to be tomorrow morning. I have too much to do today."

"That's fine, sweetie. I love you."

Did she just say 'I love you?' I thought to myself. "Same here," I said.

When the next morning came, I was kinda dragging my feet to get to mama's house. I though to myself, *What in the world does she want to talk to me about?* All these years, she's acted like I was an interruption in her life. All my mama ever cared about was the men that were constantly coming in and out of her house. She had a revolving door that swung so much, I thought that it was gonna swing right off the hinges.

This is the same woman that slept with her sister's husband and she even messed around with my dad's best friend for several years when I was a child. And for all of my life, she made it clear that her life was much more important than mine.

Men have always been crazy about her because of her beauty. She knew how to swivel those hips to make the men's nature rise. She was very seductive with exotic lips, sparkling hazel eyes, long black hair that swept the middle of her back when she walked, with glistening pecan-colored skin that didn't have a scar on it.

But her clothes were very sluttish because she always wore very short skirts, high heels and revealing blouses that showed off her cleavage and flat stomach. She was something else.

It took me longer than usual to drive to East Cleveland to see my mama, simply because I really wasn't looking forward to seeing her. But when I finally reached her doorstep, I noticed that something was different.

For starters, her blinds were closed and my mother has *never* closed her blinds. She never has done that, no matter what time of the day it was. And when I looked at her porch, she had stacks and stacks of newspapers at her door where the paperboy had thrown them. They weren't even touched.

I ranged her doorbell and after a long wait, she finally opened the door. When I saw her, I almost cried. She was wearing a black sweater around her very frail body and she barely had any hair on her head. When her eyes finally met mine, I saw that her eyes were so sunken into her face that she looked like she was knocking on death's door. I didn't know what to say.

With a soft-spoken voice, she asked, "Well, aren't you gonna give me a hug?"

After staring at her, I finally gave her a hug and tried my best to fight back the tears. But I lost the fight. I cried like a baby when I hugged her. Her bones seemed like they were gonna crumble in my arms.

She ushered me inside and said, "Come upstairs with me."

When I walked into her house, I noticed that she hadn't done any dusting in a very long time. There was dust, even on the plastic fruit that was sitting in a bowl on her dining room table. And considering that her blinds were closed, the house was very dark and gloomy.

There wasn't one light on and the silence in the house was very loud. When we walked upstairs to her bedroom, I almost lost my breath, looking at the display of medicine bottles sitting on her nightstand. Then she crawled into her bed that she was obviously laying in before I came.

She took a deep sigh and said, "Sweetheart, I'm dying. I don't have long to live."

"What? I don't understand this. Mama, you've always been very healthy."

"Well, a few months ago, I was diagnosed with cervical cancer. The doctors said that it was too late to try to do anything about it because I'm in the last stage of it. So I told the doctors that I didn't wanna live my last days at the hospital and that I wanted to spend them at home."

I wiped the tears from my eyes and said, "Mama, I'm so sorry that you are going thru this. You don't deserve this."

She grabbed my hand and said, "Yes I do, Rita. I've lived a life with no boundaries. I did any and everything that I was big and bad enough to do, regardless of whether or not it would hurt anyone. God is paying me back for all of that."

"Don't say that, mama."

"Baby, it's true. There's absolutely no way that a person can live their life the way that I did and think that they won't reap what they sow. That's why I didn't get upset when the doctor told me that there wasn't anything that they could do because I knew that this was God's way of letting me know that I had to pay for all of my wrongdoing. See, when God is trying to get your attention, he will get your attention by any means necessary. I've done a lot of wrong to so many people and that includes my sister, Betty. I knew better than to sleep with her husband and I knew that it would hurt her tremendously. But I did it anyway because I was selfish and thoughtless."

"But mama, that was so, so many years ago. I was a little girl when that happened. None of that even matters anymore. Besides, you and Betty haven't even spoken to each other since that took place."

"Well, not exactly. I reunited with Betty around the same time that I found out that I had cancer. She knows that I'm dying."

"How did she react when she saw you?"

"We cried when we saw each other and she gave me a big hug and told me how much she loved me."

"She did? I would've thought that she wouldn't want to ever see you again."

Mama smiled and said, "I thought so, too. But once we sat down and talked for a while, I realized that there was something really different about her. It was like she had a glow about her. She told me that her husband died four years ago, she sold her liquor store and decided to give her life over to the Lord. Now, she's a minister and she speaks at churches all over the world. I couldn't believe it, Rita. She told me that she missed me and that she loved me so much."

"Wow. Did you guys talk about that situation that happened between you and her husband?"

"Of course. But to my surprise, she said that she forgave me and that she still loved me very much."

"Really?"

"Yes. But honestly, I was really reluctant to hear what she had to say about God because I thought that I did way too much wrong to ever have God in

my life. I thought that I wasn't good enough for God to love and forgive me,"
Mama started to cry and then she said, "But when my sister ministered to me,
I realized that God has always loved me and that He still does. Rita, I could've
been dead, long, long time ago. But God loved me so much, that He was willing to show me mercy even when I was out there in the world, doing wrong.
I realized just how wonderful God is. So after reuniting with Betty, she led
me to Jesus and now, I'm saved. I found a church home but nowadays, I'm
too weak to get out of bed so I study the Word at home and a friend of mine
stops by my church and buy me a copy of each sermon so that I can listen to
them. Rita, I've never been so happy in all my life."

"Mama, how can you say that you're happy when you're dying?"

"Because I've made peace with God and if he decides to call me home
tomorrow, I'm overjoyed in knowing that I will be in heaven with the Lord.
I'm not scared to die, Rita. I will have everlasting life in heaven and nothing
on this earth is better than that."

"But mama, why did you wanna see me?"

"Because I want to warn you, baby. Get right with God."

I was a lil' defended but anxious to know what she meant. "What makes
you think that I'm not right with God?" I asked.

With tears still in her eyes, she said, "Because I know you, baby. You have
always been like me, which is why we have never gotten along. Your ways are
my ways. The minute you became grown and on your own, I noticed that you
were picking up all of my bad habits and I want to warn you before you end
up with a life full of suffering. Put God first in your life so that you can really
experience the goodness of Him."

"But mama, I can't change my ways. I'm in too deep."

"Baby, you are never in too deep that God can't clean you up."

"But I'm a wife of a Pastor. I'm a first lady of the church. Shouldn't that
be good enough for God?"

"Sweetheart, there are gonna be a lot of first ladies and pastors that will
go thru a lot of hell because of their wicked ways. Your title will not save
you from God's wrath. When you decide to accept Christ into your life and
devote your life to Him, that's when you will be able to see Him working
in your life and you will see yourself changing for the better. He knows that
you're not perfect and He won't ask you to be. All you have to do is open your
heart to Him."

"But I do things in the church. I help organize church meetings, I make
sure that the choir is wearing the colors that they are supposed to wear, I serve
breakfast every Sunday…"

"Do you do all of that out of obligation of being the first lady or do you
do it because you love God?"

I really didn't know how to answer that. Surely, mama was not someone that I needed to be listening to. She's done wrong all of her life and now all of a sudden she thinks that God is on her side. Does she honestly think that God will just forget about her past and be willing to accept her, faults and all? There's no way.

Ten

(Shawn)

"HI, SHAWN. HOW are you doing?" my cousin Darlene said to me as she sat down in my office at the church.

"Fine. How much do you need?" I quickly asked. I already knew that she only came to my office to see if she can get some money from me. She *never* visits me unless she wants something.

She asked, "What makes you think that I want something?"

"Because I know you."

"Well, at least I did ask you how you were doing, Shawn. You didn't even bother to ask *me*."

I took a deep sigh while looking up at the ceiling and I asked, "Darlene, how are you doing?"

"I'm fine. Same ol' stuff. The kids are walking around with long faces, though."

I heard myself ask, "Why?"

"Well, because they can't go to camp this summer. I can't afford to send them. So they'll be spending their summer vacation at home. It's a shame that they can't go but I have bills to pay. If I just knew how to get the money, I would love to send them. I feel kinda bad that they can't go, but..."

"Darlene, the answer is no."

"No? I didn't even ask you for anything."

"But I know that you're about to. That's why you're throwing out lil' hints and giving me a sob story."

"A sob story? How can you talk to me like that?!"

"Because it's the truth, Darlene. At least twice a month, you ask me for money for this and money for that. Several times, I have helped you with your rent, light bill, gas bill, food, milk and diapers. It's time that you stand on your own two feet and be responsible."

"Excuse me?! What makes you think that I'm not being responsible?! Who are you to tell me what to do?! You don't have all the answers, Shawn. Just because you're some *high and mighty* Pastor, don't mean that you're better than me."

"I never said that I was better than you."

"But you're acting like you are. I may not have a bunch of money like *you* do but that doesn't mean that I'm a piece of crap. I'm trying to take care of these kids, Shawn. You're not facing the problems that I'm facing. It's hard out here and ain't nobody even trying to help me out. The least you can do is give me help instead of acting like I'm a burden."

I felt myself getting a migraine. Darlene has that affect on people. I said to her, "I want you to listen to me; Darlene, I've given you lots of advice on how to better your situation because I love you. But instead of listening to me, you popped out more babies and kept on dealing with the same ol' no-good men, who filled your head up with lies. When you told me that you wanted to go to college, I was the main one in your corner. I paid for your books and put money towards your tuition. You were in school for two weeks, dropped out and when I asked you why, you came up with some lame excuse, saying, 'Shawn, I was just tired.' When you made the foolish decision to buy an entertainment center with your rent money, I was the one that came to your rescue and prevented you from being evicted. I tried to get you to see a financial advisor so that you would know how to take care of yourself, financially. You went to *one* meeting, got mad at the man because he was try-ing to tell you what you needed to do to better your financial situation and you never went back. All your life, you expected for things to be handed to you and never wanted to work for anything. Darlene, you are almost twenty-nine years old. When are you gonna get your life together?"

"You go to hell! You don't have the right to turn your nose up at me! I'm doing the best I can, trying to take care of these kids by myself."

"I'm not turning my nose up at you. I'm giving you some tough love because you need it. Stop using your kids as an excuse for not wanting to work hard and make something of yourself. There are many women who have children but they are not sitting at home, waiting for someone to give them a handout. Many single moms have been determined to go to school and make something of themselves so that they can create a better life for their children."

"Are you sayin' that they're better than me?"

"No I'm not, Darlene. What I'm sayin' is that they were willing to do whatever was necessary to get their lives together because they didn't wanna be just another welfare case. They wasn't expecting for other people to take care of them. Look at the type of example that you are setting for your kids; they see that you have six baby daddies, one of them is in prison for murder and the other five are drug dealers. None of them help you with the kids and they don't even bother to spend time with them. Many times you have left the kids at home by themselves while you went out to the club with your friends and didn't come home until the next morning. Don't you know how dangerous that is? You put your friends and stupid men before your own children. Don't you realize that you are not setting a good example for them? If you don't try to change your situation, your two sons will grow up thinking that it's okay to make babies all over the place and not take care of them. They will think that being a thug is how they are supposed to be. They will think that it's okay. And your four daughters will think that it's fine to have a bunch of kids by different men that are not father material and that it's normal to expect handouts and not work. Is this how you want your kids to end up?"

She sighed and said, "No but it is what it is. Once my kids get grown, they're on their own. They will be entitled to make their own decisions. I won't be responsible for their actions."

"But you are responsible for them, *now*. And the way you live your life will have a major impact on your kids and not in a good way. Whether you believe it or not, you *are* responsible for how your kids turn out because you're their parent and for a long period of time, they will only know only what they've been taught."

"So what are you sayin', Shawn? Are you trying to say that I'm not a good mother?"

I sighed again and said, "What I am saying is that you should want to live a better life for your children and stop looking for someone to carry you."

"Shawn, you must've forgotten where you've come from. You didn't always have it together."

"Darlene, I can't ever forget where I've come from because everything that I've been thru, it made me who I am. I remember when I was out there in the streets, getting into all kinds of trouble and messing around with a bunch of women and treating them as if they were nothing. But after a few years of making bad choices, I realized that if I didn't change my ways, I would either be dead or in jail. And now, my life is so much better because I decided back then, that I *wanted* to live a better life. God has put me in a position where I can be a blessing to others and that includes you. But don't act like I owe you something, Darlene. I don't owe you anything. Where were you when I was struggling and had to go several days with barely any food to eat? I had to work very hard to get where I am and I'm not ashamed to be successful. Things turned around for me because I decided to make the choice to change.

I can't make that choice for you. You are the only one that is responsible for your successes and failures."

"Thanks for the after-school special," she said, sarcastically, "But I don't have time for all of this."

"See, that's your problem. You don't wanna listen to nobody. You create problems for yourself and then you expect everyone else to fix them. I'm not paying for your kids to go to camp and that's that. With all the money that you spend on getting your hair and nails done, you could've had the money to send them, yourself."

"Whatever, Shawn. I gotta go," she said as she stormed out of my office and slammed the door behind her. I put my head down on my desk, drained from all the energy it took for me to sit and talk to her crazy behind.

Out of all of Aunt Thelma's kids, her daughter Darlene was the one that everyone had high hopes for. In high school, she never got into trouble and she graduated at the top of her class. She got involved in many extracurricular activities, she studied the violin and she was even the captain of a chess club.

With such a brilliant mind, she was immediately accepted to Princeton University on a scholarship. I even remember how excited she was when she received her acceptance letter from them. After she graduated from high school, she decided to get a summer job so that she would have money in her pocket before she moved to New York to attend Princeton. She was on the right track in all aspects of her life.

That is, until she met a brotha named Raheem. She met him at a block party and he got into her head so bad that he was able to persuade her not go to college. In less than two weeks, she moved in with him and became pregnant. Aunt Thelma was extremely devastated.

But see, that's how the devil works; whenever your life is on the right track and you're on your way to being successful, that's when the devil steps in and set up all types of wicked schemes to distract you so that you can lose your focus.

Once Raheem found out that Darlene was pregnant, he threw her out of his apartment and she had to move back in with her mom. After her baby was born, another baby was on the way by a dude named Tariq that she met at a gas station. That's the one that's in jail for robbing and murdering a lady on E.55ᵗʰ Street.

Then there was baby daddy, number three; His name was Donte' and he was friends with Tariq. As soon as Tariq was sent to jail, that's when she hooked up with Donte' and had her third baby. She moved in with Donte' and he used to beat her for breakfast, lunch and dinner. Then he met another woman and forced Darlene to get out.

She again had to move back in with her mom but after a few months, Aunt Thelma got sick and tired of putting up with Darlene and her three kids. So she made Darlene apply for Section 8 so that she could move out and get her own place. After several months, Darlene and her kids moved out of her mama's house and into a two-family house on the west side of Cleveland.

But that didn't stop her from making more babies. There were three more baby daddies and they all treated her like crap, just like the previous men did. So here was a young, intelligent woman who had the world in the palm of her hands but she let all of her great opportunities fall thru the cracks because she let men become her distraction.

But over the years, me and the family have tried to help Darlene get her life back together but she's never became motivated enough to change her situation. All she did was make excuses for herself and make it seem like her problems are supposed to be *everybody's* problems.

Just like me, her brothers and sisters got sick and tired of bailing her out of trouble as well, so nowadays they really don't have much to say to Darlene. I just hope that one day, she wake up and smell the coffee and realize that it's *her* choice to live her life the way that she wants, whether it's in poverty or prosperity.

Life is crazy. Just when you think that you've seen everything, that's when life shocks you again. I conducted a church meeting with the leaders in the church, just to go over the budget to see if we could do some things differently that will help the church get a lil' better, financially.

See, I knew that the year 2002 would be just around the corner and I just wanted the church to start the New Year on the right track. And so far, the meeting was going very well and we were all on the same page. What I realized, was that the meeting went so well because Brenda wasn't there, which was *very* odd.

Brenda has always showed up to the church finance meetings, especially when it came to the church's money. And although her husband Taurus was present at the meeting, it seemed like his mind was elsewhere. I was gonna ask him about Brenda's whereabouts but the minute that I was going to, Brenda came storming thru the door and stood right in front of Taurus.

Then she asked him, "Did you tell the church what you did?"

Taurus stood up and whispered to her, "Baby, please don't cause a scene."

"Cause a scene?! You cheated on me and I'm not supposed to cause a scene?!"

Certain church leaders gasped and others mumbled under their breath. I said to her, "Brenda, let's talk into my office. Let's not bring this in front of everyone."

She said, "Why?! So that Taurus can continue to be a dog in private? Are you scared to let me tell everyone that the main Elder of the church is cheating on me?! You have no idea how badly this hurts! I've never done anything like this to him!"

I looked over at Taurus and he was looking down at the ground. I was so disappointed in what I was hearing. "Taurus, is this true?" I asked him.

Brenda intervened and said, "Yes, it's true! I have the evidence right here!" She reached into her purse and pulled out a pair of pink panties and let them hang on the tip of her finger for everyone to see. Then she threw them in Taurus' face.

"Brenda, that's enough!" Taurus yelled.

I looked over the conference room and I said, "This meeting is over. I need everyone to leave right now. Brenda and Taurus, I need you both to sit down."

When the room became empty, I looked over at Brenda and she was on the verge of tears. Brenda has always been a strong woman that has never showed an emotion towards anything so seeing her hurting like this, really made me sympathize with her. Even though Brenda is a moody, opinionated and aggressive person, she has always had a soft spot for Taurus.

Taurus looked over at Brenda and said, "Baby, I'm sorry. It was just one night. Stop overreacting."

Brenda reached over and sucker-punched Taurus right in his face. I stepped in and said, "Brenda, calm down."

After she took a deep breath and wiped the tears from her face, she looked over at Taurus and asked, "How can your cheating behind look me in my face and tell me to stop overreacting? You could've infected me with something! You're in this church, foolin' everyone into thinking that you are this God-fearing person that loves your family but yet you pulled this stunt behind my back. Had it not been for the kids exposing you, I would not have known anything and that's the thing that hurts the most. There's no doubt in my mind that your triflin' behavior would've continued if I hadn't found out anything. And for all I know, you're still messin' around on me!"

"Wait a minute, Brenda. What do you mean that the kids exposed him?" I asked.

She sighed and said, "The kids were the ones that found those nasty panties in his car."

I looked over at Taurus and he then gave me a look as if to say, 'I didn't mean for all of this to happen.' I said to Brenda, "I totally understand that you're hurt and angry. You have every right to feel the way that you are feeling right now and I will totally understand if you're confused about what you should do about this matter. But for right now, I want to speak to Taurus in private."

"Why are you giving him special treatment?"

"I'm not giving him special treatment. Believe me, I know that there's no excuse for what he did to you. He was wrong and God will deal with him on that. But as a man, I do know that sometimes we do stupid things because we really don't know how to express our feelings when we're unhappy about something. I'm not making any excuses for what he did but I want to talk to him, man to man."

She sighed and said, "Do whatever you want, Pastor. But as far as I'm concerned, I don't want anything to do with him." She then got up out of her seat and stormed out of the conference room, leaving me and Taurus to speak to each other.

I looked at Taurus and asked, "Brotha, why? I just wanna know why."

He looked at me and said, "Don't you remember how happy Brenda and I used to be? You remembered how we were when we first got together; we used to be crazy about each other. She used to tell me how much she loved me and how she thought that I was the most wonderful man in the world. Man, I felt needed. But now, she's a handful. We barely make love and I didn't feel appreciated anymore. She started to treat me as if I was one of the kids and then our marriage started to feel more like a business relationship. In the past, I've tried to explain to her that we needed to sit down and talk about some things but she never wanted to hear what I had to say. She would just blame *me* for things not going right in our marriage. What am I supposed to do?"

"You could've talked to me, Taurus. I would've understood and tried to help you save your marriage. I'm your friend. You could've told me that you were dealing with these issues in your marriage and I would've been more than willing to give you advice on what to do."

"I know but I was too ashamed to tell you that I was having problems in my marriage."

"Why? We've been friends for years. You shouldn't be ashamed to tell me anything. Rita and I have been thru some things in our marriage but I'm not ashamed at all. Things happen and sometimes, you may not even know why you're experiencing these things. But every couple goes thru some things. That's just how it is. Sometimes, it can get overbearing but that's no excuse to step out on your wife. I understand that you messed up and you're not perfect, but you're still in a position of leadership in the church. When you took on that responsibility, you knew that you had to lead by example."

"I know. This is the worst thing that I've ever done. I really messed up."

"I agree. But it's not the end of the world. You did mess up but I'm here to help you get thru this."

"Are you for real? You're not gonna turn your back on me?"

"Of course not. What kind of Pastor would I be to treat you like that? We *all* have issues in our life that we need to work on and as Christians, we have to learn to help one another get back on the right track. I'm not sayin' that its' gonna be easy but nothing is impossible with God. Anyway, I guess that you're not staying with Brenda so are you staying with someone right now?"

"No. I'm staying in a lodge."

"Oh, I see. Well, did you wanna stay with Rita and I? You know that I have an extra bedroom."

"Thanks but I'm okay. I just need to be by myself for a while."

"Are you sure? You're not gonna do anything stupid to yourself, are you?"

He gave a half-smile and said, "Of course not. I just need to take this time to get my mind right."

"I understand. Well, come by my house tomorrow and let's sit down and chat. I'm gonna help you thru this. And so is God."

Eleven

❖

(Joy)

MONICA AND I haven't spoken to each other since May, ever since we got into that heated argument in that restaurant. So I figured that I would be the bigger person and try to make up with her. Besides, she's my best friend.

I wasn't trying to tell her how to live her life; I was just trying to be a good friend and get her to see that she deserved to be treated a lot better than how that idiot was treating her.

So I decided to call her but her phone was disconnected. That's never happened before. Monica always kept her phone on at all times. But since I couldn't reach her, I called her mom instead.

Her mom answered the phone on the first ring and I could tell by the soft tone in her voice, that something was wrong. So I said, "Mrs. Truman, I had been trying to get in contact with Monica but her phone was disconnected. Is she over at your house?"

"No, sweetheart. I'm afraid not," she reluctantly answered.

"Oh. Well, can you give her a message for me?"

"Well…uh…I don't think I'll be able to do that."

"But why? What's wrong, Mrs. Truman?"

She started to cry and then she said, "Monica is in the hospital. Me and the family don't even know if she's gonna make it."

I felt my knees trembling and I started to breathe heavy from panicking. I asked, "Mrs. Truman, what's wrong with my friend? Why is she in the hospital?"

She took a long, deep breath, trying to get her composure together before answering my question. Then she asked, "Have you ever met Todd?"

"Yes," I answered, "About a month ago, she introduced him to me and my boyfriend. But I think that he's bad news."

"Well, you thought right. He hurt my daughter."

70

"What are you talking about?"

She sighed and said, "According to the neighbors, Todd and Monica got into a very heated argument inside the apartment. They said that they heard Todd yelling at her and calling her all kinds of names and that Monica was pleading with him to leave. He refused and the next thing they heard was Monica screaming and crying and things bumping up against the walls. They said that it sounded like he was trying to tear the place down. Somebody called the police and when they got over there, Todd opened the door but when he saw that it was the police, he tried to slam the door back but the police over-powered him and they got into the apartment. They said that his shirt was covered in blood and there was a bloody baseball bat, laying in the middle of the floor. There was blood all over the walls and they saw Monica slumped over in the corner of her living room, with lots of blood coming from her face."

"Did they arrest Todd?"

"Yes. He admitted that he beat her and they arrested him on the spot. He's in custody and he has been charged but that doesn't make me feel better about a damn thing. He's still alive while my beautiful daughter is laying in a hospital bed, hanging on for dear life."

"Mrs. Truman, when did this happen?"

"Two weeks ago."

"She's been in the hospital for two weeks?!"

"Yes…in a coma. Seeing her like that, really hurts me and the rest of the family. I just keep on praying that everything is gonna be okay and that she will have a full recovery. I'm just waiting on God to open her eyes."

I felt that I was gonna cry but I held back the tears to be strong for Mrs. Truman. "What hospital is she in?" I asked.

"She's at Cleveland Clinic. She's in the Intensive Care unit."

After I got off the phone with Mrs. Truman, I immediately started pray-ing to God. I didn't want Him to take my best friend away. We have known each other for years and have been thru everything together. When I broke my leg running track in high school, she used to come over to my house and eat dinner with me and my mom and make me feel better so that I wouldn't fall into a depression.

When this guy named Steven stood me up at the prom, she got all her male friends together and they beat the hell outta him and made him pay me back for all the money that I spent on my dress, hair, shoes, jewelry and make-up.

People used to think that we were related because we were so close to each other .I used to stick up for her in high school when girls wanted to fight her because of her dark-chocolate skin and her dreadlocks.

We were so close to each other that we even knew when one of us was happy, sad or if we were dealing with an issue. So for her to be in the hospital on the verge of death, it was like I just got slapped in the face. How dare he do something like this to my best friend!

See, Monica always had a problem picking the right boyfriends. Always. I remember that there was this guy named Andre' who used to steal money out of her purse to support his drug habit. He was a hot mess. The last straw was when he broke into her apartment and stole everything except the hair on her head.

With all the boyfriends that she had, they mistook her kindness as a sign of weakness and that's the reason why they've always walked all over her. But none of that matters right now. I'm not here to judge her. I just want my friend to be okay. She didn't deserve this.

On my way to the hospital, my heart was beating out of my chest by the thought of what was to come. I didn't know what to expect when I walked into her room. But when I did, the sight was too much to bear.

Monica was laying in the hospital bed with all kinds of tubes, sticking out of her body. Her eyes were black and blue and swollen shut and her head was bandaged up.

She had deep scratches on her nose and her lips were swollen. I couldn't believe what he did to her. It was like looking at a monster. I sat down next to her by her bedside and noticed all the scars on her arms and from the looks of her hands, she at least tried to fight back.

I spoke softly into her ear and said, "Monica, this is your best friend. I just want you to know that I'm here and that I love you. Please forgive me for the way that I acted towards you. I just want you to have the best because you *are* the best and you *deserve* the best. I want you to know that everything is gonna be okay. When you recover, girl, we are gonna throw a big, big party for you. Things are gonna be so much better. You just wait."

"Baby, what's wrong with you? Why aren't you eating your dinner?" Clay asked. We were eating fried tilapia at his dinner table at his apartment.

I replied, "Um, remember my friend, Monica?"

"Yeah, I remember. Have you guys made up?"

"Well, not exactly."

"What do you mean?"

"She's in the hospital. Her boyfriend beat her up really bad. She looks so bad, Clay."

"Are you serious?"

"Yes, I am. He beat her beyond recognition."

He leaned back in the chair and said, "Are you okay?"

"Yeah, I'm fine. It's just that this kind of news is a lot to handle."

"Humph. Well, I know about news being hard to handle; I met my father today, for the first time."

"What? How did you meet him?"

"He ran into my mom at a grocery store and she told him some things about me."

"Wow. How did you feel when you saw him?"

He took a sip from his glass and said, "I didn't feel anything. I said hello and then he had the nerve to say, 'Aren't you gonna give me a hug?' It was really awkward."

"Did you ask him where has he been all these years?"

"Nope. I already knew that he wasn't around, simply because he didn't want to be. There have been plenty of ways that he could've had a relationship with me. He knew how to contact my mom."

"How do you know that?"

"Because he knew where she worked and lived. She's been working at the same job and living in the same house, since I was born. If he wanted to be in my life, he had ample time to do so. The only reason why we met is because my mother *asked* him to meet me. Not only that, my mom showed me copies of letters that she sent to him years ago, telling him about me. Not once did he ever write back. Instead, he told his wife and my mom received a letter from her, telling my mom to leave my father Joseph alone. She even went as far as to tell my mom that he has a family of his own and that he doesn't need to add another kid to the three that he already has."

"Wow. That's awful. So what did you guys say to each other when y'all met?"

"Not much. He was sitting there, acting as if I oughta be thankful that he took time outta his day to meet me."

"What do you mean?"

"He said, 'Clay, I took off from work, just to see you. I don't usually allow anything or anyone to get in the way of my money.' So I said to him, 'Well, don't let me get in the way of your paycheck. By all means, you can leave.'"

"Humph. I can't believe that he acted that way."

"Well, he did. After about forty-five minutes of pointless small talk, he finally left."

"Hmm. So I guess there won't be a reunion, huh?"

"No way. He made a choice not to be a part of my life, years ago. So as far as I'm concerned, he can *stay* gone."

Since Clay is almost finished with college, his family decided to throw a small gathering for him. It was a cookout at his mom's house and it was very nice. It also gave me a chance to meet his aunts, uncles and cousins.

And what made the party even more wonderful is that Clay introduced me to his family, as his girlfriend. That made me feel so good. Now, I know that I'm really a special part of his life.

After the gathering was over, Clay took me home but before I got outta his car, he said, "I got a job offer in New York."

I looked at him as if he was crazy. I said, "You got a job offer, *where?*"

"In New York. They want me to start as soon as I finish college."

"I can't believe this is happening."

"Aren't you happy for me?"

I looked at him and said, "How can I be happy? The man I love wants to go to another state. How in the world are we gonna have a relationship, with you being far away?"

"I never said that I was definitely going, Joy. It just so happened that I was offered a job there. I haven't decided whether I was gonna take it or not. I was hoping to talk to you about it and see if you would be cool with it."

"Cool with it? Clay, long distance relationships don't work. If you take this job and move away, our relationship with crumble."

"Not if you come with me."

This dude must be outta his mind, I thought to myself. I said, "Excuse me? I can't come with you, Clay. I'm still in college."

"But you're half-way finished. Besides, you can transfer to a college, down there."

"Clay, are you listening to yourself? I have my friends and family, *here*. I don't know anybody in New York."

"Neither do I. But what if I never get this opportunity again?"

I sighed and laid my head back on the headrest. Then I said, "Clay, you have the right to make your own decisions. I can't get in the way of that. I guess that we don't have any other choice except to have a long distance relationship and see how long we can continue to do that. Right now, I'm gonna go inside and go to bed. Goodnight." I reached over and gave him a kiss.

Then as I was getting out of the car, he blurted out, "I love you. Always remember that."

I looked at him and said, "I love you, too." Then I closed his car door and went upstairs to my apartment where I cried myself to sleep.

The next morning, I was still upset to the point where I couldn't even eat anything. I didn't want to do anything except stay in the bed with the covers over my head and sleep, sleep, sleep. I should've known that as soon as something good happened in my life, it wasn't gonna last long.

How can Clay even consider taking this job? Doesn't he love me enough to stay? The more I thought about it, the more upset I became. I didn't want him to go. But on the other hand, if he decided to stay in Cleveland because of me, there could be a possibility that he'd resent me because I was the reason that he missed out on an opportunity to live his dream.

So I'm thinking that maybe I shouldn't stop him from taking the offer. If it's meant for us to be together, it will happen. I'm just gonna be cool about the situation and see what happens.

With that being said, I decided to get my behind outta bed and go over to my mama's house to see how she was doing. Besides, I knew that she probably cooked breakfast and since I didn't feel like cooking, I figured that I would go over there and eat.

When I arrived, mama was sitting in the kitchen with a Kleenex box and used tissue, sitting next to her on the table. There was no cooked breakfast and she didn't even look up when I came thru the door.

I slowly approached her and I said, "Mama, what's wrong?"

"Nothing that I can't handle," she replied.

"What do you mean? It must be something devastating, otherwise you wouldn't be crying. Please tell me what's wrong."

She wiped her nose with a piece of tissue and said, "You may not be ready for this."

"Mama, I'm an adult. I've been ready for a lot of things."

"But you might not be ready for this kind of news."

I was starting to get a lil' frustrated and I said, "Mama, how do you know if I'm ready or not if you don't tell me?"

She took a deep sigh and said, "Here it goes; you have a sister."

"Mama, what are you talking about?" I asked, with a puzzled look.

"A young lady by the name of Summer, called me and said that she is Shawn's daughter. She lives in Cincinnati and she located my phone number by going thru some old things that her mom had. She's the same age that you are. I can't believe that I'm finding all of this out, now."

"Mama, are you serious?"

"Yes, sweetheart. I can't believe that Shawn kept this secret from me. I knew that we had problems in our relationship when we were together but I would've never thought that he would cheat on me. I'm so angry and I don't even know what to do about it. Why did I have to find out like this? All these years went by and he's never even bothered to tell me anything about this other daughter."

"Mama, I know you're angry but everything is gonna be okay. Does this girl know about me?"

"Yes, she does. She knows that you and her are both the same age and that you live in Cleveland. She said that she wants to meet you. She gave me her number and…"

"Mama, I don't think that I want to meet her. I mean, I have grown up without a sister and as far as I'm concerned, I don't need one now. Who does she think she is, calling you and interrupting our lives with this mess? We don't need this."

"Joy, this whole ordeal is not her fault. She's not responsible for Shawn's actions, she didn't ask to be born and she didn't choose her parents. Your father is to blame for this whole mess. He kept this secret hidden for years."

"But mama, how do you know that this girl is telling the truth?"

"Because she knew a lot of things about me and your father. She knew that my name is Natalie and she even knew how her mom and Shawn met and how many times he came to Cincinnati to see them. The whole time that he was going back and forth to Cincinnati, he told me that he was going there to visit some of his friends. And I was so stupid to believe him."

"Mama, you wasn't stupid. You and dad were young when y'all met and made me. Have you told dad that this Summer person called you?"

"No…but I will. Right now, I'm just trying to get my thoughts together. Cheating is bad enough but for him to get another girl pregnant at the same time that I was pregnant with you and didn't even bother to tell me about this other daughter, that's the thing that angers me."

"Did she tell you whether or not she has spoken to dad?"

"She said that she hasn't seen or heard from him since she was ten-years old."

I sighed and said, "Well, I guess when it rains, it pours."

"What do you mean, Joy?"

"Clay has been offered a job in New York and he's been thinking long and hard about accepting the offer, which means that he will be miles away from me. I don't want him to go, mama. How can he just consider moving there when he's in a relationship with me? Then he had the nerve to think that I would drop everything that's going on in *my* life, transfer to a school in New York and live there. I don't wanna lose him but at the same time, I have a life of my own."

Mama put her arms around me and said, "You do what's best for you, Joy. But I will say that I don't recommend that you leave your life behind, just to be with a man. That's not how I raised you."

"I know but what do I do?"

"Continue to live your life. And if it's meant to be, you two will be together."

Twelve

(Taurus)

CHRISTMAS IS ABOUT a month away and I'm afraid that I won't be able to see my kids for the holidays, considering that Brenda wouldn't allow me to spend time with them on Thanksgiving Day.

When Thanksgiving Day came, I called and called Brenda and she wouldn't answer the phone. I left voice messages and she wouldn't return any of them. And I didn't stop by the house because I didn't know what to expect. I felt that if I showed up unannounced, there could've been a possibility that she'd cause a scene. So I stayed clear of the house.

So on Thanksgiving Day, I went over to my mama's house. She had a couple of relatives over there and after they left, I stayed behind to help her clean up.

While loading the dishwasher, mama said, "Brenda told me what happened. I hope that you're not over here to get some kind of sympathy."

"Mama, it only happened once," I explained.

"Boy, I'm your mama. I know when you're lying. It didn't just happen once."

"I know that what I did was messed up but I do love my wife."

"Humph. Spoken like a true cheater. You're crazy for putting your wife thru this. What about your kids? What if your son Dillon grows up being a cheater like you?"

"Mama, please. You don't have to kick me while I'm down. I already feel bad."

"Well, you *should* feel bad. There's no excuse for what you did. You are just like your daddy."

"Mama, my dad is dead and gone. Show him some respect."

She looked at me as if I was crazy and she said, "Respect?! Don't tell me to show your father some respect! He didn't show *me* any respect! That man put me thru many years of turmoil and you're starting to do the same things that he's done to me."

"Well, in *my* case, Brenda just seemed to be a handful at times and I really didn't know how to handle it."

"So instead of trying to work out the issues with your wife or seek counseling, you decided to stick your…"

"Mama!"

"Well, it is what it is. I'm your mama and I will always love you but if you're wrong, you're wrong. And if Brenda decides to take you back, you need to be willing to do whatever is necessary to get back on her good side. And that may take a while because when women get betrayed by the men they love, most of them always have it in the back of their minds that their man will betray them again. You are no exception to the rule. You *may* love your wife but please understand that love is not supposed to hurt. And by all means, don't sit up here and try to justify your actions for what you did because if the shoe was on the other foot, you most certainly would be feeling the same way that she's feeling, right now. Or worse. See, so many of you men try to fix problems in your marriages with the tool that you have in your pants. So like I said, you're not gonna get any sympathy from me."

That sounds just like something that my mama would say. She's still bitter because of how my dad treated her for years. He used to cheat on her with every woman that was in one inch of him.

A couple of women that he messed around with, ended up having kids by him but my mama refused to let any of the kids come to the house because she couldn't cope with the fact that my father was a cheat. So to this day, I have no idea who my siblings are or how to get in contact with them.

Yeah, my father was something else. If he wasn't smoking and drinking with his buddies, he was messing around with loose women. I remember when I was five-years old, my father had to pick me up from school because my mother had to go to a doctor's appointment. I was riding in his car and he took me over to some woman's house.

I asked my father, "Why are we here?"

He answered, "I have to take care of something. Just go in the living room and watch some cartoons. We won't be here long."

Then he followed the attractive woman to her bedroom and closed the door. We were over there for what seemed to be an eternity. I heard a lot of bumping around in her room but as a small child, I didn't know that I was actually hearing the sound of my father having sex with this woman.

Because of his infidelity, he stayed in arguments with my mom, begging her not to leave him and promising her that he would change. And she always believed him. But day after day, week after week, month after month and year after year, things remained the same.

Dad continued to stay out late at night and sometimes, he didn't come back until the next morning. Sometimes, I'd hear my mom in her room, crying over what she was going thru with dad. But one night, my father left the house and he didn't come back. The next morning came and there still wasn't any sign of him. The second day came without any signs of dad and that's when my mom got really scared.

She called the police and told them that her husband was missing and so they went out and searched for him. Some of the people in the neighborhood were even looking for him.

Almost a week went by and that's when my mom received a call from the police, telling her that they found my father's body behind a trash dumpster of an apartment complex. His throat had been slashed from ear to ear and part of his head was cut open. My mother almost had a nervous breakdown when she found out.

About a month later, the police caught the person who did it. According to the police, the man who killed my father was a man named Wesley Johnson.

It was said that Wesley killed my father because he found out that my father was messing around with his wife and to add insult to injury, Wesley found out that the baby that his wife was carrying, was not his and that it was my father's child.

So he tracked my father down and killed him. I guess my dad's ways finally caught up to him. But see, I'm nothing like my father. I mean, okay, I got caught slippin'. But I love Brenda so much, that I made sure to never let her find out anything.

And had it not been for my nosy kids, she still wouldn't have known anything. But what's done is done and now I have to figure out how to get my wife back. I'm not saying that I won't ever cheat again. Next time, I'll make sure to cover up all the evidence.

It's two a.m in the morning and I just can't sleep. My kids mean so much to me and if I can't spend Christmas Day with them, it will break my heart. And although I knew that Brenda was still angry at me, I knew that I needed to get in contact with her so that I could see my kids.

I knew that I was risking the chance of getting cussed out or punched in the face, but that was a risk that I was willing to take in order to see my kids. So since there was absolutely no chance of me getting any sleep, I stayed up and watched TV until about seven a.m, which is about the time that Brenda gets out of bed.

My plan was for me to keep calling her phone until she picked it up but to my surprise, she answered on the first ring. "What do you want?" she asked, in a low tone.

"Brenda, I think that we need to talk," I stated, trying not to sound nervous.

"If you want to talk to someone, you can talk to my lawyer."

"What? Brenda, what are you talking about?"

"I filed for divorce yesterday, Taurus."

I felt a huge lump in my throat and my stomach started to hurt, badly. *Lord, this can't be happening,* I thought to myself. "Brenda, please don't do this. I know that I made a mistake, but…"

"But? There are no buts, Taurus. You did the unthinkable and I don't trust you anymore. If there's no trust, I can't stay married to you."

"But look at what you're doing to the kids."

"*You* need to look at what you're doing to the kids! Were you thinking about the kids when you were messing around?! Don't you dare act like this is my fault. This is the consequence of doing wrong for just a few minutes of pleasure. And knowing you, I'm pretty sure that it was *just* a few minutes of pleasure."

"That's hitting below the belt, Brenda."

"Below the belt is what got you in this mess."

I took a deep sigh and said, "We really have a lot to talk about. And I'm willing to work things out for however long it takes because I most certainly don't want us to get a divorce, at all. We've been together for too long to let that happen."

"Well, that's life. I was expecting to stay married to a *faithful* man. I wasn't expecting for my husband to hurt me like this."

"Well, can I at least see the children for Christmas? There's no need for them to have to pay for what I did by keeping them away from me."

"We'll see," she said and quickly hung up.

I was sitting in my chair with the phone still in my hand. I felt worse than I did before I spoke to her. See, I thought that this whole thing would blow over in a matter of weeks and she would forgive me and take me back. I mean, that's usually how it supposed to happen. It's not supposed to end in a divorce. I understand that she's hurt and angry but her filing for divorce, is just going too far.

Thirteen

(Rita)

I WAS PLANNING on spending a nice, quiet evening at home by myself, with nothing but a glass of wine and a Maxwell CD playing to keep my mood mellow. But twenty minutes into my quiet evening, I got a phone call from my sister Marilyn, saying that she wanted to come over and see me today.

"Girl, not today. I just want some time alone," I explained to her.

"But Rita, I have a surprise that I want to show you," she pleaded.

"Marilyn, Christmas is only a month away. Show me your surprise on *that* day."

"C'mon, Rita. I can't wait that long. I really need to show you my surprise, right now."

I sighed and said, "Alright, Marilyn. It betta be good, too."

"Oh, it is. I'll be over there in a few minutes."

After about forty-five minutes, my doorbell rang. I gathered up all the energy to pull my butt off of the sofa to answer the door and when I did, my sister was at my doorstep with a tall, dark-skinned man next to her who had the body of a football player. Her face had such a major glow and she was giddy like a high school girl.

"Marilyn, who is this?" I asked.

She smiled at the man next to her and said, "Rita, this is Allen. We're engaged."

"What?! Girl, come in here," I said, ushering them into my house. Then I asked, "What is this about you being engaged?"

She smiled from ear to ear and said, "Girl, it was love at first sight. I never knew that love could be like this."

"Um…Allen, can you excuse us for a second? I need to speak with Marilyn," I said, grabbing her hand and taking her into my bedroom so that we could talk. When I closed my bedroom door, I gave her a look as if she was completely out of her mind. "What in the world is going on?" I asked her.

"What do you mean?" she asked.

"One day, you were trying to work things out with Paul and now all of a sudden, you're engaged to a guy named Allen? This doesn't make sense."

"Maybe not to you but it does to me."

"How?"

"Because I know that I have real love, Rita. *Real* love. Yes, I did love Paul and I wanted to spend the rest of my life with him, even though I knew that he didn't want to be married to me anymore. I've tried everything to make things work but for most of our marriage, I had to spend many days by myself because he was spending his days with someone else. I had to face the fact that he did not love me."

"Marilyn, just because you guys are having problems in the marriage, doesn't mean that Paul doesn't love you."

"It means more than what you think, Rita. When he moved out, it was at that moment that I felt like the loneliest woman in the world. I was in love with a man who wouldn't love me the way that I wanted to be loved because I allowed him to treat me like I wasn't important. I've cried many tears over that man, Rita."

"But can't you work it out?"

"Work *what* out? Rita, are you listening to me? Paul and I are over. If the other person is not willing to try and they don't want you anymore, you have no other choice but to let them go. So I did."

"And then you met Allen?"

"Yep. Once I finally let Paul go, that's when I met Allen. I met him thru a friend of mine. Not only that, but I joined his church. You know that I was never the type to go to church."

"You what?"

"Girl, you heard me. I remember sitting on the couch, crying over Paul and it was like God spoke to me and said, 'Everything is gonna be alright. Just trust in Me.' I heard Him clear as a bell, Rita. It was almost scary. So I wiped my tears and decided to start my life over. I deleted Paul's number out of my phone and I threw away anything that reminded me of him. I even sent him a long letter, explaining to him that as soon as our divorced is finalized, we no longer needed to stay in contact with each other for anything unless it had something to do with our son."

"Hmmm. Has he tried to reach you since then?"

"*Humph.* Of course. He called me and said that he didn't care whether we kept in contact or not. And just to get me upset, he had the nerve to tell me that his girlfriend was pregnant. I told him that I felt so sorry for her. Then he hung up in my face."

"So you're really serious about letting Paul go?"

"I've already *let* him go. I'm completely done with him. It took me a while but I've finally opened my eyes and realized that God wants me to have His best. And His best is not for me to be with a man who doesn't love me. There's no future in that. So I prayed to God that He would help me get over the hurt. And He did. Three days later, I met Allen. The first night that we met, we must've stayed up for hours on the phone, just getting to know each other and finding out what we both wanted out of life. And although we've only known each other for a short period of time, it feels like I've known him all of my life. I find myself being so open and honest with him."

"Are you really happy with this guy?"

"Yes, I am. Once I decided to let go of the trash that was in my life and I allowed God to take control, He blessed me with a wonderful man who only wants me and treats me like I'm the best thing that's ever happened to him."

I let out a deep sigh and I said, "Well, if you're happy, then *I'm* happy. I wish you well and I hope that you two have a wonderful marriage. Sometimes, I wish I *hadn't* got married. It's not all that it's cracked up to be."

"Well, maybe you feel that way because of the marriage that *you're* in. But just because *you're* not happy, doesn't mean that *I'm* not gonna be happy. Besides, your husband Shawn may not be perfect but what man is? He may not do all the things that you would want him to do but he's still a good man, Rita. He still loves you and respects you. At least he doesn't beat you and step out on you with other women. It's *you* that's doing all the cheating. And honestly, he doesn't deserve that, Rita."

"Wait a minute. Who are you to be counseling me? You don't have all the answers."

"But that doesn't matter. What I'm telling you is the truth. Shawn may be a lil' weak but he does love you, Rita. And if you take that for granted, you're gonna lose him."

"Oh, please. That man ain't going nowhere. And if he does, I'll be alright. I'll simply get another man."

"Like who? Taurus?"

"Well, why not Taurus?"

"Duh! Because he's not yours, Rita. Love the man who loves you. I wanted to stay with Paul because I didn't want to be lonely. But I started to understand that I was lonelier than ever, dealing with a man that didn't love me. Being with Allen makes me realize that there *is* someone for everyone."

"You tell that mess to the millions of women that are single. I'm pretty sure that they wouldn't agree with you."

"And that's because they keep on believing that big lie that there are not enough men to go around, which is one of the reasons why men have been treating women like a piece of gum on the bottom of their shoe. That big lie is the reason why women are more desperate than ever to get a man and are willing to take whatever a man dishes out, just so they can say that they have a man. That's why you have women giving away their goodies as if it's government cheese because they figured that that's the best way to get a man. But honestly, that is absolutely the worst way to try to get a man because most men see that as a lack of self-respect. And when you don't respect yourself, you most certainly won't get it from a man. I know that because I used to be that way. I used my body to try to keep Paul home but it didn't work. But once I listened to God's voice, everything changed because I started to seek more and more of Him. And of course, once you put God first, He will put *you* first. As for you, I can't tell you what to do. You're a grown woman. But I will say that you have a lot that you need to go to God about. But it's up to you whether you do that or not. That's between you and God."

I rolled my eyes and said, "So now that you think that you heard from God, you think that you have the right to preach to me?"

"Rita, I never called myself a preacher. Girl, I don't even know one Bible scripture by memory. But I do know that when you hear God's voice, it's like nothing you've ever heard before. It's calm, comforting and right. I was so, so honored that He spoke to me and showed me how much he loved me, even though I was living a life full of mess. I thought that I did way too much wrong to ever have God in my life. But I was so wrong. Ever since that day that I heard from Him, God's been helping me clean my life up and get some things in order. And I am not looking back."

I gave Marilyn a hug and I said, "Well sis, I'm glad that things are working out for you. Let me know when your guys decide on a wedding day."

She smiled and said, "I will. We're planning to get married next year."

I was fuming with anger when I found out that Taurus had sex with some woman and Brenda had the nerve to bring the hepha's pink panties up to the church, during a meeting. Everyone knew about it.

I was angry because I knew that the pink panties weren't mine. I hate pink. So that meant that he was messing around behind my back with someone else. Doesn't he know how dangerous that is? He could've passed a disease to me. So after finding out where he was hiding, I went over to his lodge.

He answered the door and said, "What is it, Rita?"

"We need to talk," I answered, as I barged into the door.

"About what?"

"About us! Who the hell was you messing around with that was wearing pink panties?! They most certainly wasn't mine."

He laughed and said, "You've got to be kidding. You're confronting me as if I owe you an explanation. I don't owe you anything, Rita. I'm not married to you. If I want to sleep with someone else, there ain't anything you can do about it."

"Excuse me? Who do you think you're talking to? If you loved me..."

"Love? Are you really using that word? Rita, we are both married and have other obligations. We may be heavily involved with each other but there was *never* any love. At least, not on *my* part. You knew the situation when we started messing around with each other. There's no doubt that we're attracted to each other but there was never an opportunity for us to really have something special. I care about you but I can't give you all of me."

I sighed and said, "You're right. You're absolutely right. And I'm sorry that I jumped down your throat. I'm sure that you're going thru enough, as it is."

"Yeah, I am," he said as he sat on the bed, "Brenda wants a divorce."

My face lit up with delight but I made sure that he didn't see it. "She wants a divorce, huh?" I asked.

"Yep. I'm hoping that once she cools down and we spend all this time away from each other, she will start to miss me and take me back."

I put my arm around him and said, "Well, just in case she doesn't take you back, you will always have me. I care about you, Taurus."

"And I care about you, too," he stated. Then we slowly kissed each other on the lips, which led to us rolling around in the bed, feeding our sexual hunger.

Fourteen

(Shawn)

THIS IS THE saddest day of my life. Chris and I have been friends for many, many years and we've been thru so much together. Although he was doing things that I definitely didn't agree with, I still loved him like a brother. I knew that his wife Lisa was extremely hurt and angry because of his infidelity but I never thought that she would snap and take his life.

When I received a frantic call from Chris' mother saying that Lisa blew his head off with a shotgun, I immediately dropped to my knees. I couldn't believe that it happened. Of course, Lisa wasn't at the funeral because she was in jail being charged with murder but it's a good thing that she wasn't there because Trina, the church's secretary, had the nerve to be present. That would've only added to Lisa's fury.

One part of me was angry with Lisa for taking the life of a dear friend of mine but another part of me, sympathized with her. After being a good wife, a good mother, a hardworking person in the church and the community, she didn't deserve to be married to a man who didn't appreciate her. Honestly, I didn't even know that Lisa could even get that angry to the point where she could kill someone.

She was sweet, very soft-spoken and never had a bad word to say to anyone. But I guess that when a person is fed up, they are fed up. Chris' mom was crying so hard that I thought that she was gonna have a nervous breakdown. But I put my arms around her to give her comfort.

Chris was her only son out of the five kids that she had so I definitely understood her grief. Rita attended the funeral with me but she didn't seem to show any kind of passion. Instead, she said something like, "Oh, well. It is what it is."

According to Chris' mom, Lisa came home one night and caught Chris in the bed with Trina. So Lisa grabbed the shotgun and when she did, Trina ran while Chris was still sitting in the bed. And that's when Lisa shot him.

"So what happens now to his church? What about his kids?" I asked her.

She answered, "Well, I really don't know what's gonna happen to his church but as far as the kids, I'm gonna seek full custody of them. I don't think that it's a good idea for Lisa to have them in her care. Besides, she probably will be in prison for a long time."

I gave her a hug and said, "Well, Ms. Waters, if you need my help for anything, just call me. I will do whatever I can to help you."

"Thanks, Shawn. And thank you for being such a good friend to Chris. He didn't have many friends but I'm glad that he had at least one. I know that he wasn't perfect and he was doing things that he shouldn't have gotten involved in but he was still my son and I loved him. I was hoping that one day, he would finally change some things in his life so that he could be a better leader for his church but he didn't get a chance to prove that he could do it. What am I supposed to do without my son?"

"You have to keep on living. Always tell his children how much their daddy loved them. Protect their young ears from negative things that people might say about their father because although he might have been living a double life, his kids don't need to know that, right now in their young lives. They're too young to understand. What they're gonna need is your love, support and protection."

"You're right, Shawn. We'll keep in touch, okay?"

"Sure. Take care of yourself."

"Why didn't you tell me? I can't believe you did this," Joy stated over the phone, the minute I answered it. It was almost six o'clock in the morning.

"What are you talking about?" I asked, just barely awake.

"Why didn't you tell me that I had a sister named Summer?"

When she asked that question, I quickly jumped out of bed and was pacing the floor, trying to figure out what to say. "Well...um..."

"Well, um? Is that all that you have to say to me, dad? Here I am, twenty-years old and I never knew that I had a sister. Why did you keep this secret from me? She found out who my mom was and where she lived and now this girl wants to meet me. What am I supposed to say to her? I'm not even sure if I want to see her."

"Joy, I..."

"Joy *what*! What exactly can you say to me, right now? She is the same age that *I* am! Do you know how upset my mom was? You're a pastor and you're always preaching about how people should be honest but yet you were carrying this secret around with you for years. Is that your definition of being honest?"

"You watch your mouth!"

"Why? Is my truth about how I'm feeling right now, too much for you? You cheated on my mom while she was pregnant with me. How could you do this?"

I took a deep sigh and I said, "Joy, I know that this is a lot for you to handle and I'm really, really sorry that you had to find out like this. I wish that I had been the one to tell you and I truly regret that I kept it a secret from you. Believe me, I wasn't trying to hurt you or make it seem like I was being untrustworthy. But I just didn't know how to tell you and your mom."

"Is that the best answer that you can give me?"

"Joy, what is it that you want me to tell you? I'm not trying to make up an excuse for what I did but you have to understand that I was very young when you were born. And so was your mom. We were both eighteen-years old. I was too young to even think about having a committed relationship and so, yes, I cheated on her."

"Was my mom not good enough? Did you have to cheat on her?"

"No, but things happen. Natalie is still a wonderful woman and she did a beautiful job, raising you. But we just wasn't right for each other. So I met Summer's mom and...well..."

"I can't believe how nonchalant you are. Do you realize what just happened? I just found out that I have never been the only child! I have a sister! How do you think I feel to have my life interrupted like this, due to a twenty-year old secret?! This is all your fault! I don't ever want to speak to you again!"

"Joy, you don't mean that. You're just angry."

"Yes, I do mean it. I don't want anything else to do with you."

Joy slammed the phone down in my ear and I was left holding the receiver in my hand. I wasn't upset at how she reacted; I was upset at how long I kept it a secret. If it was the other way around, I probably would feel the same way that she felt. So I wasn't angry at her anger.

On the other hand, I'm glad that Joy finally knows that she has a sister. I was so wrong to keep this from her but I just didn't know which way to reveal it to her. But of course, what you do in the dark, will be brought to light. I was a coward.

So now, I guess I'm gonna have to deal with the consequences of possibly being isolated from Joy and having to hear Rita's mouth when she finds out about it. And I just know that she's gonna find out about this.

My friend Candace came to church again but she came with a male friend. His name was Stanley and he seemed to be very interested in her. Rita seemed relieved to see her with a man on her arm. I guess because she felt intimidated that Candace and I knew each other. Rita actually came up to her and gave her a big hug and found out that Candace's male friend is actually her *boyfriend*. I was happy that she found love.

During dinner, Rita said, "I'm glad Candace got her a man. He seems like a really nice guy."

"Yeah, he seems like a cool person. I hope it works out for her," I stated.

"Where was Joy? I didn't see her today. She was nowhere to be found."

"Well...um...she's not feeling well." I lied. Joy was so angry with me that she didn't want to even come to church.

"How do you know that she's not feeling well?"

"Because we've talked."

"Oh. So anyway, have you heard the latest news?"

"About what?"

"Brenda went on a weekend cruise with this guy that she just met. It's all over the church. She showed some of the church members a couple of intimate pictures that she took with him. I didn't see the pictures but someone told me about them."

I sighed and said, "Rita, why are you telling me this?"

"I don't see why I wouldn't. What's the problem?"

"Brenda and Taurus are going thru a tough time in their marriage, right now. They most certainly don't need the church members gossiping about them."

"Well, *she* was the one who showed the pictures."

"It doesn't matter. If she did go on a cruise with a man and take some sexy photos, you all should be able to understand that she's acting out because of what Taurus did to her. Did any of you at least bothered to pray for her or pray *with* her?"

"Of course not. Most of them don't even like Brenda. Including me."

"See, that's the problem. That's why the world looks at us Christians as if we're nothing but hypocrites because we *talk* about loving one another but we don't do it. Whether you like Brenda or not, she is still your sister in Christ and like many of us, she's going thru some issues, right now. So she needs prayer just like all the rest of us."

"Why are you taking up for her?"

"Because if you're not helping, then you're hindering. If you're talking about her behind her back with all the rest of them, you're adding to the problem. As many times as I've preached on unconditional love, there is still a massive amount of hate, circulating around the church. We're so quick to point out other people's problems and whisper behind their backs, that all of us forget that we have problems, too. And most of the time, our problems are a lot worse than the person that we're whispering about."

"Shawn, first of all, why would anyone want to pray for her?"

Getting frustrated, I said to her, "Rita, did it ever dawn on you that a lot of people in the church can't stand you either? Don't sit up here and act like you are so well-loved by everyone. Now, to answer your question, there is a scripture in the Bible that tells you to 'Love your enemies.' You're supposed to pray for them and treat them like gold."

"Yes, I know that. I also know that if you love your enemies, God will get them back for what they did to you."

"Although that's true, that's not all that that scripture is about."

"Then what is it about?"

"In that scripture, 'Love your enemies', it's about that word, 'love'. Love is a very, very powerful thing, Rita. Although God can punish your enemies, the *love* you demonstrate to your enemies can get them to see the God in you and they may start to have a positive change because of that. And before you know it, they may start to love you because of the love that you demonstrated to them. So even though you may not like Brenda, love her and make it your business to pray for her, despite her faults. And pray for yourself as well."

Fifteen

(Joy)

WITH THE DRAMA that I faced with dad and this so-called sister of mine, I almost forgot that my friend Monica was being discharged from the hospital, two days before Christmas.

I was so, so thankful that Monica was strong enough to pull thru and get out of the coma. God really does answer prayers. I wasn't there at the hospital when Monica opened her eyes but her mom called and told me that she was out of the coma.

Mrs. Truman said to me on the phone, "Hi, Joy. God gave her another chance."

"Huh? What do you mean?" I asked.

"I'm talking about Monica. She's out of her coma. I was here when she opened her eyes."

I dropped to my knees and thanked God, over and over again. This type of good news made me forget all about the argument that I had with my father. Monica has never been thru something like this so I knew that if she survived this, she'd never be the same.

Although Monica was allowed to go home, she still had to endure a lot of therapy because of all the damage that Jeff did to her; her wrist was broken, one of her ribs were fractured, her left leg was broken and so was her nose. But her family was still able to bring her home and Mrs. Truman paid for a private-duty nurse to come to the house to help Monica recover. So that was a good thing.

However, there was talk that Todd was out on bail and he was looking for Monica. But Mrs. Truman thought that it would be a great idea for Monica to stay with her so that she could take care of her and help Monica to recover.

So since Monica wasn't at her own apartment, Todd had no idea where she was residing.

But that didn't stop Todd from being absolutely vicious; this jerk broke into her apartment and stole her TV and two-thousand dollars that she stashed away in her bedroom. So Mrs. Truman didn't think that it would be a great idea for Monica to go back to that apartment after she recovers.

So she made arrangements for Monica to stay with her as long as she needed to and then once Monica recovers from her injuries, she would help Monica find an apartment in a better area, far away from the old apartment complex. I knew that Monica and I hadn't spoken since our argument but I knew that now was the time for us to talk and work things out.

We've been friends for too long to let our friendship go down the drain. So I showed up to Mrs. Truman's house to see Monica and to my surprise, Monica was very happy to see me. To see her smiling was the most wonderful thing in the world.

"Hi, Joy!" she greeted me, "I'm so happy to see you."

I gave her a hug and said, "I'm so glad that you're home."

I stayed over for a while and ate dinner with her and her family and afterwards, I helped Monica get to her room. We sat on her bed and she reached inside her nightstand and pulled out a small pink journal. I looked at her and saw a tear fall down her cheek.

"What's wrong?" I asked.

"Life is a crazy thing, Joy. I remember writing in this journal when I was eleven-years old. On a couple of the pages, I wrote down the type of husband that I wanted, once I grew up."

"And what was the type of husband that you wanted?" I asked.

She sighed and said, "He was everything that I wished I had. The kind of husband that showed me the most important thing, which is love. But since my real father was never around and I never had a positive male figure to show me how a man is supposed to love a woman, I thought that the way that I was being treated by men, was the true definition of love. But love doesn't break your bones."

"You're right, Monica. But what you also need to know about love is that it first starts with you."

"What do you mean?"

"You must first learn to love yourself."

"But Joy, how in the world do you do that?"

"You have to get to a point where you accept the way you are, flaws and all. And that may take some time for you to get to that point. You have to be able to look in the mirror and love what you see. Learn to say something positive about yourself everyday and don't expect for other people to do it for you because honestly, you don't need anyone's approval to feel good about yourself. And you most certainly don't need approval from a man. Accept the fact that you are not perfect and you don't need to be perfect in order to be with someone special. It's called self-love, Monica. And it doesn't start on the outside; it starts on the inside."

"I understand. And let me just say that I'm really sorry for the argument that we had. You are my best friend and I didn't mean to be so angry with you. I knew that you were telling me the truth about Todd but I just didn't want to believe the truth. Not only that, I was a lil' envious of your relationship with Clay. I saw how well he was treating you and I wanted that same treatment from Todd. Clay seems like a wonderful person."

I smiled and said, "Yeah, he is...but...well..."

"Well what?"

"I don't know what the future holds in regards to my relationship with Clay."

"Why do you say that?"

"Because he's been offered a job in New York and he's thinking about taking it."

"So what's the problem?"

"Monica, if he takes this job, that means that he will have to move and I don't want that to happen. But on the other hand, I don't wanna be selfish and try to keep him from pursuing his dream. I'm just scared that if he moves to New York, it's gonna be hard for us to have a relationship because he's gonna be far away."

"Why don't you move to New York, too? That way, you two don't have to worry about being far apart."

"I don't wanna move to New York. There's nothing there for me."

"You don't know that. Besides, Clay is too good of a guy to let go of, Joy. Don't be a fool. He's handsome, got no kids, friendly, educated and he's obviously crazy about you. If you let that go, another woman may take the prize. Do you want that to happen?"

I sighed and said, "No, but I'm still in college. I can't just up and move."

"But you can once you *finish* college. Since you've been taking courses in the summertime, you only have one more year to go before you get your degree, right?"

"Yeah, but..."

"So there it is. Once you finish college, you can move to New York and start your life there, with Clay by your side. And while you're trying to finish your last year of college, you two can make every effort to see each other on the weekends and on the holidays. It shouldn't be a problem, considering that Cleveland is not that far away from New York. Before you know it, a year will pass by and you will be finished with school and be able to start your life in New York without anything holding you back."

"But what about my family?"

"Joy, your family will still be your family. But they have their own lives. You need to start yours. If you tell them that you wanna move to New York after you graduate to start a life for yourself, I betcha they will understand."

"You think so?"

"Of course. Why wouldn't they? You don't wanna be sixty-years old and looking back on your life, saying, 'I wish that I had did this and that, but.' You get what I'm saying?"

I smiled and said, "Yeah, I do. And I'm gonna go ahead and make the decision to move there after graduation. I guess it's time to put fear aside and make the right choices for my life."

"Well, you're not the only one; I'm going back to school to get my degree in sociology."

I was extremely shocked. "Are you serious?" I asked, "What brought on that decision?"

"After getting out of the hospital, I realized that if I didn't start to change my life in a positive direction, my life would just get worse and worse. When I think about it, I know that I could've been dead. But since God gave me another chance, I'm gonna make my life mean something. Never again will I ever allow myself to be put in a situation where a man has my life in the palm of his hand. I have too much to live for."

"You sure do, Monica."

"Hello?" I said when I answered the phone.

"Hi…um, can I speak with Joy?" the mysterious voice asked me.

"This is Joy. May I ask who's calling?"

"This is Summer. I'm you sister from Cincinnati."

"How did you get my number?" I asked, quickly getting upset.

"Um, I asked your mother for it. I don't mean to bother you. I'm in Cleveland, visiting some relatives and I wanted to meet you. I just wanted a chance to talk to you…if that's okay."

"Talk to me about what? What do we have to talk about?"

"Well…um…I just want to get to know you, Joy."

"What's there to know? My name is Joy and I live in Cleveland. End of story."

"Joy, please give me a chance. It was hard for me to even pick up the phone to call you because I didn't know what to expect. I just want one chance to meet you. I'm not trying to interrupt your life or make you have a relationship with me. So do you think that we can meet for breakfast? It's my treat. Just tell me where you wanna go."

Humph. Well, since she wanted to treat me to breakfast, I didn't see anything wrong with that. And I most certainly didn't wanna pass up a free meal.

So I said to her, "Okay. Well, there's this one breakfast place on the corner of Broadway Avenue. Do you know where Broadway Avenue is?"

"Yes, I do."

"Okay. Well, I'll meet you there in about an hour."

"No problem. I'll see you then."

I had no idea what to expect once I met Summer but when I saw her, I was amazed at how much we looked alike. It was unbelievable. We had the same green eyes and long, sandy-brown hair. When we saw each other, we gave each other such an awkward hug, that it seemed phony.

"Nice to meet you, Joy," Summer stated.

"Same here," I replied.

We walked into the restaurant together and when the waitress seated us, there was so much tension between Summer and I that it was making me extremely uncomfortable. We would glance at each other and then turn our heads in opposite directions.

To go ahead and break the ice, I said to Summer, "I don't know if you've ever been here or not but they do serve a good breakfast."

"Oh, I see," she asked, "So how old are you?"

"I'm twenty-years old. And you?"

"I'm the same age. So I guess that we were born the same year."

I sighed and said, "Look Summer, I understand that you wanted to meet me but I'm not sure that I'm ready for this. My dad cheated on my mom with *your* mom and when I see you, that's the first thing that comes to mind. Don't you realize that you are a product of my father being a cheat?"

"First of all, it's *our* father. And secondly, what makes you think that *you're* not the product of our father being a cheat?"

"Because my father loved my mom."

"Well, apparently he loved my mother too. Otherwise, he wouldn't have spent as much time with her as he did."

"Well, he actually *proposed* to my mom. Can you say the same?"

"Well, I guess that it doesn't matter, considering that dad didn't end up marrying your mom."

"At least he loved her enough to propose. Your mom didn't even get that far."

"And how do you know that? Were you there? I don't think so. You have absolutely no idea what went on between my mom and our father. And to be honest with you, you shouldn't be making that your concern, simply because it's none of your business and it's none of my business. I don't care to know what happened back in the day with your mother, my mother and our father. All I want is to get to know you because you are my sister. You have no reason to attack me or try to make it seem like my mom was a tramp because unless you were there to really know what happened, you really don't know anything."

"Well, what I do know is that I don't wanna get to know you. As far as I'm concerned, I've been my father's only child for twenty years and I'm not willing to share the spotlight with someone who claims to be my sister. So you can order breakfast without me."

I grabbed my purse and stormed outta the restaurant, without even looking back. I thought at that moment that it was all over but as soon as I drove away, I started crying uncontrollably. This whole matter was gonna be hard for me to get over. Clay called me twice that night but I was so upset that I couldn't even talk to him.

When it got late and I was tired of crying, I went to bed and stared at the trees outside my window. I think I fell asleep for about thirty minutes and then I woke up, tossing and turning. I couldn't seem to get Summer off of my mind. I was struggling with whether I should accept her into my life or just leave the matter alone.

Finally, I rolled over on my back and I said, "God, what do You think I should do? After the way I acted towards her, she probably don't wanna ever see me again." Then suddenly, He revealed it to me: call her and work it out.

It was about midnight but I figured that she wouldn't be asleep. And I was right. When I called her, she picked up on the first ring. I said, "Joy, this is Summer. Are you busy?"

"No," she answered, "Are you calling to insult me some more?"

"No. As a matter of fact, I'm calling to apologize. My attitude was completely out of line. And you were right; whatever happened between our parents, has nothing to do with us. So I am truly sorry for how I acted towards you. It's not that you did anything wrong. It's just a lil' hard for me to accept the fact that my dad…*our* dad wasn't perfect."

"I understand. And believe me, it's not easy for me to accept this either. I never thought that I had a sister."

"Me either. But I knew that we were definitely related because when I laid my eyes on you, it was like I was looking in a mirror."

She laughed and said, "I felt the same way."

"Well, how long will you be in Cleveland?"

"I'll be here until after New Year's Day."

"Oh, okay. Well, I would love to see you on Christmas Day if you're not too busy with your other relatives."

"That would be wonderful! Let's hang out on Christmas evening."

"That will be cool. I look forward to seeing you, Summer."

"I look forward to seeing you, too. Have a goodnight."

Sixteen

────◆·◆·◆────

(Taurus)

"So how are things going?" my manager Kevin asked me on the phone. Kevin has been my manager for ten years and has always worked hard to make sure that each of my books became bestsellers.

"Fine," I answered, in a nonchalant manner.

"Fine? Just fine? What's the status on this new book that you're working on? Is it almost complete?"

"Kinda."

"Taurus, what's wrong?"

"Nothing!"

"Well apparently, *something's* wrong. I haven't heard from you in over a month."

"Look, I'm going thru some things right now and they've been rather emotional."

"Emotional? What are you, a woman?"

"Kevin, you just don't understand. I'm going thru some things."

"Did somebody die?"

"No."

"Are you in the hospital?"

"No."

"Then whatever it is, you can get thru it. You have to stay focus. Is your manuscript at least halfway done?"

"No. But I'm still working on it."

"C'mon, Taurus. You have a deadline to meet on this book and your deadline is almost up."

"Kevin, I'm gonna have to call you back."

After I hung up the phone in Kevin's face, I cut my cell phone off and I rolled back over and went to sleep. I didn't wanna have any connection with the outside world. That's how I been since I moved into a lodge. I even kept the drapes closed because as far as I was concerned, there was no need for me to see the sunlight because I was too depressed to desire it.

I remember when I used to make fun of people who called themselves depressed. I thought that they were just people who were crazy and were in desperate need of attention. But that's not the case. I started to realize within my own pain that the most intelligent person can experience depression when things start to become too much to handle.

And I can definitely understand that now; I can go days without taking a shower, all I do is watch TV in bed, I eat even when I'm not hungry and I find an escape thru my situations, simply by sleeping thru it everyday. Through it all, I think that I gained at least ten pounds...and I don't care.

Since Brenda hired a divorce lawyer, I figured that I needed to do the same. So I hired a divorce lawyer named Mitchell, who was straight-up with me and that led to me becoming more depressed. He said, "Mr. Nate, I really don't believe that this divorce will rule in your favor."

"Why do you say that?" I asked.

"Well, you yourself told me what your children found in the back of your car. Mrs. Nate has the evidence of your infidelity and now that she knows that you've cheated on her, you can best believe that she's going thru *all* of your belongings that are still in your house, to find whatever else that she can find to have more proof of your infidelity. And if you were careless enough to let a pair of panties stay in your car, there's no telling what else that you left behind that Mrs. Nate may notify her divorce lawyer about. Your case is not gonna look good to the judge."

"So what do you suggest I do?"

"Beg."

"Beg?"

"Yes. Beg her to take you back. Beg her like your life depended on it. If she asks you to kiss her feet, offer to suck her toes as well."

"Naw, man. I don't beg anybody for anything."

"Mr. Nate, you either do that or lose everything you worked for, in a divorce settlement."

"Are you serious?"

"Absolutely. From what you told me about Brenda, it seems like she is a very strong-minded woman so more than likely, she will try to get you for everything you got. She probably won't be willing to compromise a lot."

"But Brenda is a very successful hairstylist. She doesn't even need my money or anything else. She's a wealthy woman."

"It doesn't matter. When a woman is emotionally hurt, she will try to own your mama if she can get away with it."

Christmas morning came and to my surprise, Brenda called me. I immediately answered the phone and said, "Merry Christmas, sweetheart."

"Yeah, whatever," she said in a nasty tone, "Look, your kids have been asking about you and so I was gonna bring them over to you so that you can visit with them for a while."

"Oh. Well…uh, why can't I just come over *there* to see the kids?"

"Because I don't want you here."

"Brenda, don't you realize how this separation is affecting the children?"

"The children are fine. They know that we are not living together anymore and that we are getting a divorce."

"You told them that we are getting a divorce?! Why!?"

"Why not? There's no need of me lying to them about what's going on between their parents. I simply told them that mommy and daddy are no longer gonna be married."

"I can't believe you did that."

"Well, believe it. Anyway, I will be bringing the kids over to you in a few minutes."

After she slammed the phone down in my ear, I got so angry that I wanted to just throw my TV thru the wall. My children are my life and the worst thing for Brenda to do is drag them into an ugly divorce or turn the kids against me. I want to protect them from this, as much as possible.

When my kids showed up to my lodge, it took all of my strength to hold back the tears. I didn't want my son and my daughter to see my pain. I hugged them for so long and so tight that I didn't wanna let them go. Brenda just stood there with her arms folded, staring at me with such a cold look that it felt like she was shooting a dart at me with her eyes.

"Thanks for bringing the kids by," I said to her.

"Humph," she said.

"Daddy, we miss you," Kiera said as she sat on my lap.

I gave her a kiss on her cheek and said, "I miss y'all too."

"So are you gonna come home?" Dillon asked.

I looked at Brenda and then at him and I said, "I'm working on it."

Brenda whispered in my ear, "I'm only giving you one hour with them."

I looked at Brenda as if she was crazy and she gave me a look as if to say, 'I'm not joking.' For the hour that I was spending with my kids, I felt like

Brenda was supervising me. She kept her eyes on me the whole time and her arms remained folded. I offered her a seat and she quickly refused. And when that one hour was up, she took the kids and left immediately.

It felt like a part of my soul was going out of the door. I sat right there in my chair, staring at the door. It was at that moment that I knew that my life was messed up. Everything that I worked hard for was slipping thru my hands and it seemed like everything was spinning out of control.

And just when I thought that things couldn't get any worse, Rita called me. At first, I didn't answer her call but she kept on calling and calling that I decided to go ahead and answer it. "Merry Christmas," she said, as if she didn't mean it.

"Same here," I stated in the same manner.

Then she sighed and said, "Well, I hope you're sitting down."

"Why?"

"Because I have some news that's gonna knock your socks off."

"Did somebody die?"

"No."

"Then your news can wait. Goodbye,"

"Taurus, I'm three-weeks pregnant," she blurted out.

It was like my heart stopped. "You're what?"

"I'm pregnant. I found out two days ago. I had been trying to reach you to let you know."

"I don't know why you're telling me this."

"Because there's a possibility that the baby may be yours, Taurus! Why do you think I'm calling you?"

"Well, I doubt that the baby is mine."

"Are you serious? Taurus, we've had sex several times."

"And? I'm sure that you had sex with your *husband*, several times. And I'm pretty sure that you still are."

"Taurus…"

"Look! Just leave me alone. I don't wanna hear anymore about it."

When I hung up the phone, it felt like there was a dark cloud hanging over me. Everything seemed to be getting worse and worse. I mean, what if I *am* the father of Rita's baby?

If so, that would completely ruin my chances of getting back with Brenda and my friendship with Shawn would be completely over. The last thing I need is an unwanted baby to be in the picture.

Seventeen

(Rita)

UNBELIEVABLE. I WASN'T expecting Taurus to act like that. He treated me as if I was some kind of tramp. One would think that he would have more respect for me, considering how long he's known me.

His attitude really messed up my mood for Christmas morning and I knew that if I didn't talk to someone and release some steam, my whole Christmas day would be ruined. So I called my best friend Yvette, whom answered her phone on the first ring.

"Merry Christmas, girlfriend!" she delightfully shouted thru the phone.

"Girl, I'm so pissed. If I was to spit on the ground, it would catch on fire," I said to her.

"Oh, my. What's wrong? Did you and Shawn get into a lil' spat?"

"Humph. If only it was that simple. Girl, I found out that I'm pregnant."

"So why are you pissed? Bringing a child in the world is a blessing. You should be rejoicing."

"Well, I'm not."

"Why?"

"Because there's a possibility that Taurus is the father and when I explained that to him, he totally disrespected me."

"Oh, my goodness. Does Shawn know that you're pregnant?"

"No. I haven't told him yet."

She was silent for a minute and then she said, "Um, Rita, all I can do is pray for you."

"Are you serious?! Is that all you have to say to me?! How come you didn't pray for me *before* all of this happen?! Now, all of a sudden, you wanna have a prayer life."

"First of all, don't get angry with me as if I'm the one that caused this whole mess. *You* were the one that just had to have your cake and eat it too. Secondly, what makes you think that I wasn't praying for you before all of this happened? I have been praying for you, ever since the first day you told me about Taurus because I knew that you were headed for trouble. I tried to warn you but you wouldn't listen to me. I told you that if you didn't leave Taurus alone, your world was gonna be turned upside down. But you laughed at me and said, 'Girl, *I'm* in control of this. Nothing's gonna happen that I don't want to happen.' Now that you're up to your neck in mess, you wanna blame everyone except yourself."

"Are you sayin' that this whole ordeal is *my* fault?"

"Who else fault is it, Rita? You were the one that created this whole mess for yourself. Instead of appreciating the love that you had at home, you chose to mess around and as a result, you're now faced with the fact that this baby that you're carrying, may not belong to your husband."

"Yvette, I'm not perfect, okay? Sometimes, things just happen."

"You honestly believe that? Rita, all of this happened because of the wrong that you were doing to Shawn. I'm being honest with you because I'm your best friend and I care about you. And if I were you, I would tell Shawn."

I almost dropped the phone out of the sheer shock of what she suggested that I do. I asked, "Yvette, are you crazy?"

"No, I'm not. I'm being very serious with you."

"Yvette, I can't tell him what's going on. It would hurt him."

"Yes it will but you need to be honest with him. If you *don't* tell him and he finds out years later, it will hurt him even more."

I started to cry and then I said, "But what if he leaves me?"

"Isn't that what you wanted in the first place? You hate being a first lady and you obviously hate being married to Shawn. Remember all those times when you kept complaining about what was going on in your marriage and that you wished that you weren't married anymore? Well, you're finally getting your wish."

"Are you trying to be funny?"

"No, I'm being realistic. When you do wrong and hurt others in the process, you are bound to get what's coming to you. It doesn't mean that your life is over, it just means that you're gonna have to deal with the consequences for the choices that you've made. But honestly, Shawn loves you so much that he may decide to work things out, no matter how hard it may be for him to do so. But whatever his decision is, you need to deal with it."

"But what if he decides to throw me outta the house with no place to go? Are you sayin' that I'm supposed to deal with that?"

"Yep."

"Why? It ain't like he's perfect."

"*No* man is perfect, Rita. As far as I'm concerned, you have yourself a good husband. He may not be the best husband in the world but no matter how he is, you should've showed your appreciation for the love that he has tried to demonstrate to you. There is no perfect marriage, Rita. But if the good outweighs the bad, then the bad really won't make much of a difference. But no matter what the outcome may be when you tell him, I'm still gonna be your friend and help you get thru this drama."

After I got off the phone with Yvette, I wiped the tears off of my face and quickly pulled myself together. Shawn and I were having company come over for Christmas and I most certainly didn't want anyone to notice that I was crying. After reapplying my make-up, I went straight into first lady mode and put a smile on my face.

As I was heading downstairs, I heard talking and laughter. I recognized the voice to be Shawn's brother, Sheldon. "Hey, Rita! How are you doing?!" he loudly asked when he grabbed me and gave me a big, bear hug.

The smell of alcohol was so strong on him, that it almost made me faint. I looked around the living room and I didn't see his wife. I found that to be awfully strange that Lavetta wasn't with him. Everywhere he goes, Lavetta tags along. But I did see Shawn and Sheldon's damn mama, Grace. She was sitting in a corner, shaking her head in disgust at Sheldon.

As Sheldon staggered back to his seat, Shawn had a look of disappointment on his face. Sheldon has been trying for several years to kick his alcohol addiction but he'd always relapse. He's been to the same rehab place a lot of times but after a few days when he's released, he'd always go back to drinking.

Shawn whispered to me, "Sweetheart, can you leave me alone with my brother for a second? I need to talk to him."

Sheldon overheard him and said, "You don't need to talk to me about anything!"

"Sheldon, calm down. I just wanna…"

"Wanna do what?! Preach at me?!" Sheldon yelled as he got up off the couch, staggering over to Shawn.

"I just wanna help you," Shawn explained. "You're my brother and I hate seeing you like this."

"So you hate me, Shawn? Is that it?"

"No, Sheldon. I love you and I wanna help you."

"No you don't! You just wanna point the finger at me! Well, I ain't stayin' around for that! I'm leaving!"

As Sheldon staggered to the door, he fell face first on the floor. Shawn took a deep breath and asked me, "Baby, can you help me carry him to the guest room?"

"Are you crazy, Shawn?" I asked him. "Sheldon is a very tall and built man. I can't possibly help you carry him *anywhere*."

"Okay, well just help me drag him into the guest room."

So I did. Shawn and I dragged him into the guest room and let him lay there on the floor. It seemed like he immediately fell asleep as soon as we dragged him into there. Shawn closed the guest room door and when we went back into the living room, we saw that Grace was crying.

Shawn walked over to her, gave her a hug and said, "Mama, it's gonna be alright."

She wiped a tear from her eye and asked him, "But why does he keep on drinking when he knows that it hurts the family? How long is he gonna keep doing this?"

"Mom, I don't know but I'm not gonna give up on him. I'm gonna help him get thru this."

"You can try to help him all you want to but if he doesn't want help, it's not gonna work."

Just then, the phone rang and I answered it. Unfortunately, it was Joy. That was the last person that I wanted to talk to. But to my surprise, she was extremely pleasant. She said, "Hi, Rita! Merry Christmas!"

I carefully said, "Uh…hello, Joy. Merry Christmas to you, too."

"I'm so glad that you were the one that answered the phone because I have a big surprise for my dear, sweet father and I wanna bring it to him. He is gonna love it."

I couldn't recognize if she was being genuinely sweet or sarcastic but I heard myself say, "Okay, well that's very nice of you."

"Thank you. I'm sure you gonna love my surprise, too. You're gonna be extremely shocked."

"Wow. Um…okay. Well, I guess I'll see you later."

"Yeah. I'll be over there, later on this evening."

Eighteen

(Shawn)

THIS WAS NOT how I expected Christmas Day to turn out. I expected for there to be peace, love and happiness. But instead, I get drama. The only good thing that came out of it, was the holiday dinner that Rita cooked. She definitely did a great job on that. Since Sheldon was intoxicated, he didn't eat dinner with us but mama did.

"Baby, this macaroni and cheese is absolutely delicious," I said to Rita, while we were at the dinner table.

She smiled and said, "Thank you, honey. I'm glad that you like it."

Then my mom blurted out, "Well, I think that the turkey is kinda dry and I think…"

"Mama, be polite," I interrupted, "Rita went thru a lot of trouble to prepare this dinner." Rita then glanced at mom and rolled her eyes.

"So who was that on the phone?" I asked Rita.

"It was Joy. She said that she had a surprise for you. It must be a good surprise because she seemed rather excited to give it to you. She claimed that I would like the surprise, too."

"Hmm. So did she say what time that she was coming over?"

"She didn't give an exact time but she said that she would be over later on, tonight."

After we ate dinner, mama complained that it was getting late and that she wanted to go home. So I told Rita that I was gonna take mama home and that I would be back in a few minutes.

Rita's face expression let me know that she was relieved when I told her that. Although it was obvious that there was still some tension between Rita and my mom, I was still rather pleased that an argument didn't break out between the two of them.

"Mom, I know that this Christmas didn't turn out the way that you wanted it to but I'm glad that you came over and ate Christmas dinner with us," I said to her, while I was driving her home.

"Thank you, son. But I just wished that Sheldon had never showed up. I wish that he would just die."

"I can't believe you just said that. No matter how Sheldon is, he is still your son."

"Well, he's definitely not the son that I'm proud of. If I'd followed my mama's advice and got that abortion like she urged me to, I wouldn't have to be bothered with his triflin' behind. Ever since he was born, I always knew that he wasn't gonna be nothing but trouble. I'm so ashamed of him."

"Well, maybe that's the reason why he turned out to be the way that he did."

"Excuse me? Are you saying that I'm responsible for him being a disgrace to this family?"

"All I'm sayin' is if you'd showed him at least half of the love that you showed me, maybe his life would have turned out a lot better. When Sheldon and I were kids growing up, you were extremely hard on him about every wrong thing he did. You never praised him for the good things that he tried to do and the only time you showed him any kind of affection, was either on his birthday or a holiday."

"Shawn, I gave that boy the love that I felt was necessary; I gave him *tough* love."

"You gave him *no* love."

"You can say what you wanna say but as far as I'm concerned, Sheldon is the way he is because he *wanna* be that way. I'm not responsible for his actions. He's a forty-one year old, grown man."

"I'm not trying to make excuses for his behavior. I understand that he's grown but when you don't get the love that you should've received as a child, you won't know how to love or how to accept it when you become grown. It doesn't mean that it's impossible for him to change but it's gonna be harder for him to do so because he only knows what you've taught him. But you shouldn't be ashamed of him. Even crack addicts have mothers and their mothers still love them."

"Humph. People need to learn to love themselves and stop waiting for someone else to love them."

After I dropped mom off at her home, I drove home thinking about mom and the things she'd said. I realized that she was repeating a cycle; her mom treated her the same way that mom treated Sheldon. My mom was the youngest out of four daughters and she was the only one that didn't go to college and was the only one that became an unwed mother.

When she was a child, she was the one that her parents didn't pay much attention to. And as a result, she wasn't loved. In her family, my mom was the black sheep because everyone else had their college degrees, owned big houses and they were all *married* with children. So when she used to come around her family, they treated her like an outcast.

She was hurt for many years because of it but what she doesn't realize is that she allowed history to repeat itself with Sheldon. When it comes to me, I am the apple of her eye but when it comes to Sheldon, she can go for years without even calling him to see how he's doing. She doesn't even ask about his wife.

When I arrived back home after dropping mom off, Rita was in the kitchen, putting up all the food and cleaning the dinette table. "Would you like some help?" I asked.

"Yes, please," she answered.

I went ahead and put the dishes in the dishwasher and just when I was getting ready to sweep the crumbs off the floor, the doorbell ranged. Rita went to the door and answered it. When I walked into the living room, I was extremely taken off guard when I saw Joy in the living room with a young lady that looked like my second daughter, Summer. I wanted to just run and hide.

"Merry Christmas, dad! Rita, I was told that dad hasn't seen his other daughter Summer in years and so I thought that he would be more than delighted to reunite with her. So in other words, you have another stepdaughter, Rita. Dad, I'm sure that you and Summer have a lot to talk about. So go ahead and talk," Joy explained, in a very sarcastic manner.

Rita looked at me in total shock and I saw the anger in her face. She said, "Shawn, you had another daughter that I didn't know about? Why would you keep something like that from me?"

I said to Rita, "Baby, I'm sorry. I didn't know how to tell you. This was your surprise, Joy?"

"You better believe it, dad."

Rita threw up her hand and said, "I can't deal with this. I'm going to bed. I don't know how you even thought that you could keep a secret like this from me."

As Rita stormed off to our bedroom, Joy sarcastically blurted out, "Merry Christmas, Rita."

I looked at Joy and said, "Look, I don't know what it is that you're trying to prove but…"

"What I'm trying to prove is that you're a liar."

"Hey! Don't ever speak to me like that! Now, I understand that you're angry because I never mentioned to you that you had a sister but causing this type of scene is not the way to handle this."

"Oh, really? How was I supposed to handle it? Was I supposed to keep it a secret, just like you did?"

"No, but we could've handled this in a better way."

Then Summer blurted out, "Look, just take me home, Joy. Maybe it's just not meant to be. I see that I made a bad mistake trying to get in contact with my father. I just want to forget the whole thing."

Joy sighed and said, "Are you sure?"

"Yes, I'm very sure."

Joy gave me a hard look and said, "You always preach about honesty. Practice what you preach, dad. Practice what you preach." After that, her and Summer left the house.

That whole night, I kept on tossing and turning in bed because God kept trying to speak to me about this whole ordeal with Summer but I didn't want to hear Him. Although I was upset at how Joy went about this, I knew that she really wasn't the one to blame for it. *I* was the one who tried to keep my daughter Summer a secret.

As a result, Joy sees me as a hypocrite, Rita went to bed extremely angry and I'm pretty sure that Joy's mother knows about Summer and is angry as well. And it's my fault. I was wrong for acting as if Summer didn't exist, just because I don't speak to her mother anymore.

By leaving Summer out of the picture, I realized that I was being extremely selfish. When you hide the truth from people instead of being upfront, *everyone* gets hurt. I wasn't thinking about nobody's well being but my own and not thinking about what was best for Summer.

She does have the right to want a relationship with me and find out if she has siblings. I didn't have the right to take those opportunities away from her, all because I wanted to keep her a secret. She's my daughter. She's a human being. She deserves to know the truth. And I knew that God was trying to tell me this.

The next morning, I woke up to the sound of Sheldon throwing up in the bathroom. I guess that he was finally feeling the effects of all that alcohol he consumed. When he walked back to the guest room, I followed behind him. He sat on the bed and I sat in a chair across from him.

"So how are you feeling?" I asked him.

"Is that a trick question?" he asked as he began to wipe his mouth with a piece of tissue.

I smiled and said, "Well, if you know that you can't handle liquor well, then why drink it in the first place?"

"Because it gives me what I need."

"Which is what?"

"An escape."

"Escape from what?"

"From everything, Shawn. Lavetta left me and…"

"Wait a second. Lavetta left you? Why?"

He sighed and said, "For certain reasons. One of them is that I got fired from my job and couldn't provide for her anymore."

"Oh, wow. I'm sorry to hear that, man. Have you been looking for work?"

"Of course I have but it's very hard out there. But I have been looking for work, everyday."

"Well, why did you get fired from your job in the first place?"

He put his head down and said, "Because I came to work, drunk. Like a fool, I was walking right in front of my boss, staggering to my work area."

"Oh, no. Sheldon, you have got to do something about this drinking problem."

"Don't you think that I have tried?! But the drinking helps me to forget that my mom never approved of me, it helps me to forget that my dreams are gone down the drain and it helps me to forget that my wife is disgusted with me because I can't get her pregnant."

"You can't get Lavetta pregnant?"

"No. After I had that car accident, the doctors told me that I wouldn't be able to have children. Obviously, he was right because Lavetta and I have been trying for two years to have a baby and we still don't have any. Every time she takes a pregnancy test and it turns out negative, she gets angry at me. Man, that tears me up inside."

"Hmm. Have you guys thought about adopting?"

"Yeah, but it's not the same as looking into the eyes of your own child and seeing yourself inside of them. And I want to be able to give that to her but I can't."

"I understand. But Sheldon, things will get better."

He started crying and then he said, "Shawn, I have to look up to see down. Everything is fallin' apart and I don't know what to do about it. I know that a lot of it is my fault but I am trying to fix things. But it seems like when I try to fix things, it never works out. And to make matters worse, Lamar is calling another man, daddy."

Lamar is Sheldon's fourteen-year old son from his first marriage. "Sheldon, what are you talking about? You know doggone well that Lamar knows that you are his father," I said.

"Well apparently, I must not be good enough to be his father anymore because ever since his mom Sheila got married to that square-head punk named Greg, Lamar's been calling *him* daddy.

"And how do you know that?"

"Because one day, I was talking to Lamar on the phone and when he put me on hold, I overheard him calling Greg, daddy. But I don't blame him, though; I blame Sheila for allowing him to call Greg that. For all I know, she probably was the one who talked Lamar into doing that, trying to turn the boy against me. You know how she is. She barely lets me spend time with Lamar. I guess she feels that since Greg is such a big-time wealthy lawyer that I'm not good enough to be Lamar's father anymore. I mean, I may not be rich like Greg and can buy Lamar the world but that's still my son. No matter what happened to my marriage with Sheila, I've always tried to maintain a good relationship with my son. Sheila's only been married to Greg for three years and all of a sudden, Lamar is calling *him* daddy? You don't know how badly that hurts me. She got my son looking up to another man. I love my son, Shawn. Nobody has the right to take my place as his father. Nobody. I understand that Sheila has her own life and that's fine. But my son is still my son."

"You're absolutely right, Sheldon."

He wiped the tears from his eyes and said, "Shawn, I'm just tired of being rejected. I don't know what to do anymore."

"Have you spoke to God about what you're going thru?"

"God? Man, are you crazy? God ain't trying to hear nothing I got to say. I wouldn't even know how to begin."

"You just open up your mouth and talk to Him, the same way that you're talking to me. He wants to help you but He wants you to come to Him. Believe me, He loves you and He cares about what you're going thru. All you have to do is accept Him into your heart and you will start to see things turn around for you."

"But Shawn, I've done so much wrong in my life and I ain't perfect and…"

"Sheldon, God knows all of that. He ain't asking any of us to be perfect because He knows that we can't be. Besides, if we humans were perfect, there wouldn't have been any reason for Jesus to die for our sins."

"But since I never bothered to have a relationship with God, what makes you think that He would want to have a relationship with me?"

"Because God is not like us humans. That's what makes Him God. See, we humans are the ones that can be unforgiving and treat people as if they are not worthy of a chance to be better in life. *We* are the ones that like to hold things over a person's head, not realizing that *all* of us have done wrong in our lives. But God can take the lowest of the low and turn them into a polished stone. So don't even think that you've done too much wrong to be a friend of God. And as far as mom, you don't need her approval for anything because she is not the one that can put you in a heaven or hell. So what she thinks about you, really don't even matter. *She's* the one that's gonna have to answer to God for the way that she's treated you, all of your life. I'll tell you the truth, Sheldon; if you start to seek a relationship with God by simply opening up the lines of communication with Him, it will be the best decision you ever made in your life."

Nineteen

(Joy)

IN THE MORNING, there was a knock at my door and when I answered it, it was Summer. "Hi, Summer. Come on in," I said to her.

When she walked in, she said, "I can't stay long. I just wanted to say goodbye."

"Goodbye? Are you going back to Cincinnati?"

"Yeah. I gotta get back to work. But I just wanted to let you know that I'm glad that I had the chance to meet you and I hope that I get the chance to see you again."

I gave her a hug and said, "I hope to see you again, too. I'm glad to know that I have a sister. I've always wanted one."

"Me too. I'll call you when I've made it home."

Just when she was getting ready to walk out the door, I said to her, "Summer, I'm really sorry for how things turned out with dad. I was angry with him but I didn't mean to make you feel uncomfortable. Maybe someday you and dad will be able to have a relationship."

She smiled and said, "Maybe. I'll talk to you later, Joy."

"Take care. Goodbye."

Later that night, Clay called and asked if we could talk over dinner. We hadn't spoken to each other since that night in the car when he told me about the job offer. I did miss him a lot and I was so glad to hear from him. I was very calm when he called me but I was jumping for joy, on the inside. I didn't know what to expect at this dinner but I definitely knew that I was going.

When he arrived at my place, he gave me a beautiful bouquet of red roses. "Wow, Clay! Thanks so much. They're beautiful," I stated, before giving him a kiss on the lips.

"Nobody deserves them more than you," he said, with a warm smile on his face.

Lord, how could I have ever thought of ending things with him? I thought to myself.

He took me to this wonderful restaurant on Coventry Street and I really enjoyed myself. He knows that I love that area because it's eccentric. People of the arts and of different races stay in that area, which makes it so beautiful. I've always wanted to move to that area but the cost of living was a lil' steep for me.

When the waiter seated us at the table, Clay took my hand into his and said, "I really miss you. I know that we have a lot to talk about but I'm willing to work things out."

I smiled and said, "Me too. I thought about a lot of things and all I know is that I want this relationship to work."

"I do, too. I love you, Joy. You are such an amazing woman and I never met anyone like you."

"I feel the same way, Clay. And I'm sorry that I got so upset with you and…"

"You don't have anything to be sorry about. I understand that you were scared of what the distance may do to our relationship."

"Yeah, I was. But in relationships, you have to learn to make sacrifices. That's why I decided to move to New York once I finish school."

He smiled and asked, "Are you for real? You're willing to move to New York?"

"Yeah. I don't want us to have a long distance relationship and I most certainly don't want to put you in a position where you have to choose between your career and loving me."

"But you know that I would've put you first, if push came to shove."

"Yes, I know. But after giving it some thought, I felt that it wouldn't be right for you to spend four years in school only to pass down the opportunity to do what you went to school for, all because you're in a relationship. I want to support you in everything that you do and if your dream is in New York, I want to be with you."

"But aren't you sad of what you may be giving up if you move to New York?"

I sighed and said, "Well, I do have my family and friends here but it's not like I can't visit them. Besides, I have to start living my own life and quit making life choices based on how others feel. I have to do what makes me happy and being with you, makes me happy. Not only that but after I finish college, I will be working on my career as an art buyer. And what better place to start a career like that, than in New York!"

He reached across the table to give me a kiss and then he asked, "Are you sure you wanna do this?"

I gave him a warm smile and I said, "I have no doubts about this."

He got out of his seat and walked over to me. Then he got down on one knee and said, "Well, I have no doubts for wanting to spend the rest of my life with you. So Joy Waters, will you marry me?"

When he popped open the black velvet box to reveal the most beautiful ring I've ever seen, I cried tears of joy. Then I asked, "Clay, are you serious about this?"

"I had to apply for a loan to get this ring so believe me, I'm very serious."

I giggled a little and then I asked, playfully, "If I marry you, do I have to deal with you farting in the bed when we're sleeping?"

He laughed and said, "I'll try my best to hold it in."

We both laughed and then I said, "Of course, I will marry you." He slid the ring on my finger and I gave him the biggest kiss as if he was going off to war.

The next morning, I called my cousin Carmella and told her about my engagement and she was real quiet. So I said to her, "Hello? Are you there?"

She sighed and said, "Yeah, I'm here."

"Did you hear me say that I'm engaged?"

"Yeah, I heard you."

I was getting a lil' upset at how nonchalant she was. I asked, "Well, aren't you happy for me?"

"It's not that I'm not happy for you, Joy. I just hope that you know what you're getting yourself into. I mean, you're only twenty-years old."

"Going on twenty-one. And what difference does that make? *You* were only twenty when *you* got married, so what's the problem? Besides, we're not gonna get married right now, Carmella. I still have to finish college. I told you about it because I thought that you would've been happy for me."

"Well, I just want you to really give it some thought. Otherwise, you're gonna be in the same boat that I'm in."

"And what boat is that?"

"Honey, you don't even wanna know."

"Yes, I *do* wanna know. What's going on?"

She sighed and was quiet for a second. Then she said, "Joy, I'm pregnant and when I told Mark, he had the nerve to say, 'We can't afford a baby, right now. So I suggest that you get an abortion.' When I refused, he packed his bags and left me. He even changed his phone number. I haven't seen or heard from him in almost two months. I called his mama and asked if she'd seen him and she said that she has but that she didn't want to tell me where he was staying."

"Did she actually say that?"

"Yes. She said that he needed some time to himself. Can you believe that? I'm the one that's been trying to hold our marriage together and he has the nerve to flee? He needs some time to himself? When he got laid off from his job, did I leave because I needed some time to *myself?* Absolutely not. While he was at home scratching his balls and doing nothing, I went and got a second job to take care of the bills."

"Did he even bother to find another job?"

"Hell, no. He gave me some ridiculous story that he needed to find himself. What in the hell does that mean?"

"Girl, I don't know. Look Carmella, I'm sorry that things are not working out for you but that doesn't mean that I'm gonna go thru the same things."

"Maybe you won't but it doesn't mean that you shouldn't be cautious. You may wake up one morning and not even know the man that you're married to. Never in my wildest dreams did I ever think that I would go thru something like this but I am. It's like I'm in a bad dream. Just be careful, Joy."

I knew that Carmella was just trying to warn me but I loved Clay and he loved me. Period. He ain't perfect and he can be moody sometimes but he's never given me a reason to doubt his love for me.

"Clay is a wonderful man, Carmella. You even know him, yourself. *You* were the one who reunited us," I explained.

"And?"

"And so you should know that Clay wouldn't turn on me like Mark turned on you."

"Humph. Well, since you feel that you got it all together, I'll leave the matter alone. Congratulations on your engagement, Joy."

After getting off the phone with Carmella, I went to hang out with Monica and to break the news to her about my engagement. She said, "Oh, my God! This is so wonderful! Do you need me to help you plan the wedding?"

I smiled and said, "Of course I do, girl. In fact, I want you to be my maid of honor."

"For real? Are you sure that you don't wanna make Carmella your maid of honor. I mean, she is the one that reunited the both of you."

"But nowadays, she's depressed and I really don't want her raining on my parade."

"Why is she depressed?"

"Because of some things that she's going thru with Mark. So because of what she's going thru in her own marriage, it's gonna be hard for her to be happy for me."

"Oh, I see. So have you told your mom and dad about your engagement?"

"No, not yet. I wanna find the right time to tell them, face to face."

"That seems like the right thing to do. So I take it that you're gonna move to New York?"

"Absolutely. As soon as I get my degree."

"Well, let me just say that I'm very happy for you and I think that you are making a great decision."

"Thanks, girl. So what happened with the situation with Todd?"

"Oh, girl. I forgot to tell you what happened with that. Girl, the police found his body floating in Lake Erie."

"What?! How did that happen?"

"People were saying that he went to a party on the lake with a group of his homies and he got drunk and fell in. All the people that were there were partying so hard, that they didn't even know that he fell in the lake."

"Wow. That's really awful."

"Yes, it is. On one hand, I'm sad that a person lost their life. No matter what I went thru with him, I never wished death on him. But on the other hand, he continued to stalk me and send me death threats after I broke up with him. He found out that I moved in with my mom and he had the nerve to show up and cuss my mama out because she wouldn't allow him to see me. Sometimes, I was scared to even walk outside. So in a way, I'm relieved to know that I don't have to worry about him anymore. I no longer have to live in fear. I asked God to protect me from this man and I guess that God did what He felt was necessary in order for me not to be scared anymore."

I woke up with a smile on my face, thinking about my wonderful man. I'm usually very grumpy in the mornings and like complete quietness but I jumped outta bed, turned the radio on to the gospel station and made me a plate of bacon with hash browns.

The sun was shining thru my kitchen window and I was humming a song from Yolanda Adams, while eating my food. I was definitely looking forward to meeting with Monica this afternoon to go over some ideas for my wedding.

My phone ranged and to my surprise, it was Taurus' wife, Brenda. We don't talk and I didn't give her my number so I didn't know why she was calling me. But I still answered the phone and said, "Hello?"

"We need to talk, woman to *young* woman," she said, in a calm manner.

My heart started beating fast. I asked, "About what?"

"You'll know once we sit down and talk."

"Well, what if I don't want to meet up with you?'

"Honey, don't play with me. You either meet up with me or I'm gonna get really ugly. And believe me, I really don't think that you want that to happen."

"First of all, how did you get my number?"

She giggled and said, "Sweetie, that's the last thing you need to be worried about."

For some reason, I was a lil' frightened that if I didn't go along with it, she would probably do something crazy. So I said to her, "Okay. Fine. We can meet up and talk but it can't be today because I already have plans. How about we meet up in Beachwood on Friday afternoon?"

"Fine. I'll see you, Friday afternoon," she said.

After she slammed the phone down in my face, my whole mood changed from happy to curious. What in the world did she wanna talk to me about? I was wondering if maybe Taurus told her something about me and now she got her panties in a bunch. If so, it doesn't matter because I'm in love with Clay. So what's done is done.

Twenty

———◆·•·◆———

(Taurus)

AFTER THINKING ABOUT what the divorce lawyer told me, I realized that I had to work very hard to try to win my wife back. My goal was to butter her up so good, that she'd allow me to move back into the house, tonight. So I stepped out on faith and packed up all of my belongings, to prepare myself to move back into the house.

After that, I threw something on and left to go get a manicure, pedicure and a haircut. I even went as far as to get a facial, which is something that I don't normally do. I wanted to look my absolute best for Brenda.

After the pampering was done, I drove to Beachwood Mall to buy the best, black suit that I could wear for the evening. Once I did that, I drove to our favorite restaurant to make reservations and then I picked up a large bouquet of long-stem red roses. I even went as far as to order a limo to pick me up from my lodge and drive me over to my house to surprise Brenda and to pick her up to take her to dinner.

I knew that the kids would be staying with Brenda's mom for the weekend so I knew that I didn't have to worry about them being a distraction. When I got back to my lodge to get myself ready, I rehearsed everything that I was gonna say to Brenda to win her back. I wanted the night to be perfect and for it to end up with us being in each other's arms.

The limo was at my door at eight o'clock that night and I walked outta my lodge with the bouquet of flowers in my hand. "You look sharp, sir," the young limo driver said to me as he opened the limo door for me.

I grinned and said, "I was hoping that I would. I'm trying to make-up with my wife."

"Well, I'm pretty sure that she will appreciate your effort."

"I hope so," I said to myself.

On my way to surprise Brenda, I was very nervous as if I was getting ready to propose to her. I was hoping that she would smile when she saw me and as a matter of fact, I prayed to God on my way to her. When the limo driver reached my house, I saw her Jaguar sitting in the driveway. So I knew that she was home.

When the limo driver got out of the car to open my door, he said, "Good luck."

"Thank you," I replied.

My legs were shaking as I walked up to the door with the bouquet of roses in my hand. I took a deep breath and ranged the doorbell. When Brenda opened the door, she had a blank look on her face. Then she asked, "Taurus, what are you doing here? Why are you dressed up like you're going to prom?" Then she looked over my shoulder at the limo and asked, "What's with the limo?"

I gave her the bouquet of roses and I said, "I wanted to surprise you, Brenda. I know that I did you wrong but I still love you and I wanna come home. You proved your point and I just want to make everything up to you. I made reservations at the restaurant where we had our first date so that we can talk and work things out. I'm willing to do anything I can, to save our marriage."

All of a sudden, I heard a man's voice from inside the house, saying, "Baby, is everything alright out there?" Then some big, buffed brotha came to the door and put his arm around *my* wife's waist. Then he looked at me and then at Brenda and asked, "Who is this?"

She looked at him and said, "Cecil, this is my husband, Taurus."

He gave me a look but he didn't say anything. I asked Brenda, "What the hell is going on?"

This Cecil person blurted out, "What do you *think* is going on? Brenda and I are together."

I got angry and I said, "Brotha, I wasn't even talking to you! And what kind of man would want to mess with someone else's wife?!"

"What kind of man would want to *cheat* on his wife?!" he had the nerve to ask.

"Man, you stay outta my business!"

"You stay away from Brenda! She is now *my* business."

Then Brenda shouted, "Wait a minute! Just stop! Cecil, it's okay. I can take care of this. Let me talk to Taurus for a second."

The brotha looked at me as if he wanted to hit me and then he slowly crept back into the house. Then Brenda looked at me and said, "I think that you need to leave."

"Brenda, I can't believe this. I went through all this trouble to win you back and…"

"I didn't ask you to."

"I can't believe that you're cheating on me with this dude. Is *he* the reason why you're filing for divorce? Is *he* the reason why you haven't been willing to work things out? Here I am, trying to fix what I messed up and you up here, playing house with some other dude. Are you bringing this man around my kids?"

"Let me tell you something: what I do is *my* business. You didn't consult with *me* when you were messin' around so therefore, I don't have to consult with *you* if I decide to do the same. And as far as the kids, they are well taken care of, without you. They are fine. *Everything* is fine."

"How can you say that everything is fine when you have a man up in our house, sleeping with you?"

She laughed and sarcastically remarked, "Awww, poor baby. I've bruised your pride because another man is taking care of business. Poor you."

"Don't play with me, Brenda."

"Go to hell, Taurus! I can't believe that you're standing up here, playing the victim. Are you kidding me? *You* are the reason why things are the way that they are."

"I know this but…"

"But what? I'm sorry, Brenda? I didn't mean it, Brenda? Is that what you were gonna say to me, over dinner? Well, you can save that because I don't wanna hear it. What you did to me was very hurtful. I honestly thought about taking you back but once I found out who the skank was that you were messin around with, I knew that there was absolutely no way that I could take you back and love you the same way that I did before I knew about your infidelity."

"I don't know how you found out who it was that I cheated on you with but it doesn't even matter. What's done is done, Brenda. I can't change the past. If I could, I would've never even *looked* at another woman, let alone, sleep with one outside our marriage. The other woman is out of the picture and I don't ever want to see her again. She meant nothing to me and she never did."

"Humph. Well, I'll be sure to ask her when I go see her, on Friday."

I took a hard swallow and I said, "What?"

She had a sly grin on her face and she said, "Oh, you definitely heard what I said. I know exactly who she is. See, you called yourself trying to be a cheater and in the midst of that, you were leaving tracks."

"I don't know what you're talking about."

Oh, yes you do. While I was going thru your things last night, I found a Valentine's Day card that Joy gave to you. Inside of it, she wrote, 'Baby, I love you and I'm so glad that you're my man. Thanks for the necklace.' I should've blown your brains out when I had the chance."

Wow. I was so busted and there was absolutely nothing that I could say to get myself out of that one. I remember when Joy gave me that card. That was before she met Clay. How stupid I was to leave that card in the house. That was *really* stupid. I was staring at Brenda, trying to think of a good lie but nothing came about.

I sighed and said, "Look Brenda, I…"

"Just shut up, Taurus. We're through. I knew something was going on between you two and you had the audacity to try to get me to believe that it was just my imagination. Her fast behind kept staring at you in church as if she wanted to put you between two pieces of bread and eat you. Every time I saw her at church, the hairs on the back of my neck, stood up. And what makes the matter worse is that my kids love her. They'd always run up to her after church and give her hugs. Now, I find out that *she's* the other woman. Was I not good enough? She's not half the woman that I am and ain't got what it takes to have the class that I have. Maybe our marriage wasn't perfect but I most certainly didn't deserve this type of treatment. I was still a good woman to you, Taurus. Does Joy take care of your kids? No. *I* do. And when a couple of your books didn't make it to the bestsellers' list and people thought that your career was over, *I* was the one that helped you to gain your confidence back. It was me that helped nurse you back to health when you caught pneumonia. I know that at times, I was a bit much but I didn't deserve to get my heart broken. What in the world were you thinking, cheating on me with a woman that goes to our church? Did you forget that she is the Pastor's daughter? You didn't think about how this would affect me and your kids and how it would hurt the Pastor, if he found out. All you cared about was your own satisfaction and you think that you can just show up to my house with some stupid flowers and a limo and think that's all you have to do, to make things right."

"Well Brenda, at least I tried."

"Well, try this: go home and leave me alone." After she said that, she gave me back the bouquet of roses, walked back into the house and slammed the door.

When the limo driver saw me walking back to the limo, he had a puzzled look on his face as he got out to open the car door for me. He asked, "She turned you down?"

"Just take me home," I answered.

Twenty-one

(Rita)

MY SISTER MARILYN called me early Saturday morning and said, "I think mama doesn't have much longer to live, Rita."

I jumped outta bed and asked, "What are you talking about?"

"Well, I'm over at mama's house and she's kinda going in and out of consciousness and she absolutely refuses to let me call a doctor.

"I'm on my way over there," I stated.

I threw on a pair of jeans, an old shirt and tennis shoes and hot-tailed it out the door. When I reached mama's door and went inside, Marilyn was sitting on the couch, wiping tears from her eyes. I walked over to her and put my arm around her to console her, which made her cry even harder.

"Is mama upstairs?" I asked in a whisper.

She sniffed and said, "She's gonna be gone any day now, Rita. And there's nothing I can do to fix it."

I gave her a hug and said, "It's gonna be okay. Everything happens for a reason. Let's just make her last days the most peaceful days that she ever have."

After speaking with Marilyn, I went upstairs to mama's bedroom and her eyes were looking up at the ceiling, half closed. Then she asked, "Where's Marilyn?"

"She's downstairs, crying her eyes out," I replied.

Mama rolled her eyes and said, "That girl has always been so dramatic."

"Well mama, she's just worried about you. I am, too. We don't want you slippin' away."

"Chile, please. I have terminal cancer. I can slip away in five minutes. But don't y'all worry about me, sweetheart. I'll be going home to be with the Lord and I won't have to suffer anymore."

I sighed and said, "Sometimes, I wish that *I* was with the Lord."

"Why do you say that?"

"Mama, my life is so messed up. I'm pregnant."

"You're pregnant? How is that a mess? I'm sure that Shawn is absolutely thrilled that he is gonna be a father."

"I haven't told Shawn."

"Why?"

"Well…um…I don't know who the father is. I cheated on Shawn."

She shook her head and said, "That doesn't surprise me."

"Why do you say that?"

"Because I know you."

"Well, Shawn had got so involved in the church that I was feeling left out. Spending time with me didn't seem to be a priority to him anymore and so…"

"Rita, Rita, Rita. I tried to warn you to get yourself together but obviously you didn't listen to me."

"But mama, I just wanted to have what I was missing at home. Do you honestly think that I wanted to cheat on Shawn?"

"Well, obviously so because you did. Didn't you learn anything from my mistakes? Look at me, Rita; everyday that I'm in pain, it's an ugly reminder of the pain that I've caused in other people's lives. And all those men that I dealt with in my past, they are not even around. I knew that you were trailing down the wrong path and I tried to get you to stop and turn around. But now, you have a baby in the picture and so now you have to figure out if Shawn is the father. And if he's not the father, why would he ever want to trust you again?"

"Well, it's not like he's perfect, mama. I found out that he has another daughter by the name of Summer. The girl lives in a totally different area code. She's the same age as his other daughter, Joy. I know that he had other relationships before he met me but he still should've told me about her. I couldn't believe that he kept her a secret from me."

"But yet, you're keeping your affair a secret."

"It's not the same, mama."

"How so?"

"Because it's just…"

"Did he apologize for not telling you about her?"

"Yes he did but…"

"Rita, this daughter of his named Summer is a daughter that he obviously had *before* he even knew you. So therefore, he didn't go behind your back and conceive this girl. Yes, he was wrong for not telling you about her but now you know about her. So get over it. Everyone has at least one secret in their lives because sometimes it's hard to be honest with people, simply because people are so damn judgmental. And considering the fact that Shawn is a pastor, I'm pretty sure that people are *always* judging him. Maybe he felt that you would do the same thing. It's all out in the open now, so let it go. Don't go pointing out the dirt on someone else's porch when you have dirt on yours. Let's be honest; your life is like a soap opera."

"My life is nothing like a soap opera. What's I'm going thru, is real life. This is serious."

"I know it is but what can you do? Absolutely nothing."

"But what if Shawn is not the father, he finds out and he leaves me?"

"Well, can you blame him? I guess you won't have any other choice but to move on with your life if he does decide to leave you."

"But mama, what if I find out that I *can't* move on with my life?"

"You're a strong woman, Rita. You always have been. If you're put in a position where you're backed into a corner, you'll do what you have to do to keep your sanity."

The whole time that Shawn was teaching Bible study, I couldn't even look him in the face because of my shame. Usually on the second Wednesday of the month, Shawn gets someone else to teach Bible study but Deacon Plunder was sick with the flu and so Shawn taught Bible study himself.

Out of everything that he was saying, he caught my attention when he said, "Sometimes, the truth hurts but when the truth comes out, there is a piece of freedom attached to it. See, that's the wonderful thing about God; if someone finds out everything you've done in your past, God still has your back and you can walk with your head held high, knowing that God has washed away your sins and you don't have to live a life of guilt. Yes, you may have to go thru some things for the wrong that you've done but as it says in His Word, He will never leave you nor forsake you."

After Bible study was over, I was headed towards the restroom when I ran into Taurus. He whispered to me, "Can we talk?"

"Where?"

"Around the corner, near the staircase."

As I walked near the staircase, I checked around the corner to make sure that no one saw Taurus and me. Then I asked him, "What do you want? Just a few days ago, you treated me like I was a cheap whore. Now, you wanna talk."

"Look, I wanna talk about this baby you're carrying. Are you sure that you're really pregnant?"

"Of course, I'm sure. I can't believe that you would even ask me that."

"Well, are you gonna go thru with this or are you gonna get an abortion?"

"I don't wanna abort the baby, Taurus. The child has no fault in this."

"But I might be the father, Rita. And honestly, I don't want to be the father of your child. I think that you should get rid of it."

"You are such a selfish bastard. This baby is a human being and he or she does not deserve to die, all because we were messin' around."

"Look, if you have this baby and Shawn finds out that he's not the father, he's gonna be furious and he's gonna want to know who the father is. This type of news will cause a lot of mess. Get rid of it, Rita."

"He or she is not an *it*. Stop saying that word."

"Does Shawn know that you're pregnant?"

"Not yet."

"See? If you get the abortion, he will never have to know."

"No. I'm not doing it."

"Rita, why?"

"Because there's a possibility that I might be carrying a baby that belongs to him."

"But what if the baby is mine?"

"Then I will deal with it. Now if you will excuse me, I have to go to the bathroom."

As soon as I walked away and turned the corner, Shawn's friend Candace was standing right up against the wall. She looked me straight in the face and said sarcastically, "Wow. It's amazing how thin these walls are."

"Excuse me?" I asked.

"You heard me. I heard everything that you and Taurus were talking about. Humph. I can't stand women like you."

"Women like me? You don't even know me."

"But I know your type; you are the type of woman that has a good thing and messes it up."

"Oh, I bet that you want my good thing, don't cha? That's why you've joined Shawn's church. See, I know your type too; you're the type that will try to take what doesn't being to you, such as my Shawn. I knew it the minute you slithered into this church."

She giggled and said, "Why is it that insecure women always think that every woman wants their man? Understand that not every woman wants your man. And that includes me. Just in case you haven't paid much attention to the ring that I wear on my left hand, let me inform you that I'm *engaged* to a wonderful man of my own, the same man that you were so obviously relieved to see me with. See, you were so busy watching me but *you* were the one that was doing dirt with Shawn's long-time friend. And he has the nerve to be an

126

Elder. If you wanted to be cheater, why in the world would you cheat with someone who's affiliated with your church? Are you really that stupid? What kind of woman are you?"

"I'm the kind of woman that minds her business. I suggest that you do the same."

"Hmmm. It would be a shame if your lil' dirty secret got leaked out and Shawn and the whole church found out about it."

I got close to her face and I said, "Honey, don't play with me. I will mess your whole life up."

She gave me a sly grin and said, "My life could never be as messed up as yours. But you can wipe the sweat from your forehead because I'm not gonna tell Shawn, anything. He's not my husband and that's not my place. But every dog has its day and you are no exception to the rule."

Twenty-two

(Shawn)

I DO BELIEVE that the past is the past. However, I do believe in tying up all loose ends when it's necessary. So I took it upon myself to call Joy's mother and talk to her about my daughter, Summer. I knew that Natalie found out about her and so I wanted to call and apologize to her for not telling her that I had another daughter.

When I called her, I said, "Hi, Natalie. I hope that you're doing well."

She sighed and said, "I'm fine, Shawn."

I knew from the tone in her voice that I needed to choose my words, carefully. So I said, "Well, I'm calling because I know that you already know."

"Know about what?"

"Know about my other daughter, Summer."

"Imagine my surprise when she walked on my doorstep."

"That's what I wanted to talk to you about. I'm sorry that you had to find out that way. I was very young at the time and…"

"Shawn, I'm not gonna hold a grudge against you. We were both young and we didn't know much about having a committed relationship. But what I'm upset about is that you kept this a secret for so long and Joy had to grow up without any knowledge that she had a sister. You kept that from her and you were wrong for that. Now, at twenty-years old, they both are trying to build a relationship with each other, whereas if you'd been honest from the start, they could've already established a close relationship with each other when they were kids. They could've had so many experiences together but you ruined that for them."

"You're right, Natalie. I don't disagree with anything you're saying. But at that time, I didn't know how to tell you that I had got another woman pregnant, at the same time that you and I were seeing each other. Can you honestly say that you would've stayed with me if I'd told you the truth?"

She sighed and said, "I don't know. I mean, yes I would've been extremely upset to find out that you cheated on me and made another child outside of our relationship. However, I would've eventually come to grips with it. Shawn, you and I were best friends before we became a couple so therefore, you should've felt comfortable enough to tell me anything because our friendship has always been more important to me than the relationship that we had."

"I feel the same way. I guess that's why we were able to have a smooth break-up and still remain friends."

"That's right. Even after you married someone else, we've always had a good friendship so there was no need to keep a secret like this from me. And be honest, Shawn; if this girl hadn't showed up on my doorstep claiming to be your daughter, it would've still remained a secret."

"I guess you're right. But I'm glad that the secret is out and I definitely regret that I've never said anything about her before. She is such a beautiful girl."

"Yes, she is. And she seemed to be very sweet."

"Yeah. Rita knows about her."

"How? Did you tell her?"

"No. Joy showed up to my house with Summer. And that's how Rita found out. She didn't take it lightly at all."

"Humph. That doesn't surprise me. Anyway, I gotta go but I'll talk to you later."

"Okay. Take care."

My Aunt Thelma called and left a frantic message on my voicemail, saying that she needed to speak with me as soon as possible. I was a lil' worried by the tone in her voice that something was terribly wrong. So instead of calling her back, I decided to show up at her house.

When she opened up the door for me, I notice that her eyes were blood-shot red as if she'd been crying. "What's the matter, Auntie?" I asked.

She sat on the couch, took a puff from her cigarette with her eyes closed and said, "Shawn, I don't even know where to begin."

"Just take your time," I said to her.

She wiped the tears that were falling down her face and she said, "I don't understand how I could raise all of my kids the same way and all of them turn out just fine, except for Darlene. I just don't understand."

"Is Darlene in some kind of trouble?"

"Not yet but she *will* be. That's why I called you because I was hoping that you could talk some sense into her."

"What seems to be the problem?" I asked.

"Well, she met this fool named Doonie and…"

"Doonie?"

"Yeah."

"Is that his real name?"

"Shawn, I don't know. All I know is that he's trouble. He's a drug lord and he's talked Darlene into allowing him to stash his drugs into her house and use her house as the place where he conducts his business. She don't even realize how dangerous this is. She got my grandchildren around that mess. So I went over to her house to try to talk some sense into her. Shawn, she got so mad with me that she asked this Doonie guy to physically escort me outta her house. And he had the nerve to say to me, 'Don't come back here, if you can't respect me.' Shawn, she could end up in jail and I don't want that to happen to her. Please talk to her."

"Where did she meet this man?"

"At a nightclub, where she has met most of her boyfriends."

"Well, you know that Darlene has a hard time listening to people when it comes to her life. And she most certainly doesn't listen to me."

"Just try to get thru to her, okay? Do what you can to get thru to her, Shawn. I love her and my grandchildren too much to just mind my own business."

"I understand. I will do the best that I can."

"Thank you, sweetheart."

Later that night, I drove over to Taurus' place to drop off his Bible tote bag that left at church at Wednesday night's Bible study. Besides, I wanted to take a few minutes to talk to him about Brenda. I wanted to know if things were getting better in their marriage or if they were still on their way to having a divorce.

When he opened the door, he was wearing a shower cap and a white robe. I said to him, "Hi, Taurus. I didn't mean to show up unannounced but…"

He walked me into his lodge and said, "Man, don't worry about it. I wouldn't mind the company. I was just getting ready to take me a shower but you can come in and sit in the living room until I come out of the bathroom."

What a beautiful lodge it was! There was a high ceiling in the living room with a large crystal chandelier hanging from it, the floor was covered with a black and white Persian rug, African art pieces hanging on the wall and a beautiful view of Cleveland that I was able to see thru his huge, picture window.

I sat on the couch and watched some TV as I was waiting for Taurus to finish his shower. His cell phone was sitting on the coffee table in front of me, making a funny bell sound. I took a quick glance and saw that he had a text message from my wife. I thought to myself, *why in the world would Rita be texting Taurus?*

Curious as to why, I flipped open his phone and the text message said this: *Taurus, I thought about what you said and I might go ahead and have an abortion because if the baby turns out to be yours, how will I explain that to Shawn?*

I felt like I was in a bad dream. Rita was pregnant and didn't tell me?! Not only that, but the man that I knew as my dearest friend, might be the father?! I thought that maybe I read the text wrong so I read it again. And again. *This couldn't be true,* I thought to myself. I knew that Rita and I were having problems but she didn't have to do this to me.

The more I sat on the couch, the angrier I became to the point where I jumped up and wanted to so something about it. And I did. I stormed into Taurus' bathroom and I snatched him outta the shower by his neck, flinging him from one corner of the bathroom, to the next.

He slipped away from my grasp and ran out of the bathroom but I was on his heels. I chased him all over his lodge until he had no other choice but to run outside. I chased after him as people were looking and gasping at the fact that Taurus was outside, butt-naked. When I caught him, I slammed him to the ground and tried to beat his head open.

Two people ran up behind me and pulled me off of him. As I was trying to get outta their grip, I said to Taurus, "Man, you were supposed to be my friend! How could you sleep with my wife?! Were you that stupid that you thought that I would never find out?! She's my wife! You crossed the line, Taurus! God's gonna have his way with you!"

He picked himself up off the ground and said, "Shawn, I am so, so sorry. I didn't mean for this to happen. I just…"

Before he had a chance to finish his sentence, I swung and punched him in the jaw. He fell up against someone's car and slid down to the ground. I stood over him and said, "Brenda was smart for kicking you outta her life. I think that I'm gonna follow by her example; I want you outta my church and outta my life, for good."

"I'm sorry, Shawn. I'm really sorry."

"Sorry? Is that all you gotta say? Man, I treated you like a brother and you turned around and slept with my wife. You have lost your mind. But since you want Rita, you can have her."

I walked away from him and headed towards my car. I heard Taurus trying to talk to me but I didn't turn my head to even acknowledge him. As far as I was concerned, there was nothing he could say to me to fix what he messed up. At this point, all I wanted was Taurus' head on a platter.

I sped off to my house, so full of rage that I ended up running a bunch of red lights. When I finally reached my driveway, I put my car in park and tried to think about what to do next. God was speaking to me and telling me to be calm before I enter the house but Satan was *screaming* at me to grab my gun from my glove compartment and walk in the house and shoot Rita's head off.

After about an hour, I calmly walked into my house and there was Rita, sitting on the couch. She was reading a book with a blanket wrapped around her legs for warmth. She didn't even look up at me when I walked in the door. But I definitely got her attention when I walked up to her and snatched the book out of her hands and threw it across the room.

She looked at me in total shock and asked, "Shawn, have you lost your mind?!"

I answered, "Not yet but I'm just getting started."

When I walked away from her, I headed upstairs and I heard Rita's footsteps behind me. She kept on screaming, 'Shawn, what is wrong with you?!' But I wouldn't answer her. I went into our closet and gathered up all of her things and placed them on the bed to be put in garbage bags.

Then she screamed, 'Why are you doing this?!' But I still wouldn't answer her. I just kept on grabbing her things and placing them on the bed, even all of her things that were in the drawers, all of her perfume bottles, cosmetics and knick-knacks. Rita started to cry but her tears were not moving me.

Then she grabbed me by arm and cried, "Shawn, what did I do?"

Still burning with anger, I looked at her and calmly answered, "I know everything."

She looked at me and I could tell by the look in her face that she knew what I meant. She cried harder than ever and said, "Shawn, I'm so…"

"Please, don't say it. I don't wanna hear it. The only thing that I wanna hear is silence in my house when you leave, tonight."

"Baby, please don't do this. I know that I messed up but I still love you."

"Rita, you don't love me. You don't even love yourself."

"But Shawn, I didn't mean for this to happen."

I laughed and asked, "Do you and Taurus read from the same script?"

"Shawn, I'm serious. I really wanna work this out."

"I don't believe you at all. The worst part is that you allowed a baby to be a part of all of this. You were careless, thoughtless and selfish. And that's not the type of wife that I want. And I most certainly don't want a wife on my arm that may be carrying some other man's child. We can't pretend like everything is gonna be okay. It's over, Rita."

She kept crying and pleading but I turned a deaf ear to her. I grabbed all of her things, placed them in garbage bags and placed them outside on the front porch. Rita was sitting in the hallway, shedding tears while I was packing up her things. After that, I called her a cab.

Then I walked over to her and I said, "I'm gonna call for you a hotel room for the night. After that, you're on your own. I thought about having the cab driver drop you off at Taurus' lodge, since you love him so much. But I figured that after what I did to him tonight, he probably don't want nothing else to do with you."

After about thirty minutes, I heard a horn blowing from outside and I knew that it was the cab that I called for. I looked at Rita and she looked at me and asked, "Is it really over? Just like that?"

I opened up my front door and I said to her, "Just like that."

She looked at me with tears streaming down her face and slowly walked out of my house. When she turned her head to look back at me but I slammed the door in her face. As far as I was concerned, that was the end of her and the beginning of better things to come.

Twenty-three

(Joy)

FRIDAY COULDN'T GET here fast enough. Whatever it was that Brenda wanted to meet with me about, I wanted to go ahead and get it over with. I can't stand this woman and I didn't want to be bothered with her.

She picked an eating area outside of Beachwood Mall for us to chat and I arrived there first. While I was waiting, I ordered me a glass of cranberry juice. About ten minutes later, Brenda showed up.

Although I don't like her, I do have to give homegirl her props when it comes to her sense of style. Girlfriend came to Beachwood Mall, looking like she was on her way to a fashion show in Paris.

She was wearing all winter white; a winter white fedora with a winter white pants suit, made of wool. The only splash of color was the red lace turtleneck that matched her red, high-heel boots. She walked towards me as if she was on a runway.

Then she sat down in a chair across from me and just stared at me. Then she asked, "Who do you think you are?"

Startled, I said, "Excuse me?"

She pulled a Valentines Day card outta her purse and slid it to me. The she asked, "Did you honestly think that I wasn't gonna find out about you messin' around with my husband?"

I looked at the Valentines Day card and I remembered giving it to Taurus, a year ago. I looked at her and said, "Well honestly, I really didn't care whether you found out or not."

"I'm sure you didn't. You're young and dumb as hell."

"Honey, I'm not as dumb as you think."

"You're *just* as dumb as I think. See, you did the most disrespectful thing that you could ever do to a married woman. And what you fail to realize is that you're gonna get back what you've dished out. When I found out that Taurus was cheating on me, I felt that pain thru every part of my body. But honestly, I don't think that I felt that pain in vain because there's something to be learned in everything that you go thru in life. And one of these days, you're gonna feel the same pain that *I* feel because you were a part of this mess. See, I know that you're in love with some fella named Clay. You've been bringing him to church and talking about him to everyone that's been willing to listen. And according to that lil' cheap-looking ring that you got on your finger, you guys are obviously engaged. Well, let's say that he decides to cheat on *you* with a woman who is just as scandalous and cheap as you are. How would *you* feel? How would you feel if she left her funky panties in your *bed*, just like you left yours in Taurus' *car*?"

I grinned and said, "First of all, Clay loves me like crazy. He will *never* cheat on me."

She giggled and said, "Clay is still a man and can be tempted just like everyone else. Although Taurus has his issues, I most certainly didn't think that he was gonna cheat on me. Especially with the likes of you. But he did. If he was really in the need of cheating, I would've thought that it would be with someone that was halfway decent."

"Excuse me? Well, if you were woman enough to be able to keep your man to yourself, he wouldn't have been with me."

"Woman enough? Sweetie, let's not go there. I have more woman in my pinky toe than you have in your whole body. You could go to college, get fifty degrees and be the president of the United States and you still wouldn't be *half* the woman that I am."

"Well apparently, Taurus thought that I was woman enough. That's why he wanted me."

She rolled her eyes and asked, "Joy, do you mind if I ask you a question?"

"Go ahead, if you feel the need to."

"What's your favorite restaurant, Joy?"

"Not sure. I have a few of them."

"Well, when you go to one of your favorite restaurants, do you order an appetizer?"

"Yes."

"Do you order yourself something to drink?"

"Yes."

"Do you order your main course?"

"Of course I do, Brenda."

"Out of the appetizer, the drink and the main course, which one would be the most important to you, in order for you to wanna go back to that restaurant?"

"The main course."

"Exactly. And that's because when you go to your favorite restaurant, the main course is the reason why you went to the restaurant in the first place. The appetizer may be tasty and tease your stomach but the main course is what satisfies your hunger. See, that's the reason why Taurus keeps on fighting to win me back because he realizes that I am the main course and can't nobody satisfy his hunger better that me."

Humph. She got a lot of nerve, I said to myself. I rolled my eyes at her and said, "Brenda, you forgot one thing while you were *trying* to make your point; sometimes, an appetizer can be more satisfying than the main course."

"But it's also the most *cheapest* meal on the menu. Anyway, please understand that although I've been made aware of your stupidity, I'm not gonna tell Shawn. With all the things that he deals with at church, he most certainly don't need to know that his daughter is a ho. So with that being said, have yourself a good day."

Brenda then got up outta her chair and sashayed away. I was so mad that I wanted to pick up a rock and throw it at her wide behind. Who did she think she was to try to make me feel like I was just some kind of tramp? But it doesn't matter; I have my man and the past is the past. Forget Brenda. Forget Taurus.

Saturday morning is usually when I go to the market and pick up fresh fruit. But on this particular Saturday, it was really packed and I really didn't feel like being bothered with the crowd. So I took a detour thru an alley to get to a grocery store to pick up a few things and as I driving thru the alley, I drove past Olivia, the choir director at the church.

I was shocked to see her in an alley. She tried to duck behind a brick building so that I couldn't see her. I backed my car up and she was leaning up against the brick building, looking like she hadn't bathed in weeks.

She had on a dirty, gray t-shirt with grease spots on the front, a pair of black shorts and no shoes on her feet. I parked my car and walked over to her. She wouldn't even look me in my face. I wanted to embrace her but I was afraid to.

I carefully asked her, "Olivia, why are you here?"

She said, "Um...do you have twenty dollars that I can borrow?"

"Borrow? For what?"

She got angry and asked, "Why are you in my business?! Just let me borrow twenty dollars."

"Olivia! What's going on with you? I'm not used to seeing you like this."

"Joy…I…you wouldn't understand."

"Oh really? Olivia, I'm not dumb. Any fool can see that you're high as a kite. So many people at church look up to you and they always speak highly of you. Do you know how many people that you are letting down by doing this to yourself? And you've promised my father a year ago that you would leave drugs alone."

"See, that's the problem. Everyone expects so much outta me. They always think so highly of me."

"You oughta be thinking highly of *yourself*, Olivia. You don't need to get high."

"Joy, I am human just like everyone else. I'm tired of everyone putting my life under a microscope and treating me as if I have it all together, just because I'm a Christian. Everyone comes up to me and feel comfortable enough to tell me about their problems and expect me to come up with the answers as if I don't have any problems of my own. Little do people know that there are many days when I wanna just end my life. There are many days when I don't wanna conduct the choir or hear any gospel songs. I just want the tears to stop rolling down my face and for the pain to go away."

"But Olivia, that pain is gonna be there until you finally confront it. When the accident happened, everyone tried to talk to you and get you to open up. But you convinced everyone that you were alright and that you didn't wanna talk about it. You have to talk about it so that it can be released. If you keep holding on to it, things won't get any better. And smoking crack is not helping anything. Let me help you, Olivia."

"Help me with what?"

"Help you get thru this whole ordeal. If you need someone to listen to you, I will. You can talk to me."

She started crying and I put my arms around her and I held her as tight as I could. Then she said, "Joy, I just don't know what to do."

"But God knows what to do. C'mon and let me take you home," I stated to her as I walked her to my car.

Without hesitation, she got in the car. As I was driving out of the alley, Olivia asked, "Can you do me a favor?"

I answered, "I'm not giving you any money, Olivia."

"No, not that. I wanted to ask you not to tell the Pastor."

I smiled at her and said, "I'm not gonna say a word. We're sorority sisters. I wouldn't betray your trust. I'm expecting *you* to tell him, yourself."

"I will. Believe me, I will."

I've always looked up to Olivia because she was always so easy to talk to and she was the type to help others before she helped herself. It was her that encouraged me to get into the AKA sorority. She introduced me to a couple of people in the sorority that helped me with a lot of things at college.

She was the first one in her family to get a college degree and start her own successful cookie business as well as being a choir director at our church. And that's where she met a man named Vincent and it was a match made in heaven. They were both into that whole organic thing, wearing African garments and always did things to help out their community.

Vincent was just as successful as she was and when they got married, everyone was happy for them. My father was the one that married them. A few months later, she found out that she was pregnant with her first child. She had a beautiful baby girl named Sarah Marie.

Olivia seemed to have everything that she wanted and everything she needed. But one day, Vincent took the baby with him over to his mom's house for a visit but on his way back home, he got into a head-on collision with a drunk driver. Vincent died instantly and the baby died on the way to the hospital.

When that happened, Olivia's world was turned upside down. She stayed locked up in her house for almost three months and when people came over to her house to check up on her, she wouldn't open the door. Then she strayed away from the church and started hanging around with people that were from the wrong side of the tracks. That's when the drugs came into the picture.

She was taking every drug that she was big and bad enough to use. One time, she almost overdosed on cocaine. I remembered that night as if it was yesterday. That night, I went over to her house, along with another sorority sister and we found her laying on the living room floor with cocaine powder on her nose and she was breathing funny.

For a while, she was really angry with us because we rushed her to the hospital. I realized that she was trying to kill herself. A month later, she moved to Akron Ohio to be with her family for a while. My father supported her decision to do so because he was very aware of what she was going thru.

After several months, she moved back to Cleveland and started to get her life back on track. My dad hired her back as the choir director and we all thought that she was better and that she healed from the loss of her husband and her baby. But I guess your problems are never gone if you bury them, instead of facing them. That's the start of moving mountains. It's time for Olivia to speak to her mountain so that it can move.

It's been almost a week since I've spoken to Clay. I left message after message on his voicemail and he hasn't returned any of my calls. So I drove over to his apartment and knocked on his door but I didn't get an answer. I drove over to his college to see if he was walking around campus but there was no sign of him.

All kinds of thoughts were going thru my head and I was getting more worried by the minute. I didn't know if maybe he was sitting in a jail cell or if he had been killed and left stranded on the side of the road.

So I called his mom and she said, "Clay went to Las Vegas with a friend of his. He should be back at his apartment, tonight."

"How long was he gone?" I asked.

"He's been gone for a few days. He called me this morning and told me that he will be back, later on tonight."

"Hmmm. Did he say why went to Las Vegas?"

"Chile, I didn't bother to ask. I don't really get involved in Clay's personal business. Anyway, I gotta go. I got fish cooking on the stove."

After I got off the phone with Clay's mother, I drove back over to his apartment and decided to wait for him to come home. I wanted some answers as to why he went to Las Vegas without even telling me. *If this is how he's gonna act when we get married, we are gonna have some problems*, I thought to myself.

With each minute that I was in my car waiting for him to come home, I was getting more and more frustrated. Finally, after about three hours, I saw his car pull into the apartment complex. When he got outta his car, a Puerto Rican girl got out of his passenger seat. I immediately jumped outta my car and headed over to him.

From the looks of it, he was extremely caught off-guard when he saw me. Then he had the nerve to ask me, "Joy, um, what are you doing here?"

"What do you mean 'What am I doing here?' I came here looking for you. I haven't been able to contact you for an entire week. I called your mom and she said that you went to Las Vegas with a friend. Is this girl your so-called friend, Clay? What were you doing in Las Vegas?"

Clay turned to the Puerto Rican girl, gave her his apartment keys and asked her, "Can you go inside? I need to speak with Joy for a minute."

Heated with anger, I asked him, "Why are you asking her to go inside your apartment, Clay? What is she doing here?!"

"Joy, I'm so sorry but…"

"Sorry? Sorry about what?"

"Consuela and I decided to work things out. We realized how much we still loved each other and so we flew to Las Vegas and got married. I didn't mean to hurt you, Joy. You are a wonderful lady and any man would be lucky to have you. But Consuela has always been the woman that I love. I am really sorry. I was trying to figure out a way to tell you without hurting you. I hope that we can still be friends."

Without even thinking, I slapped him in his face. He rubbed his cheek and said, "Joy, please calm down."

"You bastard! I opened up my heart to you!"

"Would you rather marry someone that loves only you or would you rather marry someone that loves someone else? Give me credit for at least being honest."

"Fool, are you crazy?! You weren't honest to begin with, Clay. Now I see that you made me out to be the rebound chick. I'm a human being Clay, not a toy. And if you knew that you were still in love with this girl, you shouldn't have proposed to me. That was stupid. What in the world were you thinking?"

"I thought that maybe my love for her would go away, eventually. But it never did. And when you came along, I thought that I would be able to get her outta my system by simply loving you. But that didn't work either. So one night, I called her and tried to end things once and for all but the more we talked on the phone, the more we realized that our love was real. I know that you are too angry to understand me right now but I hope that one day, you understand and agree that I did the right thing. I really didn't mean for any of this to happen. But I can't help who I love."

"Go straight to hell, Clay. You played with my heart and you had no right to do that. And as far as us being friends, that will never happen. I can't be friends with someone who can't be honest with me."

"But I was honest with you. I told you what I did and why."

"Being sneaky and honest are two totally different things. You hid your true feelings from me. And had I not showed up to your apartment, you wouldn't have told me anything about this Consuela girl or the fact that you flew off to Las Vegas to get married. As far as I'm concerned, I'm done with you, Clay."

I was too angry to even cry. When I got home, I lit some candles and laid back on the couch with a jazz CD playing on the stereo. I couldn't believe that something like this happened to me. Did I miss something? Were there signs that I didn't pay attention to? Was I that blind by love, that I couldn't see that I getting played?

Humph. Here I was, planning a wedding and preparing to tell my parents about my engagement and he was in Las Vegas, saying his vows to another woman. I thought that I had the man of my dreams but he turned out to be a nightmare.

And although I hated to admit it, Brenda was right; Clay is still a man and can be tempted, just like everyone else. But I'm not gonna shed one tear over that fool. And he is *definitely* not getting my engagement ring back.

Twenty-four

(Taurus)

IT'S BEEN ABOUT two weeks and my body is still kinda sore from the fight that I had with Shawn. I haven't even come close to going to church because I already know that everybody knows about the fight. Shawn is not the type to gossip and spread his business but I just know that everybody knows about it.

And there's no tellin' how he reacted with Rita. As a matter of fact, I haven't even heard from her since that night that she sent me a text and Shawn read the text. I hope that he didn't snap on her and do something stupid.

My manager called me again, early in the morning, to find out how the status of my new book was coming along. I really didn't want to hear his mouth but I went ahead and answered the phone, just to get it over with. As far as I was concerned, writing was the last thing on my mind.

"What's going on, Taurus? How's the book coming along?" he asked in a cheerful tone.

"Look Kevin, I think I'm gonna take a break."

"Take a break? Taurus, you can't afford to take a break. You have a deadline to meet and if you don't meet it…"

"I don't care! I have some personal issues going on and I need to get away for a while. I really don't care what happens with the book."

"Taurus, I…"

After I hung up in his face, I thought about what I told him over the phone. Humph. Maybe I really *do* need to get away for a while. So with that thought in mind, I decided to give my cousin Brian a call. He lives down in Miami and is one of the most successful realtors down there. So I figured that I would pay him a visit and leave Cleveland behind for a while.

"What's up, Taurus!" he greeted me when he got on the phone.

"Hey, Brian," I replied, "How are things in Miami?"

"Um, pretty good. Just handlin' my business."

"Yeah, I bet you are. The last time I came down there was when we had the family reunion. I remember you showing me your mansion with the ocean view."

"Um...yeah. So what's been going on, Taurus?"

"A lot of things, man. That's why I'm calling you. I want to leave Cleveland for a while. I need a break. I was hoping that I can come and stay with you for a few months."

"Well...um...I don't have the mansion anymore."

"Oh, really? Did you move to another one? A bigger one?"

"Um, no. I have an apartment," he explained.

I was silent for a second, wondering why in the world was he in an apartment. I said, "Oh, I see. I didn't know that you moved to an apartment."

"Well, it happens. But I do have an extra bedroom for you to stay in."

"Cool. I'll pack and jump on a plane, tomorrow."

When I arrived in Miami, Brian was already waiting for me. From what I've known of him, Brian has always been a sharp dresser even when he was dressed in casual wear. But when I saw him at the airport, he was dressed like he was as poor as a church mouse.

He looked like he was at least two months late for a haircut, his facial hair wasn't well-kept at all and the muscular physique that he used to have, turned into a big pile of fat. He was wearing clothes that looked like he slept in them, which was shocking because Brian has always spent time and money on his appearance.

When he saw me, he gave me a hug and said, "Nice to see you, cuz."

"You too," I said, trying not to look so shocked.

We grabbed my suitcases and headed towards his car, which wasn't the S-class Mercedes that he used to use as a chick magnet. Instead, we headed in the direction of a rusty, ten-year old Chevrolet Cavalier with the blue paint chipping off of the hood.

"Whose ride is this?" I blurted out.

He glanced at me and said, "It's mine, Taurus. I bought it from a 'Buy here, Pay here' lot."

"For what? What happened to the Mercedes?"

"It's a long story. I'll tell you later."

Brian has always been the type of dude that had much conversation. That was his forte'. But while we were heading to his house, he didn't seem to have much to say at all. He asked me about the weather in Cleveland but outside the small talk, it was pretty much silent.

When we arrived at his apartment, I was extremely appalled by the sight of it. First of all, the grass had mud spots in it, parts of the siding was hanging off of the building, there were cracks in certain windows, dirty-looking kids playing in the street and loud music playing as if everybody wanted to hear it.

Brian helped me with my suitcases and while we were walking into the hallway towards his apartment, the odor of urine hit my nose and almost knocked me out.

Not only that, a couple of thugs that were in the hallway was smoking so much weed that it was burning my eyes. So here I was, getting nauseous from the stench of pee and damn near blinded by weed smoke. *Who in the world owns this dump?* I thought to myself.

When Brian finally opened the door to his apartment, I was greeted by roaches and a rat that ran past my feet. In the living room, he had one small TV that was sitting on a milk crate, the beige carpet was filled with stains and there was one old brown couch that was sitting underneath a dirty window. There were dirty dishes in the sink and a raggedy card table used in place of a kitchen table.

He showed me to his extra bedroom, which didn't have anything in it except one mattress that was sitting in the middle of the floor. I put my suitcases next to the closet and headed back to the living room, where Brian was. He kicked his tennis shoes off his feet, sat on the couch and was flipping thru the channels on the TV.

I sat on the couch next to him and looked around the room. This place was definitely not the white Spanish-style mansion that Brian used to gloat about. This place looked like hell had come thru it. I wondered what the hell went wrong but I didn't know how to ask him.

"So how is Brenda and the kids?" he asked, with his eyes still glued to the TV.

I sighed and said, "Well, not so good."

He looked at me and asked, "What do you mean?"

"We're getting a divorce."

"Aw, man. I'm sorry to hear that, Taurus."

"Well, it's *my* fault. I cheated on her."

He looked at me in shock and said, "Wow, Taurus. I never expected you to be the one to cheat on your wife."

"Well, I did. I know that I was dead wrong but there's nothing that I can do about it."

"Did you try to work things out with Brenda?"

"Yeah, but it was painfully obvious that she had moved on with her life and that she's serious about this divorce. I can't blame her, though."

"Humph. Well, are you still messin' around with the other woman?"

"It's actually two women that I was messin' around with."

"Two women?"

"Yeah. And one of them is pregnant."

"Oh, my God. Taurus, what in the world…"

"Man, I didn't mean for all of this to happen but since I caused this mess, I'm gonna face it and deal with it, the best way that I can."

"Hmm. Well, are you sure that the baby is yours?"

"No, because she's married."

"She's married?"

"Yep…to my best friend. So he might be the father. But if she decides to keep the baby, I'll go ahead and take the DNA test to see if the baby is mine. I hope not, though."

"Does your best friend know anything about this?"

"Yeah, he knows. We got into a big fight."

"Whew! Seems like you got yourself caught in a bind."

"It's way more complicated than that, brotha."

He shook his head and said, "Well, I wish you much luck with that."

"Man, I need more than luck to get me thru this mess. I need the full attention of God."

"Yeah, we all do. It took God to get me to see that I needed to put Him first."

"Well, now that we are on the subject of you, what in the world…"

"I knew that you were gonna ask. Yes, I lost everything."

"How?"

He sighed and said, "Being stupid."

"Stupid? Can you be just a lil' more specific?"

"Well, as you know, I was one of the wealthiest realtors in Miami and I lost it all because I was selfish."

"Well, I don't think that God has a problem with people working hard to become prosperous. I mean, you can't get there by being lazy."

"True, but when you put money before God, that's when you're gonna be in trouble. Well anyway, I wasn't really wise when it came to my money. I bought any and everything that I could get my hands on, simply because I could. I threw my money away on fancy cars, designer clothes and shoes. And let's not forget about the mansion; it costs me a lot of money to keep it up. The taxes on that bad boy were insane and every week I had to pay my two maids and my chef, which was burning a hole in my pocket. And every time my friends and I would go to a restaurant or a club, I was always volunteering to pick up the tab, flashing my money around like a big clown. I was so selfish that I didn't even bother to take my money and help my community. It was all about me having money and getting more money. I was spending it on women and acting as if I would never run out. The minute I started putting God on the back burner, that's when I started getting into trouble."

"Like how? Did you get sued and lose everything?"

"Worse. I didn't do what I told God that I would do."

"What do you mean?"

"Well, before I made it big in the real estate business, I made a promise to God that if he helped me to become a successful realtor, that I would help others, be a faithful tither and not turn my back on Him. Man, when I started making good money, I think I went to church only twice and the minute I got my first check that was over five-hundred thousand dollars, I lost my damn mind. I stopped going to church altogether and I didn't give a dime back to my community. Business was good and I was living the high life. I didn't even give God a second thought. It was all about me and what *I* wanted. I had all the money in the world and that became my god. Soon, I started getting into trouble with the I.R.S because I wasn't paying my taxes and since I didn't have smart people around me to help me invest my money, all of my money was going thru my hands like water."

"So you ended up being broke?"

"More than you know. I didn't realize how many bills I had until I became broke and couldn't afford to pay them. Man, things were so bad that I was writing checks to buy groceries, knowing that I didn't have any money in the bank to cover them. Eventually, my maids and my chef quit because I couldn't afford to pay them anymore and my cars were repossessed. But what really broke my spirit was when I was evicted from my mansion."

"Awww, man. I know that was a hard pill to swallow."

"Of course it was. That is something that I will never forget. One morning, I woke up to the sound of a sheriff banging on my door, like he had lost his mind. He demanded that I vacate the property immediately and all I had on, was my pajamas. The place was auctioned off and so were all of my possessions. I had to live with my mama and certain relatives made me the laughing stock of Miami. Taurus, I was at a point in my life where I wanted to commit suicide. And I almost did."

"Really? You were actually gonna kill yourself?"

"Yeah. I was sitting on my bed, crying and drinking and I grabbed my gun from under my bed. I put it to my temple but I just couldn't pull the trigger."

"I'm glad that you didn't, Brian. Nothing is so bad that you have to end your life."

"That's true but when you've hit rock bottom and you don't see any way out, you don't think logically. When you see things crumbling in front of your eyes, you try to find a way to escape. But it was my mama who convinced me to get right with God. But at first, I felt too ashamed to talk to Him."

"Why?"

"Because I knew that I really messed up and that I let God down. But at the same time, I also knew that He was waiting and willing to hear from me. Besides, all of my so-called friends left me as soon as the money was gone so the only friend I had was God. But I'm not bitter, Taurus."

"You're not?"

"Not at all. I learned a very valuable lesson."

"Which is what?"

"Greed kills everything. When you get greedy, you become needy. But I'm slowly but surely getting my life back together. I was able to find a job so that I could move outta my mama's house and I help out three times a week at a homeless shelter. It's my way of giving back to my community, like I told God that I would do."

"Wow. So you don't have those thoughts of suicide anymore?"

"Naw, man. I started seeing a counselor at my church and it's helped me a lot. I may be living in a broken-down apartment complex but I thank God that I'm still breathing. Life is not over as long as you're still living."

Twenty-five

(Rita)

AFTER WHAT HAPPENED between me and Shawn, I stayed far away from his church. I didn't wanna deal with the snickering, staring, pointing and whispering. I've tried several times to reach Shawn but he hasn't returned any of my calls. But I don't blame him, though; it's *my* fault that this whole thing happened.

Ever since Shawn threw me outta the house, I've been living with my mom and she's been steadily hanging on for dear life. I'm amazed at how determined she is to stay alive. I never knew that she had that much strength.

I've been feeding her, bathing her and checking up on her in the middle of the night. Although I know that she is slowly slipping away, I try to add a lil' sunshine to her life by opening up all the drapes in her house that she kept closed. Now, the house doesn't look like death is living there.

Before I got heavily involved with mama's life, my sister Marilyn was the one that was taking care of mama's bills. But since I was now living with mama, I felt that it was only right that I took care of the bills, myself. However, since Shawn cancelled my credit cards and has fixed it where I couldn't get any money outta our checking account, I had to go get a job at a clothing store to provide for my mama and myself.

One particular day, I was at the clothing store putting some blouses on the rack when this dark-skinned woman walked up to me and asked, "Aren't you Pastor Owens' wife?"

I was kinda reluctant to answer her question but I said, "Yes, I am. And who are you?"

She gave me a nasty look and said, "I'm Tina Martin. I've been a member of Sweet Harmony Springstone Baptist Church for about a year now."

"Well, I don't remember ever seeing you."

"Humph. I'm sure you don't. I heard about what you've done. How could you disrespect your husband like that?"

"Look honey, I don't need you coming down here to my place of employment, getting into my business. I have work to do."

"First of all, I came down here to buy me a skirt. I didn't even know that you were gonna be here."

"Then buy your skirt and leave."

"I'll leave when I'm good and ready. You don't remember me, do you?"

"No and I don't care to."

She grinned and said, "Well, I feel the need to refresh your memory; two months after I joined the church, my husband was shot and killed, leaving me with three mouths to feed. After paying for the funeral arrangements, I didn't have any money to feed my kids. I called the church for help and they told me that you were in charge of the food ministry. When I told you the situation, you didn't even give me eye contact and you had the nerve to brush me off by saying, 'Honey, I don't have time for this right now. I'm late for my hair appointment.' You rushed outta the door and sped off in your Mercedes and didn't look back."

"So are you looking for an apology?"

"No. I don't need your apology. But I want you to know that I will definitely keep you in my prayers. Unlike you, if you need me for anything, I won't turn you away. I'll be there for you. Although you've treated me like I was beneath you, I want you to know that I don't hate you and I hope that you overcome the issues that you are dealing with."

"What makes you think that I have any issues?"

"Oh, please. *Everyone* has issues."

"Humph. Well, I hope things are well with you and your kids."

"They are more than well. I've been blessed with a high-paying job and was able to put my son thru college. Anyway, I gotta go but here's my card if you need anything."

When she gave me her card, I noticed that it had the church's logo on it and underneath her name was the title, *Food Ministry Coordinator.* "What is this?" I asked.

She smiled and said, "Well, since you're not at the church anymore, I asked the Pastor to allow me to be a part of the food ministry and he said yes. He loved my service so much that he made me the head coordinator for it."

"So I guess you think you got it goin' on, huh? You tryin' to be me?"

"I don't ever want to be you. See, me being a part of this ministry, is not a title to me. It's a commitment. I take what I do, very seriously. See, when a woman comes up to me in need of food or maybe in need of diapers for her baby, it warms my heart to be in a position where I can help her. And when she walks away, I know that God is smiling down at me because not only did I help her but I demonstrated love to her, which is the most important thing. Without love, people cannot see the God in you. Anyway, I'll talk to you later, Rita."

When she walked away, I walked to the stock room and found a little corner where I cried my eyes out. I was crying so hard that my body was shaking. "Lord, what have I done to myself?" I whispered to myself.

My world was turned upside down and I never thought that it would be like this. I thought that I had everything under control and that I could live my life the way that I wanted to, without worrying about anything. But the more things got out of control, the worse things became.

For it to be July, it was rather chilly outside. Me being pregnant has been the worst experience of my life; I've gained at least forty pounds, my ankles are as fat as ham hocks, I have back pains and I find it hard to get a good night's sleep.

While I was watching TV, my phone ranged and to my surprise, it was Taurus. I didn't know whether I wanted to answer it or not but I did, curious as to what he had to say.

When I answered the phone, he said, "I just called to see if things were okay with you."

"Why do you care? You've moved on with your life," I stated to him.

"Things have been pretty hectic, huh?"

"What do you think, Taurus? It most certainly hasn't been a pleasure trip. Everyone at church knows about this."

"See, that's the reason why I left Cleveland."

"You left Cleveland? For good?"

"No. I decided to go to Miami for a few months to get away for a while."

"Oh, well lucky you. While you've been vacationing, I've been working in a clothing store just to make ends meet."

"Make ends meet?"

"Yes, Taurus. I've moved in with my mom and I'm the one that takes care of the bills."

"I'm sorry to hear that, Rita."

"Yeah, right."

"I *am*, Rita. I know that you may not believe me but I am sorry that all of this happened. We should've never let it get this far. But since it did, I guess we gotta deal with it. What have you decided to do about the baby?"

I sighed and said, "I decided to keep it."

"You did?"

"Yes. In fact, the baby will be here, soon."

"Oh. Well, I guess I'll take the DNA test."

"You will?"

"Yeah. I at least wanna know if the baby is mine or not. Hopefully, not."

"Humph. Well anyway, I gotta go. I'll talk to you later."

When I got off the phone with Taurus, I turned off the TV and got myself ready for bed. On my way to my bedroom, I went into mama's room to check on her. I touched her arm and she was cold as ice. I immediately tried to revive her by shaking her but it wasn't working. She was gone. I cried while dialing the number for an ambulance and then I called Marilyn. She hurried over to the house in less than fifteen minutes, just when the ambulance showed up.

Marilyn and I cried and hugged each other while the paramedics carried mama outta the house. We knew that it was only a matter of time when she would pass away but we were still shocked when it happened.

After we've cried for several hours, Marilyn went home and I went upstairs in mama's room. I laid on her bed and held her bed covers, close to me as if I was holding her. My face was turned towards the window and I watched the stars twinkle in the sky until I went to sleep.

The funeral was small but it was very lovely. Aunt Betty did the eulogy and Marilyn and I said a few words. A couple of my mother's friends that she met thru the church, was also present to pay their respects.

Mama looked so peaceful in her white, silk dress. It almost looked as if she had a lil' smile on her face. I guess I would be smiling too if I knew that I was going to meet the Lord. I was sad that she was gone but happy that she wasn't suffering anymore.

After the funeral, we all had dinner at Aunt Betty's house, laughing at stories that Aunt Betty told us about the things that mama used to do as a kid. She was saying that mama used to sneak outta their parents' house to hang out with this guy named Johnnie and that mama got into trouble when she was five-years old because she stole her mama's make-up and wore it to school.

While Betty was telling us stories, I glanced over at Marilyn sitting with her fiancé, Allen. I tried not to stare but I couldn't help it. They looked so lovely together and Allen held her hand as they sat together. Humph. I remember when Shawn and I used to be like that.

Since I inherited mama's house, I took it upon myself to brighten up the place. I got rid of all those gloomy, burgundy, heavy drapes that were hanging up all over the house and I put up some white, lace curtains that gave the house a pleasant feeling when you walked in.

Although I kept all of mama's furniture, I got rid of all the carpet and decided to have hardwood floors instead. I put a few paintings on the wall and I even planted a garden made up of bell peppers, tomatoes, cabbage and collard greens.

One morning, I was walking past one of the bedrooms and I saw a stream of bright light, coming thru one of the windows and beaming down on the floor. I kept on staring at it because it was such a beautiful light, that I just had to sit down and watch it.

Tears came to my eyes and I was filled with so many mixed emotions that I didn't even know how to express them. I didn't know if it was the pregnancy or the guilt that has finally gotten to me. It's been a long time since I've prayed to God but I really had the urge to do so. At first, the words wouldn't come outta my mouth because I was crying so hard but after a few minutes, I calmed down and poured my heart out to Him.

I said, "Dear God, I haven't prayed to You in such a long time, even when I became a first lady. But I hope that it's not too late to talk to You. God, I know that You are well aware of the mess that I got myself into; my marriage is torn apart, I'm pregnant with another man's baby and my reputation is ruined at the church. I know that I don't deserve Your mercy but I pray that You will show me mercy anyway, simply because I know that You are a merciful God. Lord, please forgive me for all the wrong things that I've done to my husband and to other people. I've learned a lot throughout my mistakes and I'm gonna be a better person. And the time is now. I'm gonna turn over a new leaf and start building a relationship with You. I need You in my life. I've been wrong for so long but I wanna change. And I would like for Shawn and I to rebuild our marriage but I know that I hurt him so bad, that it may take years for us to be back in love. But if he decides that he doesn't want me back and he wants us to part ways for good, please give me the strength to move forward and respect his decision. And Heavenly Father, I'm gonna do my best to raise my baby with all the love and support that he or she needs and I'm gonna teach my child to always put You first. And I'm gonna do the same thing. In Jesus' name, Amen."

Twenty-six

(Shawn)

I HAVE TO admit that what happened between Rita and I, really made me into a stronger person. So much so, that I even had the guts to put my foot down with Brenda. I don't allow her to call the shots and try to take over my church, anymore.

Her attitude became unbearable when she found out that her husband Taurus had an affair with Rita. Brenda would come to church and take her anger out on everyone that crossed her path and she almost got into a fist fight with one of the mothers on the Mother's Board.

I understood that she was hurt and was dealing with a lot but I still had to set her straight. To my surprise, she apologized for her behavior and has been a lil' easier to deal with. Now, she takes other people's ideas into consideration and has been getting along better with some of the members in the church.

With things being so hectic, thinking about my daughter Summer actually gave me a peace of mind. I was sitting at my kitchen table eating breakfast, wondering how she was doing. I knew that I've never really built a relationship with her because of things that happened between me and her mom but I felt that it wasn't too late to start.

So I called Joy and got Summer's number from her but before I called Summer, I thought about what I was gonna say to her. I knew that we had a lot to talk about and I was trying to figure out how to get the conversation started.

When I called her, I said, "Hi, Summer. This is your father. I was thinking that maybe we can talk."

In a warm tone of voice, she said, "Well…um…it's nice to hear from you. What did you wanna talk about?"

"I first wanted to start by saying that I'm sorry."

"Sorry for what?"

"Just for everything. Sorry that I wasn't the dad for you that I should've been."

"Look, the past is the past. I'm not holding anything against you."

"I know but I should've done things...differently. It wasn't my intention to hurt you by leaving you outta the picture. Back then, I didn't know how to deal with things, in the right way. But I want you to know that I do love you, Summer. There wasn't a day that went by that I didn't think about you. I know that I can't make up for all the time that was lost but I hope that it's not too late for us to build a relationship together, right now."

"No, it's not too late. We may have missed out on a lot of time together but I still want us to be a part of each other's lives. You're still my dad."

"Yes, I am. I'm not so sure how things are going between you and Joy, but..."

"Joy and I have been talking on the phone since I've been back in Cincinnati. We're fine with each other."

I smiled and said, "That's wonderful. I'm really glad that you guys are getting to know each other. It amazes me how much you two look alike."

"Yeah. It kinda freaked me out. But I'm just glad to know that I have a sister. She's really a wonderful person."

"And so are you. I look forward to seeing you again."

"Hmmm. Maybe I'll come and see you and Joy, next weekend."

"That will be wonderful. We can all have dinner and I'll introduce you to your grandmother. You're a part of this family. Don't ever forget that."

"I won't. I can't wait to see y'all again. Well, I gotta get ready for work but I'll call you, later this week."

"Okay, sweetheart. You take care of yourself."

"You do the same, dad."

When I got off the phone with Summer, I headed over to the church to take care of some things and I found Rita standing outside of my office. I saw that her belly looked like it was gonna pop and she looked like she picked up quite a bit of weight.

Seeing her face, made me upset all over again as if I'd just found out about her infidelity, two minutes ago. Here I was, trying to get over the hurt of being betrayed by my wife and my best friend and here she was, staring me in the face.

"Why are you here, Rita?" I asked as I was unlocking the door to my office.

"Well, I thought that we should talk," she replied.

"Talk about what?"

Looking down at the floor, she said, "Well, as you know, the baby is gonna be here, soon."

"That's obvious. You're as big as a house."

She looked at me and said, "I guess I deserved that comment. Look, um, I was just hoping that you would be willing to take a blood test to at least know if the baby is yours. If you don't wanna be bothered with the process, I'll understand. I won't pressure you into it."

"I don't have a problem with taking a DNA test, Rita. If I'm the father, I'm gonna be an excellent father and give my child all the love that he or she needs. But I hope that you understand that we are over. Whether the baby is mine or not, our marriage is done."

"Shawn, are you serious?"

"You think I'm not? Rita, you did something that I never expected for you to do. Things can't go back to normal."

"Whatever happened to forgiveness?"

"Rita, I *have* forgiven you. The fact that I haven't literally picked you up and threw you outta my office is proof that I have forgiven you. But I have to move on with my life, without you as my wife."

"But Shawn, I want you to know that I'm turning my life around. I'm changing, I've learned my lesson…"

"I don't doubt that at all. Everyone can change if they want to. But let's face it, Rita; we were never right for each other. When I met you, I knew that you really didn't have a relationship with God and that you wasn't really into the church but I loved you so much, that I married you anyway. And as a result of me not listening to God when He tried to warn me not to marry you, I now have a broken heart and a bunch of unanswered questions."

"I'm really sorry, Shawn. I know that this whole thing is my fault."

"Not necessarily. It's partially *my* fault because I'm the one that decided to marry you, instead of waiting on God to send me the right woman that I was meant to have. But Rita, please understand that I don't hate you and I do wish you well in life. It's just that I can't ever trust you again. So it doesn't make sense for us to try to be together and work things out when I know that I don't trust you."

"But I only cheated on you with one person."

"It doesn't matter. You cheated on me several times, with that *one* person."

"I know but…"

"Rita, call me when you have the baby and I will take the DNA test. We don't need to talk about anything else. Have a blessed day."

She started to cry but I went ahead and walked into my office and closed the door behind me. I didn't feel absolutely any guilt by shunning her away.

She may have meant well by apologizing to me but the damage was already done.

After I had my words with Rita, I went ahead and checked my voicemail and started going over a few scriptures that I was gonna need for Sunday's sermon. Then all of a sudden, I heard a lot of commotion, outside. I was about to walk over to the window to see what was going on but before I got the chance, my phone ranged.

When I answered the phone, it was the church's secretary, saying to me in a frantic tone of voice, "Pastor, I think you need to come outside, immediately."

I dropped the phone and I quickly ran outside, where I saw Brenda in her car, trying to run Rita over. She had Rita running all over the parking lot. Brenda kept screaming, "I hate you, Rita! How could you sleep with my man! You're not gonna get away with it!"

I ran outside to the parking lot to try to stop Brenda but she was so full of rage that she almost ran *me* over. One of the deacons grabbed Rita and pulled her inside the church building and I stayed outside to try to calm Brenda down.

Before I had the chance to get Brenda outta the car, the police showed up and quickly yanked her outta the car and arrested her, on the spot. It was like a circus outside and I didn't know how to stop it. I guess this is what happens when a person snaps.

I said to the arresting officer, "Sir, please don't take her to jail. I know what's wrong and I just wanna talk to her."

After the police officer shoved Brenda into the police car, the police officer looked at me and said, "Look, I understand that you're a Pastor and like most Pastors, you wanna talk, spread peace and love. But this right here, is serious. This woman tried to run someone over with her car."

"I understand that, but…"

"She could've killed someone. What if there was a child in the way and they child got hit? She would've been looking at some serious charges. So save ya' breath, sir. She's going to jail, tonight."

The next day, I immediately drove downtown to bail Brenda out of jail. After several hours of waiting, she was finally released. She had so much pain in her eyes. I tried to make things as pleasant as possible because I knew that she was dealing with a lot.

I took her to breakfast and when the waiter brought our food to the table, Brenda just stared down at her plate and didn't eat a bite. I said to her, "If you want, I'll ask the waiter to box your food up and you can eat it at home when you're ready. I won't pressure you to eat."

With tears in her eyes, she said, "If it wasn't for my kids, I would've killed myself."

"I understand how you feel, Brenda. You trusted someone but they betrayed your trust."

"Can you believe it? *Your* wife and *my* husband?"

"But you have to move on with your life. Forgive and move on. That's the only way that you're gonna heal. I definitely know that it's a hard thing to do but if you don't do it, the problem will take over you and before you know it, you'll be doing things such as what you did in my church parking lot."

"I don't know what I was thinking when I did that. I guess that I'm just crazy."

"You're not crazy, Brenda. You just dealt with your anger in the wrong way."

"Humph. But it felt so damn good to have that tramp running from one end of the parking lot, to the other."

Aunt Thelma kept on bugging me and bugging me to talk to my cousin Darlene that I finally set some time aside to go see the girl. The reason why I was dragging my feet is because I know how Darlene is; she's stubborn and doesn't want to listen to anyone when they're telling her the truth.

I knocked on Darlene's door and one of her sons answered the door. He said, "Hi, cousin Shawn."

"Hi, lil' Tate," I answered, "Where's your mama?"

"In the kitchen."

As I walked inside and headed towards the kitchen, I noticed that there were a bunch of brothas sitting in the living room, drinking and playing cards. One of Darlene's babies was walking around, screaming and crying with half of his diaper hanging off of him. And they had the music playing so loudly that you couldn't even hear yourself think.

As I reached the kitchen, Darlene was standing over the stove, stirring something in a pot that smelled like garbage. When she turned around and saw me, she asked me, "What the hell are *you* doing here?"

"Aunt Thelma wanted me to talk to you," I answered.

She took a puff from her cigarette and said, "Well, you can save your breath because I don't wanna hear it."

"Well, good. I don't feel like wasting my breath, anyway. So have a good day."

As I was heading outta the kitchen, she asked in a loud manner, "So are you sayin' that I'm a waste of time?!"

"Yes!"

"Well, you can go to hell, Shawn! I don't need you to care about me!"

When she turned to the side, he long, dark, stringy hair was covering up her mocha-colored face so I couldn't tell if she was crying or not. I wasn't trying to get angry or hurt her feelings but sometimes, tough love is the only way that you're gonna get a person's attention.

I walked up to her and I said, "Look Darlene, if you wanna sit down and talk, we can do that. But I'm not gonna force you and I'm not gonna play any games with you. Your mom loves you and that's the reason why I'm here. She's concerned about you, Darlene. And I'm concerned about you, too. If you don't wanna do better for yourself, at least do it for your children."

She quickly wiped the tears from her face and said, "I don't need to do anything for my kids. They are fine."

"I can't believe that you are being so selfish. If you lose your freedom due to you messin' around with the wrong type of people, how are you gonna explain that to your children?"

"I don't have to explain *anything* to them. I'm grown and I can do whatever I want. They ain't payin' the bills in this house."

"Well apparently, neither are you. According to your mama, you have some fella named Doonie, taking care of that."

"At least the bills are gettin' paid. And furthermore, it's none of your business."

"Fine, Darlene. But don't you realize what you're doing to your kids? They see that you…"

"They see that you have to do whatever you need to, in order to get what you want. That's the real world that we live in so keep your motivational speech to yourself."

She took another puff from her cigarette and went back to stirring the pot on the stove. I didn't even bother to say anything else. When someone refuses my help, I let it go and move on. You can't make anybody change.

I was sleeping so, so good when all of a sudden, my phone ranged in the middle of the night. When I answered it, Rita's sister was on the other end, saying, "Rita is in labor. She's gonna have the baby, tonight."

"Is she on her way to the hospital?" I asked.

"She's already here."

"Okay. I'll be there in a minute."

I found myself putting my clothes on and rushing out of the door to get to the hospital to be by Rita's side. Everything she's done to me really didn't make a difference at this moment. I just wanted to be by her side and help her deliver the baby.

When I entered the waiting area, I saw Marilyn sitting down and she said, "I wanted to wait out here for you before I entered the delivery room."

"Did she have the baby yet?" I asked.

"Not yet but she's on her way."

Marilyn and I rushed down the hall to get to the delivery room. For this to be Rita's first child, she seemed to be doing pretty well. When she saw me, she had a smile on her face. In that one moment, I was crazy about her. I let her grab my hand and squeeze it tight, during each contraction.

Rita gave birth to a boy named David, in the month of August of 2002. When the baby came, it was the most unbelievable thing that I've ever seen. To witness a miracle like that, made me not only appreciate women a lot more but it also made me appreciate *life*, altogether. However, I knew that I couldn't allow this precious moment to cloud my judgment; I still wasn't taking Rita back and I needed to get down to business and find out if I was David's father.

Twenty-seven

———◆·••·◆———

(Joy)

THERE'S NOT A pill that anyone can take for a broken heart. For months, I have been crying over Clay from sun up to sun down. I didn't even know how to stop crying. I would get down on my knees and pray that God would help me get over the hurt but it seemed like the more I prayed, the worse I felt.

Then, it started to affect my weight; I gained ten pounds. I'm usually on top of my game when it comes to my weight. I've always been the type of person to watch what I eat but after what happened between me and Clay, I ate everything that I could get my hands on.

Being at home by myself was when things really got to me; I would just lay on the couch, watch TV and cry until I fell asleep. The apartment remained a mess, I barely hung out and I barely spoke on the phone to anyone. It may have seemed extreme but this feeling was definitely not something that I've ever experienced before.

But one night, I called Monica and I said, "Do you wanna do something wild and crazy?"

"Like what? What do you mean?" she asked.

"I wanna get that bastard back, Monica."

"Joy, don't do something insane, like take his life."

"No, I'm not gonna do that. I want him to be alive to experience what I have in mind."

"Hmmm. Do you wanna torture him or something?"

"No, but it will feel like torture to him."

After a minute of silence, she said, "Okay. I'm in."

"Good. I'll pick you up in a few minutes."

"But Joy, it's late. It's one o'clock in the morning and…"

"That's exactly what time it needs to be for what I have in mind. And by the way, wear black from head to toe."

In twenty minutes, I got myself ready for what I needed to do to make this operation a success; I dressed in black and then I pulled my hair back in a ponytail and wore a black skull cap on my head. Then I put on some dark shades and wore black leather gloves. After that, I sprinted over to Monica's house and she was sitting on the porch, waiting on me.

When she hopped in the car, she asked, "What in the world are you getting me in to?"

"You'll see," I answered, "And thanks for wearing black." On our way over to Clay's apartment, I stopped at a gas station and bought five dollars worth of gas and took the gas can from outta my trunk and filled it up. Then I told Monica to hold it while we drove over to Clay's apartment.

With a scared look, she looked at me and asked, "Are you gonna set this boy on fire, Joy?"

I laughed and said, "Girl, no. I have something better in mind."

While driving over to Clay's apartment, Monica still looked scared. Then she started praying by saying, "Heavenly Father, I don't know what my friend Joy is about to do but I ask that you watch over her. I think that she has gone straight crazy and is planning on doing something outrageous."

I laughed and said, "Girl, everything's gonna be alright. Nobody is gonna get hurt. I'm just getting my revenge."

"But you know that God will handle Clay."

"Of course He will. I'm not asking God not to. But I wanna do some work, too."

When we showed up to Clay's apartment, there wasn't a soul outside. I looked at the windows of his apartment and saw that there wasn't one light on. *He and his so-called wife must be sleep. That's good*, I thought to myself. I parked my car next to Clay's red convertible Mustang and took a good look at my surroundings, just to make sure that nobody was outside.

I looked over at Monica and I said to her, "Okay, so this is the deal; I'm gonna get outta my car and hop in Clay's car. Then I'm gonna…"

"Wait a minute. What do you mean 'hop in Clay's car'? Do you have keys to his car?"

"No, I don't."

"So how you gonna get in his car? Please don't tell me that you plan on breaking into it."

"Of course I am."

"Joy, are you crazy?! Do you know how much trouble you can get into?"

"Shhh! Keep your voice down before you blow my cover."

"Your cover? Girl, you have totally lost your mind."

"Monica, can I just finish telling you my plan? You'll understand what I'm trying to do."

She sighed and said, "Go ahead."

"Like I was saying, when I get out of my car, I want you to jump in my driver seat and let my car stay on. Put the gas can in my passenger seat. I'm gonna disable Clay's car alarm and then I'm gonna get in it and start it up. When I drive off, I want you to follow right behind me."

"Where exactly are we going?"

"You'll see. Just come on and get in my driver seat."

As she was getting ready to switch seats, she said, "Girl, this is really a test of our relationship. But I know that you're hurting, so I got ya' back."

"Thanks. I love you, too," I said to her, with a smile.

I moved fast. In less than ten minutes, I disabled Clay's car alarm and started it up, using two wires. I immediately drove off with Monica following right behind me in my car. I was shaking from both fear and excitement. But I didn't draw attention to myself. I drove all the way out to a remote, wooded area in Medina Ohio and got out of Clay's car. Monica got out of my car, still looking at me as if I was crazy.

"Girl, why in the world are we all the way out here?" she asked.

I explained to her, "Because I didn't want anybody around for what I'm about to do. Hand me the gas can, please."

Monica opened the passenger door of my car and handed me the gas can. Then she asked, "What are you planning on doing?"

I looked at Clay's car and said to her, "I'm gonna burn this sucka up. See, Clay absolutely loves his Mustang. He treats this car as if it was his child. It's his prize possession. What better way to get over a broken heart than to destroy something that you know your ex absolutely adores."

"Joy, are you sure you wanna do this?"

"Absolutely."

I let the top down on Clay's Mustang and poured gasoline all over the inside of it. After I was finished pouring the gasoline, Monica took the empty gas can and put it into the trunk of my car. Then I grabbed a book of matches from my glove compartment and lit his car up. The bigger the fire got, the better I felt.

"Come on, girl. Let's get out of here," Monica urged.

We ran to my car and took off. In the rearview mirror, I saw that the fire on Clay's car was so huge that it looked like the sun was sitting in the woods. Monica and I looked at each other and we were so amazed at what we did, that we screamed in excitement and laughed.

We didn't leave any evidence that we were involved in setting his car on fire so I knew that Monica and I were in the clear. The thought of what we did, brought a smile to my face. That night, Monica and I made a vow to each other that we would never tell anyone what we did. And for the first time in a long time, I didn't cry myself to sleep.

My father has been in rare form ever since he kicked Rita to the curb. I was a lil' pissed to find out that Taurus was messing around with her, considering the fact that I thought that *I* was the only one that he was dealing with, outside of his wife.

Here I was, thinking that I was the only woman that he wanted and the whole time that I believed that, he was banging a woman that I couldn't stand. But what's done is done. At least I'm not the one that's having a baby by that bastard.

So ever since my father found out what was going down between Taurus and Rita, my father has been tougher on people and apparently he's been tougher on my sorority sister, Olivia. She called me crying and upset and at first it was hard for me to get her to stop crying.

"What's wrong, Olivia?" I asked.

"I was honest with your father and I told him that I had a relapse on drugs, hoping that I would get some words of encouragement to help me get better. Instead, not only did he fire me from my position as choir director and told me that I couldn't get my job back but he also said that he was disappointed in me. He's never talked to me like that," she said, sobbing over the phone.

"Wow. I'm sorry that he came down hard on you like that, Olivia. He's just going thru some things, right now. I'll try to talk to him, okay?"

"You don't need to do that, Joy. He made his decision. But I'm not gonna let his attitude prevent me from doing what it is that I need to do, in order to make my life right. I'm gonna give up drugs, for good. It doesn't do anything but make matters worse."

"That's true. Well Olivia, you know that you have my support. Keep in touch, okay?"

"Of course. We're sorority sisters."

After I got off the phone with Olivia, I called dad and asked him, "Why did you have to fire Olivia?"

"Why are you in my business?" he snapped back.

"Dad, Olivia has been working at the church for a long time. She's like family. Not only that, she's my sorority sister."

"Don't you think that I know all of this? I love Olivia but I have to have my church in order. I can't be having my choir director getting high and conducting the choir. I gave her a second chance and she proved to me that she wasn't ready. Who's to say that she wouldn't relapse a third, fourth and fifth time? What if one day she'd came to church, high as a kite? I can't have that. And yes, she is like family but just like family, you have to show them tough love when it's necessary. And her being your sorority sister doesn't make her exempt from that."

"But dad, this isn't right. She…"

"Look, if you ever decide to form a church of your own, you can run it like a circus if you want to. But this is *my* church and I'm gonna run it the way that I see fit. Period. So respect my decision. I did what was best for the church."

"Oh, really? Dad, just in case you haven't been paying attention, your church is already one clown short of being a circus. Do remember the news that went around the church about your wife and Elder Taurus Nate?"

"And just like Olivia, they're gone too. And if you keep on giving me lip, you'll be next to lose *your* job."

I sighed and said, "Fine, dad. Just run everyone outta the church. I thought that the church was the place that you were supposed to go in order to get yourself right. The church is supposed to be like a hospital; you go to the hospital when you're sick so that you can get the help you need in order to get well. I understand why you kicked Rita and Elder Nate outta the church but you have people there who really do have a sincere love for God, regardless of their shortcomings. Just because they're in the church, doesn't mean that they're gonna be perfect and that they're gonna make the best decisions, all the time. But they love God and try to apply the Word of God to their lives, to live better and help others to do the same. Isn't that what it's all about? Church is where you are supposed to feel loved and that's the place you are supposed to go to when you've messed up. But if people can't even get love from the church because they're being shunned away, where do they go to get it?"

"Sweetheart, I understand where you're coming from and I know that you mean well. You are right about what you're saying but at the same time, I did what was best. Now unlike Rita and Taurus, Olivia is more than welcomed to continue to be a member of this church because I do believe that the church *is* the best place that a person should attend, to get some healing. But whether you're a choir director or an usher, you're still in a position of leadership because you are leading by example. People look up to you and watch what you say and do. And you know that many people looked up to

Olivia. But it's not good for her to be in a position of leadership if she's getting high. That's why I made the decision that I made."

"Okay, well I guess you're right. But I think that she's finally gonna get some help and really stick with it. When she realized that you meant business and that she lost her job, she seemed serious about getting her life back together."

"Well, I'm pretty sure that she will. Olivia is a very strong person. She'll bounce back."

Finally! I graduated from college. It was the most wonderful day of my life. My mother and father were present at my graduation and so were Monica and my sister, Summer. My parents threw me a graduation party but after the party was over, Monica, Summer and I went out for drinks.

I don't know if it was the alcohol talking but I said to the both of them, "I want to open up a club."

They both laughed and Summer said, "Joy, are you serious?"

"Absolutely," I said, taking a sip from my wine glass, "And I want you two to be my business partners."

They looked at each other and then at me and said, "What?!"

Monica said, "Joy, it cost a lot of money to start a business. Especially a club. There is so much red tape that you have to go thru."

"Well, let's go thru it, together. I'm serious about this, y'all. It can be a success. All we have to do is write a clear plan of how we want to create the club and find out how to get the start-up money. If we work hard and be dedicated, it can turn out to be the best decision that we ever made."

"Hmmm. I guess we could give it a try," Summer said.

"Just say that y'all come into business with me. Are y'all in?"

After a few minutes of Monica and Summer looking at each other and pondering the thought of what I said, they finally agreed to open up a club with me. I kinda figured that they wouldn't say no. It was just a matter of being convincing.

Then Summer shouted out, "I got it!"

"Got what?" Monica asked.

"The name for the club. It just came to me."

"What did you think of?" I asked, anxious to know.

Summer took the last big gulp from her wine glass and said, "Let's name it, The Big Yummy."

"The Big what?"

"The Big Yummy."

Monica giggled and said, "What in the world made you come up with that name?"

"I don't know. It's different and it's catchy. I think it's hot."

I thought about it and I said, "The Big Yummy. Hmmm. It *sounds* yummy."

Later that night, Monica and Summer went back to my place and gathered up a bunch of blankets and crashed out on my floor. I was so drunk and exhausted that I didn't even make it to my bedroom. Instead, I took my clothes off and fell asleep on the couch.

In the middle of the night, I heard Summer puking her guts out in the bathroom. I opened the bathroom door and handed her a glass of water, "Are you okay?" I asked.

She giggled and said, "Girl, I'm fine. Too much alcohol has its consequences."

I smiled and said, "I'm surprised that *I* haven't got sick. I've swallowed a whole bottle of wine. Monica is still snoring away."

"Girl, she snores like a man," she said, laughing. Then she wiped her face with a cold, wet towel and looked in the bathroom mirror with a smile on her face. Then she said, "Can I ask you something?"

"Sure. Go ahead," I said.

"What do you think about me moving to Cleveland?"

"Why do you wanna move to Cleveland?"

She looked at me and said, "To be closer to you. We've spent a lot of years apart from each other, not knowing that we were related. Now that we are building a relationship, what could be better than for us to live in the same city together, doing things together and making our bond tighter. I can easily have my job transfer me here and I can get an apartment of my own. Besides, I have relatives here in Cleveland as well as in Cincinnati so it's not like I don't know anyone here."

I smiled and said, "I think that it will be cool. Besides, if we're gonna be in business together, we're gonna be spending a lot of time together, anyway. I say, go for it."

She gave me a hug and said, "I love you, Joy."

"I love you, too," I said.

"The Big Yummy? Are you guys serious?" my father asked when Monica, Summer and I showed up at his office, presenting our business plan to him. We needed start-up money and I knew that dad would have it.

Since Summer was a certified accountant, she helped create the business proposal and she even presented a pie chart. Monica was the one that presented information on where the club should be located and what type of décor would look nice in the venue.

Daddy smiled at all of our ideas, took a very thorough look at the proposal and was rather impressed by the pie chart. I gave a wonderful introduction and I was very confident that we knew what we were talking about. We did a lot research and we were fired up.

"Dad, as you can see, we are very serious about this," I said to him.

He tapped his pen on his desk while looking at us and then he said, "I think that all three of you young ladies are very smart and have a lot of drive and I honestly do believe that y'all have a wonderful idea."

"So does that mean that you will invest into our business?" Summer asked.

"On one condition."

"And what condition is that?" Monica asked.

He sighed and said, "Don't serve alcohol."

Startled, I asked, "What do you mean? How can you have a night club without alcohol? *Every* night club serves alcohol."

"Well, form a club that doesn't serve it."

"But dad, when people come to a club, they expect there to be a supply of alcohol," Summer intervened, "It's all about supply and demand. If we don't give the people what they want, they will go somewhere else and before you know it, we'll be out of business and in debt."

Then dad said, "The same confidence that you guys had when y'all entered my office, needs to be the same kind of confidence that you're gonna need in order to do something different and be successful at it. Y'all don't need to be doing what everyone else is doing, just because it seems like the norm. Not everybody drinks and you guys need to cater to the ones that don't and you will be surprised at how many people will come to your venue. You can serve non-alcoholic cocktails and I'm almost certain that people will love them. Make a statement by standing out. People can still eat and dance and have a good time, without being under the influence of alcohol. If you make it a success, watch and see if people don't start noticing it and start opening up non-alcoholic clubs, everywhere."

Monica, Summer and I all smiled at each other at what dad explained to us and we all thought that it was worth a try. So I looked at dad and asked, "If we agree to that, will we have your support?"

He smiled and said, "You have my support and my money to help you get started. I will also hire lawyers for you guys. They will help make sure that things are on track."

The three of us looked at each and screamed with excitement. We were so excited and couldn't wait to get started. Outside of the money that dad gave us to get started, we had three key elements to make the club a success: Monica, Summer and myself.

Monica always had an eye for detail when it came to clothes, shoes and accessories. So I already knew that when it comes to the appearance of the venue, Monica was gonna make sure that the place looked fabulous.

Summer is absolutely brilliant when it comes to facts and figures. She's a wiz in accounting and would be the one to watch everything to the penny and make sure that the club was making money.

And when it comes to myself, I would be the one to hire the best people possible to serve the public and be professional at all times. It's a known fact that when people get good customer service, they come back. And that's what all three of us wanted; we wanted people to love the experience and come back. The Big Yummy is gonna be the best club ever.

Twenty-eight

---◆·❖·◆---

(Taurus)

I was back in Cleveland and received the news thru the grapevine that Rita had given birth to a boy. So I called Rita to see if it was true and to find out when we could arrange to get the DNA test done.

"Yes, it's true. I had a baby boy. I just had him about a week ago," Rita explained over the phone.

"Humph. So what's his name?" I asked.

"I named him David. That was the first name that came to mind."

Curious to know, I asked her, "So who does the baby look like? Does he look like Shawn or like me?"

She sighed and said, "Honestly, he doesn't look like either one of you. He looks like me."

"Oh. Well anyway, when can we get this DNA test done?"

"I guess that we can make an appointment for this week. Shawn has set aside a time to take the test on Thursday. I guess that you can take it on Friday."

"Well, good. At least I won't have to worry about running into Shawn when I take the test."

"Humph. Well, have you heard what happened between your wife and I?"

"No. Remember, I've been in Miami."

"I just figured that one of them nosy church members would've called you up and told you. Anyway, she tried to kill me."

"What? What are you talking about?"

"She tried to run me over with her car. The police took her to jail."

"Oh, my God. Is she outta jail?"

"Well, I heard from someone that Shawn bailed her out. But as far as I'm concerned…"

"Well, I'm glad that she was bailed out. My kids don't need to have their mom, sitting in jail. I knew that she was gonna do something crazy like this."

"You knew? What do you mean you knew?"

"Well, when she found out that we had been messin' around, she called me up and cursed me out. She said that if she found you, that she was gonna do some serious damage."

"You mean to tell me that you knew that she was gonna do something insane and you didn't try to warn me?"

"Are you serious? Rita, you are the least person that I'm worrying about. I'm headed towards a nasty divorce, risking the chance of losing everything. The last thing I'm thinking about is how to save you from catching a beat down."

"You are so damn selfish. What if she had hit me with the car and I lost the baby? *Your* baby?"

"First of all, we won't know whether it's my baby or not until I take the DNA test."

"I can't believe the way you're acting, Taurus. I gotta go. Bye."

On the day of the DNA testing, Rita was already at the testing center, holding her baby. *Thank God that he doesn't look like me*, I thought to myself. I kept looking at how very light his skin was and considering that I'm not light-skinned, I kinda figured that the baby belonged to Shawn.

"Would you like to hold him?" Rita asked me.

"Hold him for what? He ain't mine," I replied.

She sighed and said, "Please don't start that mess, Taurus. We won't know anything until we get the DNA results."

"Well, I'm not willing to hold that baby. I don't have time for a bonding moment. I just wanna take the test and get it over with."

She rolled her eyes at me and didn't say another word until it was time for us to take the test. After about twenty minutes, we finally got the DNA test done and was told that the results would be mailed to us in a few days.

Afterwards, I arrived back to my lodge to try to take me a nap that was well-deserved. I was hoping and praying that the test results would reveal that the baby wasn't mine. I mean, how in the world would I explain to my kids that I have another child by another woman? They're too young to understand.

Just when I was getting ready to take my nap, there was a knock at my door. It was my manager Kevin, saying, "I hope that your vacation made you well rested so that you can get back to work on your book."

I explained to him, "There won't be a book."

1

1 111 1

1

He looked at me as if I had lost my mind. He asked, "What are you talking about?"

"I think that I wanna give up writing for a while. I don't have the fire anymore, Kevin. I think that I just wanna try new things."

He laughed and said, "Are you serious? Do you know how much you're giving up? What are you planning to do, now? Sing? Form a band? Become an actor? Fly a plane? What in the world do you think you're doing?"

"That's for me to figure out. And I don't care what I'm giving up. I'm tired of it and I don't even know what to write about anymore. Kevin, if I complete this book, it will only be to fulfill a deadline. The sales will make it a failure because I'm not willing to push it. I want out and I don't know if I will want to go back to it, ever again."

He was silent for a second and he said, "Well, you know that there are a lot of things that you are gonna have to do in order to get out of your contract with the publishing company. You will probably have to pay back your advance money and…"

"I don't care. I'll get my lawyers on it and get the process started."

He sighed and said, "Okay. Well, I hope you know what you're doing."

After getting off the phone with Kevin, I felt like a big load was taken off of my shoulders. I didn't know what in the world was gonna be my next move but I just knew that I didn't wanna write anymore. And with me possibly heading for a divorce, the last thing that I was thinking about was writing a damn book.

I couldn't believe it. I just couldn't believe it. This just didn't make any sense. After about a week, I received the DNA test results in the mail and found out that the baby was mine. I was angry as hell. I didn't want anything to do with this baby.

Rita called me on the same day that I received my letter and she said, "Well, I received the test results in the mail. I imagine that you have, too."

"Yes, I have," I stated.

"So what are your plans?"

Her asking me that question, made me angry and I asked her, "What do you mean?"

"What do you think I mean, Taurus? Now that it's been proven that you are the father, I expect some help from you. I can't take care of this baby by myself. I need you to help me take care of him. And for the record, his name is David. You never did ask me his name."

I sighed and said, "I'll give you some money to buy some diapers and baby formula."

She laughed and said, "Do you think that's all that my baby needs? You have two children of your own so you should know that it takes more than paying for some diapers and milk to take care of a child. So you're gonna need to do more than that."

"It sounds to me like you're just looking to get into my pockets."

"Whatever. Anyway, I expect you to give me at least five-hundred dollars by the end of this week. I need help."

"You ain't lying. You definitely need help. Psychological help."

"Don't play with me, Taurus. I expect for you to handle your fatherly duties. If you can take care of two lil' brats…"

"Wait a minute, Rita. You betta watch where you steppin'. My two kids are the apple of my eye and they were here *first*, before you decided to give birth to an unwanted baby. Kiera and Dillon will *always* come first before your baby will."

"You mean, *our* baby. Outside of the money, I expect you to show David the same amount of love that you show Kiera and Dillon."

"That's gonna be *your* job, Rita. Not mine. I already have children that I love. But as far as the five-hundred dollars, you can have that."

"You are the most cold-hearted person that I know."

"Oh, really? *You're* the one that's treating your baby like he's a dollar amount. It seems to me that *you're* the one with a heart made of ice."

"Taurus, the only reason why I asked you for any money is because I'm on a limited income and it's hard for me to take care of David and take care of all the other bills, by myself."

"Rita, you act as if you're the only single mom in the world. You should've aborted the baby when you had the chance."

"Go to hell, Taurus. One of these days, God is gonna knock you on your behind and…"

I laughed and said, "The fact that you actually mentioned God to me, is quite comical."

"Taurus, just because I didn't know God then, doesn't mean that I don't know God, now."

I mailed the check for five-hundred dollars to Rita, the next morning. I didn't want to give it to her face to face because I didn't want to be bothered with potential drama. But of course, she still wasn't satisfied. Instead of getting a 'thank you' from her, she called to complain because I mailed it to her, instead of handing it to her.

But Rita and her big-headed baby was the least of my worries; I had *Brenda* to worry about. I went to see Brenda to confess to her that it was proven that I was the father of Rita's baby and to my surprise, Brenda seemed very calm. As a matter of fact, she was so calm that it was almost scary.

She said to me, "Well, it really doesn't make a difference to me. All I ask is that you tell your children that they have another brother."

Startled by her mellow response, I said to her, "What do you mean that it doesn't make a difference to you? It wasn't too long ago that you've tried to kill Rita when you found out that she might've been pregnant with my child. Now, all of a sudden, it doesn't make a difference to you?"

"That's right. I'm tired of being angry with you, Taurus. All the anger and bitterness that I had towards you and Rita, wasn't doing anything but giving me stress headaches and making my hair fall out. I'm looking forward to divorcing your triflin' behind and starting a new life for me and my children."

"So let me guess: Now that you're messin' around with this Cecil person..."

"Messin' around? Are you kidding me? Messin' around is what you and Rita did and because you two were messin' around, y'all created a *mess* for yourselves. And for the record, Cecil is none of your business. He's a special man that appreciates me. So get over it. And no, the kids are not gonna start calling him 'daddy'. I would never allow that. You are their father and I will admit that you are a wonderful father to them. But you were a horrible husband. You didn't care that you were hurting me when you decided to lay up with Rita. You were an Elder in the church. You should've known better. And now, because of your selfishness, you're not welcomed at Shawn's church and there's a bastard child in the midst of all of this. I figured that I was living a better life than *you* were so there was no need for me to waste time, continuing to be angry. I'm done with the matter, Taurus. I'm moving on."

The day that I dreaded, came upon me; the day that I got my divorce. Brenda had the most blood-thirsty lawyer that I'd ever encountered. My own lawyer kinda buckled under the pressure of him. In two months, when it was all said and done, Brenda was rewarded almost everything except the hair on my behind.

She ended up with the house, the cars and I was ordered to pay a tremendous amount of alimony and child support. I started to think that maybe I made a mistake by giving up my writing career, considering that that was my major source of income. As far as the kids, she demanded full custody and got it. I was really upset about that. I lost *everything*.

The thing that really had my blood boiling was when Brenda showed up to court with Cecil. Just thinking about him sleeping and eating in a house that *I* bought with Brenda, made me wanna kill him.

After she was rewarded everything, she walked outta the courtroom with a big smile on her face with Cecil holding her hand. The fact that I couldn't do anything about it, made me so angry that I couldn't even think straight.

With Rita constantly begging me for money and me having to pay alimony and child support on Kiera and Dillon, my finances got so bad that I had to file for bankruptcy. To pay my bills, I took a job as an English teacher at a middle school.

The most embarrassing day of my life was when a parent of one of my pupils, came up to me and asked, "Aren't you a best-selling author by the name of Taurus Nate?"

"Yes, ma'am," I answered her.

"I thought so. I have a couple of your books at home."

"Well, I thank you for your support."

"You're welcomed. But can I ask you a question?"

"Of course, you can."

"Why are you here, teaching school? Shouldn't you be driving in a Bentley, going on book tours or something?"

"Well sometimes, things happen. Life doesn't always turn out the way that you would want it to. But that's life."

"Humph. I guess so. Well, I hope that you get back on your feet."

There were days when I didn't think that I would ever be able to adapt to my low-budget lifestyle. I wasn't used to living off of generic food and eating bologna sandwiches and Ramen noodles. I used to think that people who lived like that, was beneath me. But now that I'm on the other side of the fence, I realize that you do what you gotta do in order to make it, day by day.

I couldn't afford to stay in the fancy lodge anymore so I found an apartment on the east side of Cleveland. It's a hole in the wall but at least I have a roof over my head and I'm not on the street. Sometimes, I think about the life that I once had and when I do, the first thought that comes to mind is, *If I had just kept my tool in my pants, I wouldn't be in this mess.* The minute that my lips touched Rita's, that was the beginning of my downfall. It was like eating the bad fruit from the Garden of Eden.

Brenda was nice enough to allow my kids to come over to my apartment and spend some time with me for my birthday. Kiera gave me a blue tie and Dillon gave me a pair of blue socks. The gifts were very nice but what I loved the most was that my children were there with me. I love them so much.

I put Kiera on my lap and I asked her, "So how are you doing in school? Are you staying out of trouble?"

"Yes. I made a new friend, daddy," she answered.

"You did? Where?"

"At school. Her name is Kate and we play together."

"Oh, I see. And what about you, Dillon? Are you staying out of trouble, too?"

"Yes, sir," he answered, "Mommy is letting me go to my friend's birthday party on Saturday."

"Well, good. I hope that you have a good time."

"I will, daddy."

Then Brenda tapped me on the shoulder and whispered to me, "Can I speak to you in private for a second?"

"Sure," I replied as I got up off of the couch. We went to my bedroom and I asked her, "What did you wanna talk about?"

She sighed and said, "Well, before anyone else tells you, I wanted to be the first to let you know."

"Let me know what?"

"Well, Cecil and I went and got married. We held a very private ceremony because we didn't want a lot of people to know about it."

I felt my stomach starting to hurt. I couldn't believe that she was telling me this. I said to her, "I see that you didn't let any grass grow under your feet."

"Well, I have to live my life, Taurus. Life doesn't stop just because you get a divorce."

"But did you have to go and get married so soon? How do the kids feel about this?"

"The kids seem to love Cecil and he loves them, too. He does a lot for them. He treats them as if they are his own."

"But they are *not* his own. Those kids are *my* kids. *I'm* their dad."

"I understand that, Taurus. And like I told you before, I will not turn the kids against you. But outside of my kids, I do have a life and I deserve to be happy. And Cecil does make me happy."

"Well, I don't like that you've made a decision like this. I don't even know this guy that well. I only met him once and honestly, he seemed like a jerk."

"First of all, you are making this thing all about you. It's not about you. It stopped being about you, the minute you stepped outside of our marriage. But I don't hold any grudge against you because I'm the happiest that I've ever been in a very, long time. And for your information, I didn't rush into marriage with Cecil. But there is no reason for us to wait a couple of years to get married when we already knew that we wanted to spend the rest of our lives, together. My family loves him, his family loves me and we are making this thing work. And before the kids slip up and tell you, I also want to let you know that Cecil and I are having a baby."

I almost blew my top. "You're what?!"

"I'm pregnant, Taurus. I thought that you should know."

"Brenda, be honest: Did you do all of this to get back at me?"

She shook her head and said, "See, there you go making it all about you, again. Taurus, I don't make life decisions based on what someone else does."

I sighed and said, "I guess that I don't have no other choice but to accept this."

"Humph. Whether you accept this or not, this is how it is."

After Brenda and the kids left, I found myself pacing the floor, trying to think of a way to get back at Brenda. Who did she think she was? She was making it seem as if my marriage to her, didn't even exist! How dare she bring another man around my kids!

I went to bed, tossing and turning with Brenda's words replaying in my mind. I wanted to be mad at her but deep down, I realized that I had no reason to be mad at her for anything. She has the right to move on with her life. Instead of thinking about her, I needed to get *my* life back on track and find some happiness for myself.

The next morning, I woke up and an idea hit me like a bolt of lightning: I wanted to move to Miami. I didn't have any reason to stay in Cleveland and although I love my kids, they had a male figure in their lives. So as far as I was concerned, I didn't have anything to lose by moving to Miami.

I called Brian up and I said to him, "Man, I think I'm ready to bust a move."

"Bust *what* move?" he asked.

"I decided that I'm gonna move to Miami."

"For real? What made you come up with that decision?"

"It's time for me to start a new life. Brenda has already moved on so I need to do the same."

"So are you just moving to Miami, simply because Brenda has moved on with her life?"

"Not really."

"Man, stop lying. You know that this whole idea is because of Brenda."

"Maybe so but I'm serious about what I'm sayin'. I'm leaving Cleveland."

"Taurus, running from your problems doesn't solve them."

"I'm not running from anything. If Brenda can start a new life, so can I. Not only that, I have such turmoil here in Cleveland, that I just want to escape."

"Hmmm. Well, if you are really serious about moving to Miami, then you have my support. If you want, you can stay with me until you're able to find a place of your own."

"No need, man. I'll pay for my own apartment before I leave so when I get to Miami, I'll already have a place to stay. It may take about a year for me to get everything prepared but it's a done deal; I'm moving to Miami."

"Okay, well I look forward to you coming."

"Well, tomorrow is the day. I just wanna say goodbye to my kids before I leave," I said to Brenda when I stopped by her house. It's been about ten months and I was getting ready to leave for Miami, tomorrow morning. The months flew by so fast.

Brenda said, "I don't know why you decided to make a crazy decision like this but it's *your* life."

"That's right, it is. You have yours and I have mine. I wanna see what life has in store for *me*."

"Okay. Well, the kids are upstairs. You can go up and see them if you want."

When I went into Kiera's room, she was sitting on her bed, playing with her dolls. When she saw me, she jumped off of her bed and ran to me. I gave her the biggest hug that I could and I sat down on her bed and put my arm around her.

"Are you leaving today, daddy?" she asked.

"No, I'm leaving tomorrow. But I wanted to come by and tell you that I love you and that I'll miss you. You know you're daddy's little girl, right?"

"Yeah. I don't want you to go, daddy. I won't be able to see you anymore."

"Yes you will, sweetheart. Daddy will come back to Cleveland to visit you, every chance I get."

"You promise?"

"I promise. Just promise me that you'll be a good girl and continue to do well in school, okay?"

"Okay. I love you, daddy."

"I love you, too."

After I gave her another hug, I headed off to Dillon's room, where he was sitting on the floor, playing with one of his video games. He turned his head to me and said, "Hi, dad."

"What's up, lil' man?" I asked him.

"Nothing. I'm getting ready to go to summer camp, next week. It's gonna be fun. Cecil paid for me to go with his nephew. I can't wait."

"Humph. He paid for you to go?"

"Yeah. I asked mama if I could go. She said yes and Cecil paid for it."

"Why didn't you ask *me* to pay for it? I'm your father."

"Because I know that you're busy. You're about to move far away and you won't have time for me anymore."

I thought about what he said and realized that he was hurting because I was leaving. "So is that what you think, Dillon? You think that I won't have time for you anymore?"

"But it's true. You're gonna forget about me when you move away."

"No I won't, Dillon. No matter how far I am, I will always have time for you. You are my son. You are my first born. I love you too much to forget about you."

"But if you love me, why are you leaving me?"

"Because I'm trying to get myself together. I'm not leaving because of you. In fact, it breaks my heart to leave you behind. Sometimes, adults have to make hard decisions in order to have a better life. But it's not your fault that I had to make this decision. It's just that I made some bad mistakes that kinda messed up my life and so now, I'm trying to do what I can to fix it. But I'm still your father. Always remember that. If you need me for anything, all you have to do is call me and I'll come running."

He looked at me and gave me a smile that really warmed my heart. Then he said as he gave me a hug, "Okay, daddy. Have a good trip and don't forget to call me on my birthday."

"You know that I won't forget," I explained to him.

After talking to my kids, I headed towards the front door and after I said goodbye to Brenda, she asked me, "So did you tell them about your other child?"

"No I didn't."

"Why not?"

I sighed and said, "I don't feel like the time is right. They're too young to understand and if I was to explain it to them now, they would have a bunch of questions that would be hard to answer. I'll let them know in due time."

"Okay. Well, take care of yourself."

"I will. You do the same."

The next morning, I woke up at five a.m to catch my flight to Miami. Honestly, I was really looking forward to the trip and seeing what life had in store for me.

I didn't even bother to tell Rita that I was moving to Miami because as far as I was concerned, I didn't owe her an explanation for *anything*. In fact, I went ahead and got my cell number changed and didn't give it to anyone except for a few relatives. I also gave it to Brenda, since we do have kids together.

The good part about my decision was that I was able to get a good job at a university in Miami, teaching English. My cousin Brian hooked that up for me, about a month ago before I was scheduled to leave Cleveland. I even had my apartment already set up before I arrived there.

When I jumped on the plane and it took off, I felt like the worst was over. I definitely wasn't gonna make the same mistakes, twice.

Twenty-nine

━━━━◆•◆•◆━━━━

(Rita)

THIS BABY HAS been nothing but a curse. He's almost a year old and all he does is cry, cry, and cry. Not a day goes by that I don't get a tension headache because of him. He makes me regret that I gave birth to him.

The thirty pounds that I gained while I was pregnant with him, never came off. So because of the extra weight, it's been hard to go up and down my stairs at home and I had to buy bigger clothes because I couldn't fit into *any* of my old ones.

Not only that, I haven't had at least one good night's sleep since he's been born and it's been extremely hard to find a babysitter that's willing to put up with him while I go to work. And speaking of work, money has been so tight that I had to get a second job in order to make ends meet.

Sometimes, I'd come home from work so exhausted, that I'd find myself sleeping in my clothes due to me being too tired to take them off. Then, if David catches a cold or something, I have to risk losing my job because I have to take off from work, in order to tend to him.

I think that the most horrible experience of my parenting was when I had to go to the welfare office to apply for food stamps. First of all, when I got to the welfare office, I had to deal with a woman who had a very nasty attitude and she acted as if she didn't want to be bothered. She treated me as if I was inferior.

On the flip side, I did receive some assistance for me and my baby, which made things a lil' bit easier to deal with. But my life was still a mess and I knew that it was because of the choices that I've made. Now, I'm paying for all the wrong that I've done.

Everyday, I think about the life that I once had and I find myself crying about it. I've tried not to think about it but I couldn't help it. I really did have a good life and a wonderful husband but I took it all for granted. When I look at things now, I realize that Shawn was so good to me. He may not have been perfect but he was still a good man.

Shawn was everything that I needed and wanted but I was too selfish to realize that. After hitting rock bottom, I realized that the man that was wonderful in my life, was the one that I didn't want. But the man that treated me like a piece of crap, was the one that I would've laid down my life for. What in the hell was I thinking?

But instead of complaining about how my life turned out, I deal with it the best way that I can because I know that I brought this on myself. But sometimes, I can't help but to think that there's a ray of hope, somewhere. Maybe someday, I'll find it.

My sister Marilyn has been a lot of help, though. She comes by to see the baby every chance she gets and buys him nice clothes and toys. Her son absolutely adores him and loves to spend time with him.

One day while Marilyn was over at my house, she asked me, "What's wrong with you?"

"What do you mean?" I asked back.

"You don't look too well. Are you okay?"

"I think that I'm coming down with the flu. But it's nothing serious, though."

"Are you sure? Have you went to go see a doctor?"

"For what? I ain't got no money to go see a doctor."

"What about health insurance?"

"I can't afford it, Marilyn."

"So what do you do if your son gets sick?"

"David has free healthcare. If he ever gets sick, he's covered."

"But you need to make sure that you're covered as well, Rita. What good will it be for your baby to be healthy but your baby doesn't have a healthy mom? You need lots and lots of energy to tend to a baby. If you're sick, how are you gonna be able to take care of your baby?"

I laughed and said, "Girl, you are so dramatic."

"I'm not being dramatic, Rita. I'm being real with you. Are you still getting headaches?"

"Yeah, but I've been so stressed out that I'm sure that stress is the reason why I've been getting them."

"Hmm. Well, even if it's something small, I recommend that you still get yourself checked out."

"Okay, okay. If I still feel the same after a week, I'll go ahead and see a doctor."

"You promise?"

"Yes, girl. Stop trippin'."

Every once in a while, my best friend Yvette would stop by to lend a hand but she hasn't been able to be there all the time because she's pregnant with twins. So she's been spending her days getting prepared for the new addition to her family.

Taurus, on the other hand, hasn't done a thing to help out since the day that I received the five-hundred dollar check that I almost had to beg him for, when my son was just born. That was almost a year ago.

When I tried to call him to get some help, I was surprised to find out that his number was changed. Then I found out from a certain person that was still a member of Shawn's church, that Taurus didn't even live in Ohio anymore.

So here I was, stuck with a baby that didn't have a father in his life. I never thought that I would be a single mom and the father of my baby would not be around. For Taurus to just leave the state and not say a word to me, was unbelievably cold-hearted.

One evening, I was putting David to bed and then I headed downstairs into the kitchen to wash dishes. While I was rinsing the soap off of the dishes, the doorbell rang. When I went to the door to answer it, to my surprise, it was Shawn. I haven't seen him since the day he came to take the DNA test. It was like I haven't seen him in years.

I said to him, "Wow! I most certainly wasn't expecting to see you."

He smiled and said, "I know. I just wanted to come by to see how you and the baby are doing."

I opened my door wider and I said, "Well, come on in. It's nice to see you, Shawn."

"It's nice to see you, too. Where's the baby?" he asked, sitting on the couch.

"I just put him to bed. He's sound asleep," I explained, sitting across from him in a chair.

"Oh. Well, how are you holding up? How do you like motherhood?"

"Humph. I can't say that I like motherhood but I'm dealing with it. Taurus is not around to help me take care of him so I have to do it by myself. Well actually, I do have my sister and my best friend to help me along."

"Oh, I see. Well, I'm sure that you know that Taurus no longer lives in Ohio."

"Yeah. I found out from somebody. I have absolutely no idea where he went. And it's not like I care that he's not around. I just wanted him to help me with the baby."

"Well, all I know is that he's in Miami. I found out from a source at church."

"In Miami?!"

"Yes."

"Humph. Well, it doesn't even matter. I've been taking care of David *without* his help, so I don't need it now."

"Humph. Well, I came over to give you a check for one-thousand dollars to help you take care of things."

"Look Shawn, are you trying to treat me like a charity case? I'm not a charity case, Shawn."

"I'm not saying that you are. I'm just trying to help you a lil' bit because I already knew that Taurus wasn't gonna do it."

"How did you know that he wasn't gonna help?"

"Rita, the man used to be my best friend. I knew him like the back of my hand. Well, at least I *thought* I did. If I knew him as well as I thought, I would've known that he was gonna stab me in the back, by sleeping with my wife."

I put my head down and I said, "So are you trying to hold it over my head and make me feel guilty for the rest of my life?"

"Not at all, Rita. I just want you to know that I'm here for you if you need help."

"Why do you care, Shawn? After what I've done to you, why do you wanna be so nice to me?"

"Because I still care about you, Rita. Just because we're separated doesn't mean that I don't care about what you're going thru. I have no problem stepping in to help you from time to time. I'll still be your friend."

Before I knew it, I started to cry. I tried to stop crying but I couldn't. I hurt Shawn so bad that I didn't even feel like I deserved his friendship. I wiped the tears from my face, trying to get myself together, but the tears wouldn't stop rolling down my face.

Shawn got up from the couch and came over to give me a hug. Then he said, "It's okay, Rita. Everything's gonna be fine."

I looked at him and said, "Shawn, I'm so sorry for what I did to you. I didn't appreciate you and I was so foolish. Thank you for forgiving me."

"Don't thank me; thank God for giving me the ability to forgive you."

Marilyn and her fiancé Allen changed their wedding date at least twice so I wasn't really sure if they were serious about getting married. But when I found myself sitting at her kitchen table, helping her put together the wedding invitations, I knew that she was serious.

I had to admit that I was a lil' jealous of her because she was getting ready to start a new life with a man that really loved her and her son. I was not even close to having that. All I had, was a baby and a bunch of bills.

After Shawn and I made a mutual and peaceful decision to go ahead and get a divorce, I tried to have a life and start dating again. I dated two guys and they turned out to be a total waste of my time. At first, I didn't know if maybe I was out of touch with the world or if the two guys really were jerks.

The first brotha I dated was a guy named James. He was about fifteen years older than me but had the outgoing personality and body of a twenty-five year old. And he most certainly didn't show his age.

I met him at a grocery store, while I was picking up a pack of toilet tissue. From the corner of my eye, I saw that he was staring at me. But I didn't stare back. I didn't want him to know that I knew that he was watching me.

So I continued shopping and then I felt someone tap me on the shoulder. It was him. He asked me, "Excuse me, do you mind if I ask you what your name is?"

"Um, my name is Rita. And yours?"

He smiled and said, "I'm James. I'm usually not the type to start introducing myself to strangers but I just couldn't help myself. You are such a beautiful woman."

"Humph. Thanks," I said, not really moved by his weak line.

"I know that this may seem forward but are you seeing anyone?" he asked.

"No, not right now. I'm just concentrating on taking care of my son."

"Oh, okay. How old is your son?"

"He just turned one-years old, last week."

"I see. Well, let me just say that you are a beautiful mom."

I smiled and said, "Thank you."

As I was walking away, he asked, "Do you mind if I take you out somewhere nice?"

I turned around and said, "I'm not so sure about that. For all I know, you could be a psycho."

He laughed and said, "I understand that you're cautious. And you have every right to be. But maybe we can just meet for coffee and have interesting conversation. Here's my card. Give me a call when you have time."

It took me about a week but I finally gave him a call. When he answered the phone, he said, "I'm so glad that you called. I was wondering if I would ever hear from you again."

"Well, I wanted to take you up on your offer about meeting for coffee. How about we meet downtown, tomorrow morning at nine a.m?" I asked.

"That will be fine. I'll see you then, Rita."

First of all, he was about forty-five minutes late when he finally did show up and he didn't even bother to apologize for it. That should've been my cue to leave but like an idiot, I stayed.

He had the nerve to stroll over to the table and smile at me as if I was pleased to see him. "Good morning, beautiful," he had the nerve to say.

I wasn't moved. "James, you're late. Very late."

He shrugged his shoulders and said, "It happens."

"It happens? Is that all that you have to say? You could've at least called if you were gonna be late."

"Well, you waited for me so apparently it wasn't such a big problem. Can we just move on, please?"

I sighed and said, "Anyway, how was your morning?"

"It was fine. Nothing was really happening. I watched the news, took a shower and came here."

"Humph. So do you work?"

"Um…yeah."

"Where?"

"Why?"

"James, I'm just trying to make some conversation to get to know you. Isn't that the reason why we're here?"

"I guess you're right. Um, I work at a restaurant."

"Really? What do you do?"

He took a sip of his coffee and said, "Well, I'm a waiter. I also work at a gas station."

"Oh really?"

"Yeah. I have five kids to take care of so therefore, I must work as much as possible."

"Hmm. How old are your kids?"

"My oldest son is twelve-years old, my youngest son is ten and my three daughters are seven, four and one-years old. They don't live with me, though. They live with their mothers."

"Mothers?"

"Yeah. I have three babymamas."

"Humph. Do you get a chance to see them often?"

He took another sip of his coffee and said, "Not really. If I go see them, I have to deal with babymama drama. And my mama doesn't like a lot of noise in her house, so therefore I don't bring them over there. I see them when I can."

"What does your mama have to do with it?"

"That's who I stay with."

"You stay with your mama?"

"Yep. But we don't be all up in each other's face, though. I stay in the basement and I have my own private entrance. I've been living there for about three years. So if you ever wanted to come over and spend some time with me or spend the night, you won't have to worry about my mama getting in the way."

This fool must be crazy, I thought to myself. First of all, for him to be over fifty-years old and living in his mama's house as if he doesn't want anything more, was absolutely ridiculous.

And there's the thought of him having all these young kids by different women. I was too disgusted with the whole matter. But I didn't wanna be rude and run right up outta there so I continued to stay and enjoy my cup of coffee.

He said, "With all the questions that you've been asking me, you haven't told me much about yourself."

I said to him, "Well, to make a long story short, I'm divorced and I have a one-year old son named David. I live by myself and that's really it."

"Hmmm. I'm sorry to hear that you got a divorce."

"It's okay. Sometimes, things don't work out."

He smiled and said, "Well, if things go well between you and me, I might be able to be that man in your life that can help you raise your son."

Was he kidding me? He wasn't even raising his *own* kids. And what in the world made him think that I needed his help? If anything, *he's* the one that needs help. It was obvious that this coffee date was a complete waste of my time. Sounds to me like he was looking to add another babymama to his roster.

When the waiter brought the bill over to our table, James had the nerve to say, "Do you have your half of the bill?"

I looked at him like he was crazy. I asked him, "Excuse me, are you asking me to pay my part of the bill?"

"Well, you did order a cup of coffee."

"*You* were the one who made the offer to have coffee with me. It's been my experience that if a man asks a lady out on a date, he picks up the tab."

"Well, I don't do that. I'm on a budget and I don't waste money on other people when it's not necessary. I believe that women should be independent in all aspects of their lives and not expect a man to take care of them. That also includes picking up the check at a restaurant. But I hope that I get a chance to see you again."

"I don't think that will be a good idea. You have wasted enough of my time," I stated to him as I grabbed my purse and headed up outta there.

As I was walking away, I heard him say, "You're too fat for me, anyway."

I didn't even bother to look back. I was just glad to be leaving. I didn't know that men like him, even existed. Even before I met Shawn, I never encountered a man like James, that had the mind of a dead horse.

After being on a wasteful date with James, I then met a man named Malik. He was about my age and at first, his conversation gave me the impression that he was a good guy. He was dark-skinned with a bald head and was very tall with a lean physique, like he was a swimmer.

We met at a bowling party that my friend Lola had for her birthday. While we were at the party, Malik and I sat down and got well acquainted. He said to me, "I'm gonna get something to drink. Would you like for me to buy you a drink as well?"

"Of course," I answered, "I'll take some cranberry juice."

When he came back with the drinks, he asked me, "So how do you know Lola?"

"I met her at the daycare center that my son attends. She drops her daughter off there. We kept running into each other and so we became friends. And how do *you* know her?"

"She's my cousin."

"Oh really?"

"Yes. We've always been very close."

"Oh, okay. Well, it's good to have family that you're close to."

"Yes, it is. I don't see any ring on your finger so I take it that you're not married?"

I smiled and said, "No, I'm not married. And yourself?"

"I'm not married, either. But I'm looking. I really want to settle down and have some kids."

I took a sip of my cranberry juice and I said, "Well, take your time."

"I definitely will. Do you mind if I take you out for dinner?"

"That would be nice. Give me a call."

Two days later, he called me and took me out to dinner at this nice restaurant in Shaker Heights. He looked very nice in a pair of black slacks with a leather belt and a gray button-down shirt. *Mmmm. He has a nice sense of style,* I thought to myself.

When he showed up at my door, he gave me a kiss on the cheek and said, "You look very nice, Rita."

"Thank you. I really appreciate that," I said. While we were on our way to the restaurant, we were making small talk and listening to a nice jazz CD. *He just might be the one,* I thought to myself. But at the same time, the night was still young.

When we got to the restaurant, he was the perfect gentleman; he pulled out my chair, was very attentive when I was talking and unlike James, he paid for the bill when the waiter brought it to the table.

"So is your son the only child that you have?" he asked, while we were eating dinner.

"Yep. He's my only child." I answered.

"Do you wanna have more?"

"I don't know. I never really gave it much thought. I think one is enough. It's a lot of work."

"Oh, I see. Well, I'm really having a wonderful time, tonight. I would love for us to go out again. In fact, there's a jazz concert that's gonna be going on next Saturday. Would you like to go?"

I smiled and said, "That would be great."

While we were heading back to my house, he popped in another jazz CD and I asked him, "You're a big lover of jazz, aren't you?"

He chuckled and said, "Absolutely. I have a big jazz collection. I didn't really get into it until I started listening to it at work."

"And where is work exactly?"

"Downtown. I work at a marketing firm."

"Oh, really? That seems interesting."

"It can be, sometimes. But there are times when I wish I'd joined the NBA."

"Oh, wow. Were in interested in playing basketball at some point?"

"Oh, yes. But I took my mother's advice and went to college and got a degree in marketing."

"Well, either way, it seems like you have your life together."

He smiled and said, "Well, thank you."

When we reached my house, he put the car in park and reached over to give me a kiss on the lips. I have to say that it was very nice. It wasn't one of those nasty, sloppy kisses where a guy tries to stick his tongue all the way down your throat and leave you with a mouth full of saliva.

Then I looked at him and said, "I really had a nice time, Malik. Thank you for dinner."

"You're welcomed," he said, with a smile.

"I'm looking forward to next weekend. I've never been to a jazz concert before."

"Well, I'm sure that you'll like it. As a matter of fact, here's a picture of what the last jazz concert looked like."

As he reached over and opened up the glove compartment to pull out a picture of the last jazz concert, another picture fell out and landed on my feet. I thought that it was a picture of the jazz concert but to my disappointment, it was a picture of Malik with his arm around another woman and three kids sitting next to them. It looked like one of those wallet-size family pictures that you take at Sears.

Picking up the picture, I asked him, "Um, what exactly is this?"

"Oh…um…it's just a picture that I took with an old friend of mine."

I knew that he was lying straight thru his teeth. I said to him, "Malik, I see you wearing a wedding band in this picture. And all of these kids look like you. So why are you lying? You might as well come clean."

He took a long sigh and said, "Okay, Rita. The lady in the picture is my wife. But we're separated. So it's like I'm single."

I wanted to smack him but instead I said, "Malik, if you are still married, then you are not single at all."

"But I'm separated."

"Did you get a divorce?"

"No I didn't."

"Then you're still married! I don't care how you try to dress it up, you are still a married man. Not only that, you are a *lying* man. You told me that you were waiting for the right time to get married and have kids. According to this picture, you've already established that. Just when I was getting ready to let my guard down, I find out that you were playing a game with me."

"I wasn't trying to play a game with you, Rita. But if I had told you the truth, would you have gone out with me?"

"Hell no but I would've at least respected you for being honest with me. Do me a favor and don't ever call me again. And as far as the jazz concert, go take your wife."

I immediately got out of his car and slammed the door behind me. See, after I got my divorce, I made a vow that I would never mess with a man that doesn't belong to me because I know what kind of trouble that it brings. After the mess that took place in my previous marriage, there was no way that I was gonna get myself into a whirlwind of drama, all over again.

"Rita, there's gonna be a few men at my wedding that are single," Marilyn mentioned to me while we were putting her wedding invitations together.

"Right now, I really don't want to be bothered. After going out on a date with James and Malik, I'm a lil' bit turned off from the dating scene."

"Oh girl, don't let two fools stop you from having a love life. You gotta live, Rita. Men are like pieces of fruit."

"Pieces of fruit? What do you mean?"

"When you go to the grocery store, do you just up and buy the first apple that you see?"

"No. Of course not."

"And why not?"

"Because there are some apples that may have bruises, spots and dents. Nobody wants to buy those because it's considered, rotten fruit. So you pick thru the apples to find the ones that look polished and fresh and those are the apples that you buy."

"Exactly. And that's how you have to pick the men that you deal with. Pick thru the bunch until you get the right one."

I smiled and said, "Well, I'm not ready to go thru and pick just yet. I have time."

"Oh really? The last time I checked, you wasn't no spring chicken."

I laughed and said, "Girl, leave me alone. I still got it going on."

I woke up in the middle of the night, with my head pounding off of my shoulders. It was hurting so bad that I was on the verge of tears. The headache pills that I was taking on a regular basis, wasn't working anymore so I didn't know how to stop the headaches.

I knew that I didn't have any health insurance but at this point, I didn't care that I didn't have it; I needed to take my behind to the hospital. So in the middle of the night, I called up Marilyn and asked her if I could bring David over to her house so that I could take myself to the hospital and try to find out what was wrong with me.

"What's wrong? Are you still getting those headaches?" she asked me over the phone when I called her.

"Yeah, I am. And they seem to be getting worse and worse. I need you to watch David for me while I go to the hospital."

"Sure. Of course I will. Are you sure that you don't want me to go to the hospital with you?"

"Yeah, I'm sure. I'll be fine. Whatever it is, I'm sure that it's minor and can be fixed."

"Okay, well just blow the horn when you're outside my house and I'll come outside and get David."

"Thanks, Marilyn. I'll be over there in a few minutes." As I was driving over there, David was steadily crying because I woke him up and my head was pounding like someone was taking a hammer and beating me on top of the head with it.

When I reached Marilyn's house, I blew the horn like she told me to and she came outside in her pajamas and got David outta the car. When I looked at her, she had tears in her eyes. *Oh Lord. There she goes, being dramatic*, I thought to myself.

"Marilyn, don't cry. I'm fine. Whatever it is that's wrong with me, the doctor is gonna fix it. Don't think the worst about the situation," I explained.

She wiped the tears from her face and said, "I'm not trying to think the worst, Rita. I just hope that it's nothing really serious, going on with you."

I smiled and said, "It's not. I'm on my way to get the problem fixed. Everything is gonna be fine."

She smiled back and said, "Okay. Well, call me as soon as you get through seeing the doctor. Let me know what he says to you."

"Girl, you know that I will. I'll see you later."

"Okay. Bye-bye."

As I headed on my way to the hospital, I had to admit that I was a lil' scared. I didn't know what the doctor was gonna tell me but I just hoped that whatever it was, it wasn't gonna be anything life-threatening. I had a son to take care of.

Thirty

(Shawn)

ALTHOUGH RITA AND I were divorced, we were still friends and I stuck to my word and helped her out with her son, from time to time. I thought that she was finally starting to see some light at the end of the tunnel.

But I guess that she was dealing with a tremendous amount of issues that became too much to handle and so she became stressed out. That's why it's so important for a person to focus on God because the matters of the world can really bring a person down.

I'm not a doctor but I really believe that stress was the cause of Rita having a brain tumor. But according to Marilyn, Rita tried to get some medical help to find out why she wasn't feeling well but I guess that she waited too late to get the problem fixed. According to doctors, Rita dropped dead right in the entrance of the hospital.

Nobody ever expected it. Everyone was in a state of shock and felt really bad about it when they heard the news. Even Brenda was sorry to hear that she died and even offered to help Marilyn and I with the funeral arrangements.

The most devastating part of Rita's passing was that she left behind her one-year old son, who would now have to grow up without his mom. It was bad enough that he didn't have his father in his life. Although Marilyn has been taking care of him since Rita died, it's not the same as having your own parents in your life.

At the funeral, it was a large crowd of people there. Rita always had a few enemies so I really didn't know if certain people were there to show their condolences or to see if she really was dead. But at either rate, the funeral turned out to be a very peaceful one and turned out a lot better than I expected.

I knew that Taurus found out that Rita died but he didn't even bother to show up to the funeral. All he did was send some cheap flowers as if that was the most wonderful thing in the world. Seeing those flowers made me so mad, that I took them and threw them in the trash.

Rita's death really didn't hit me until I saw her body laying in the casket. I viewed her body before I started the funeral and before anybody showed up. I finally had a moment alone with her. I really didn't know what to say but I held her hand and cried. I haven't cried in a long time.

She may have put me thru a lot in our marriage but I still loved her and I most certainly didn't want her life to end. But God allows things to happen for a reason, even if we don't understand it.

Marilyn was an emotional wreck in every way. I thought that she was gonna lose her mind. But I definitely understood why she took Rita's death as hard as she did; Rita was her only sister and she was very close to her. Not only that, it wasn't too long ago that their mom passed away. So of course, this was a lot for Marilyn to handle.

Two days after the funeral, I came over to Marilyn's house to talk to her about David. God woke me up early in the morning and laid something on my heart that I just couldn't shake. At first, I wasn't in agreement with it but when God tells me to do something, I obey Him. Well, most of the time.

When I came to Marilyn's house, she welcomed me with open arms and said, "It's nice to see you, Shawn. Me and my fiancé was just talking about how well you handled Rita's funeral. The service was wonderful, Shawn. You did a great job."

I smiled and said, "Thanks so much. It was painful for me to do it but I wanted to give her the best home-going service that I possibly could."

She invited me to sit down in her living room and she asked me, "Would you like something to drink?"

"A cup of coffee would be nice," I answered.

When she brought the cup of coffee to me, she sat down and said, "I miss her so much, Shawn."

"I know you do. But God's gonna help you get thru this."

"Yeah, but sometimes I wonder why God allows certain things to happen."

"Well, He has His reasons. Sometimes, we may not understand His reasoning but He is who He is. We just have to trust that He knows what's best."

She wiped a tear that fell down her cheek and said, "I feel so sorry for David. He's only a baby. He's too young to even understand what happened to his mother. But Allen and I are gonna do our best to raise him and tell him much about his mother as we possibly can."

"Well, that's the reason why I wanted to see you today; I wanted to know if you would allow me to raise David."

At first, she looked at me like I was crazy. Then she asked, "Shawn, why in the world do you wanna do that? He's not your son."

"I know but I want to be that male figure in his life. I'm not sayin' that I don't want you to be a part of his life but I know that taking care of David was not something that you expected to do."

"Well, it's not like David is a burden on me and my family. He's a beautiful baby."

"Yes, he is. But I've never had a son and I've always wanted one. I want to be that male figure in his life and take care of him."

"But what are you gonna do when he gets to that age and wants to know where his mama is?"

"I would do the same thing that *you* would do."

"Which is?"

"I would first tell him how much his mother loved him and that she's in heaven with God. Would that not be similar to something that *you* would tell him?"

She grinned and said, "You hit it on the nail. But Shawn, don't you realize the circumstances? This baby belongs to another man that your ex-wife was having an affair with. Don't you understand that David would be a painful reminder of that?"

"David is innocent, Marilyn. He's not at fault for how he was conceived. I'm willing to love that boy like he's my own and provide for him in the best way. I want to be the father that he needs. But I'm definitely not gonna hold the truth from him. When he gets older, I will be completely honest with him and let him know certain things about how he came about. I will let him know the truth before some stranger tells him but I can reassure you that I will not talk bad about his mother, at all. I will try to explain the circumstances in a way where he will still love and respect his mother. And I will also let him know that he has a wonderful family that loves him very much."

She thought about what I told her and then she said, "Are you sure that you wanna do this?"

"I'm definitely sure, Marilyn. I'm not sayin' that you and Allen couldn't give him a happy home but God made it clear to me that I needed to be the one to raise him."

She smiled and held my hand and said, "You have such a wonderful spirit, Shawn. I'm so amazed at how much you wanna open up your heart and raise someone else's child. And if God told you to do it, I will not stand in your way. You have my blessing."

I gave her a hug and I said, "Thank you, Marilyn. Thank you for understanding."

"Of course. I'll set up a time this weekend for you to pick him up and I'll make sure that the court turns over full custody to you."

I woke up to the sound of my phone ringing off the hook. When I answered it, my brother Sheldon was on the other end. From the sound of his voice, he seemed like he was in good spirits. I was hoping that things in his life have finally turned around for the better.

"What's up Shawn! Good morning!" he greeted me.

"Good morning to you to, Sheldon. What's got you so happy?" I asked.

"Man, have you been praying for me or something?"

"What do you mean?"

"Things have really turned around for me and Lavetta. Our marriage is better than it's ever been. Man, I am on cloud nine."

"Wow! I'm so glad that things are better for you and Lavetta. What happened that made everything alright?"

He sighed and said, "Well, I took your advice and Lavetta and I got counseling to help save our marriage. Not only that, I joined a support group to help me stay sober. With me being able to stay sober, that has also helped me communicate a lot better with Lavetta. I also listen more. Now, it's like we're on our honeymoon again."

I smiled and said, "Man, this is the best news that I've heard all week. Hopefully, the honeymoon will last forever."

"It will, man. And now, with our marriage being the way that it's supposed to be, Lavetta and I are expecting a child."

"Aww, man! Sheldon, that's wonderful!"

"Man, you won't believe how overjoyed I am. Lavetta and I have been trying and trying to have a child."

"Yeah, I know. Do you know the sex of the baby?"

"Yep. It's a girl. I'm gonna have me a beautiful baby girl."

"Man, I am so, so happy for you. I can't wait to see the baby. Let me be the one to do the christening."

"Of course, man. I wouldn't have it any other way."

"So are you still having problems finding a job?"

"Not at all. I found a very good-paying job with wonderful benefits. I'm getting paid a lot more money than I was at my last job. I will make sure not to mess things up and lose my job, like I lost the last one."

"Well good, man. I'm glad that you've learned from your mistakes."

"Thanks. And by the way, I'm sorry to hear about what happened to Rita. I know that I didn't come to her funeral but I'm still sorry that she passed away."

"It's okay. She's in a better place."

"So who's taking care of her son?"

"Well, as of tomorrow, *I* will be."

"What are you talking about, Shawn?"

"I talked her sister into letting me have custody of David."

"Man, what in the world would make you wanna take care of a child that your ex-wife conceived with another man while y'all were married?"

"Honestly, it was God. When you have a relationship with God, you will be amazed at the things you do, that you normally wouldn't do in the flesh."

"Humph. You got that right. Well, I hope everything works out with that."

"It will. I'm not worried."

"Cool. Well anyway, I gotta leave and go to the grocery store. Since Lavetta is eating for two, I have to go to the grocery store quite often."

I laughed and said, "Well, that's how it is. I'll talk to you later. Bye-bye."

"Oh, Lord. Here we go with the drama," I said to myself, when I saw Darlene stepping up on my porch. Just twenty minutes ago, I had just got in the door from picking David up from Marilyn's house.

But when I opened up the door to let Darlene in, she looked different. *Very* different. She had on a black business suit, her hair was neatly pulled back in a bun and the make-up on her face, was nicely done.

"Darlene? Is that you under that suit?" I asked, trying to be funny.

She laughed and said, "Yes Shawn, it's me. Are you gonna let your cousin in or not?"

"Of course. Come on in."

She walked in the living room and said, "I can't stay too long. I just wanted to drop off a check to you for two-thousand dollars. That's the least that I can do for you helping me out, so many times."

I couldn't believe what she just said to me. I asked, "Are you playing with me, Darlene? *What* two-thousand dollars?"

She smiled and said, "I know that we haven't seen each other in about a year but I've been doing some good things in my life. I got rid of the riff-raff that was holding me down and I started my own business. I'm a wedding planner and I'm very successful at it."

"You're a what?"

She laughed again and said, "Don't be so surprised, cuz."

"I can't help but to be. This is some surprising news."

"I know. I've surprised *myself* by the different moves that I've made."

"So…um, tell me what happened to make you…"

"Make me get my head outta the clouds?"

I laughed and said, "Yeah. What made you turn your life around?"

She sighed with tears in her eyes and said, "One day, I just took a hard look at myself and I didn't like what I saw. I really had to have a long cry and when I did, it seemed like I was able to see everything clearer. It was like I was waking up from a bad dream. When I finally saw what kind of life I was living in front of my kids, I realized that I wasn't giving *them* the life that they deserved. So I decided to do something about it; I immediately got rid of Doonie. *That* was the hard part."

"What do you mean?"

"Well, when I threw him outta my house, he turned into a monster. He started stalking me, calling me and saying all types of vicious things. But I stayed strong and started getting my life together. It wasn't easy, though."

I grinned and said, "Well, sometimes it's not gonna be easy to get rid of the wrong type of people. But you have to stay focus on what it is that you're trying to do."

"Exactly. And I did. For me and kids safety, I moved to another place that Doonie didn't know anything about and I got my number changed. I don't deal with those types of men anymore. As a matter of fact, I'm not dealing with *any* men, right now. My kids are a priority and I have provided them with a much better life."

"You know that I'm proud of you, Darlene. I'm so very proud of you. And I'm sure that Aunt Thelma is probably doing flips."

She laughed and said, "Yeah, mama is very pleased."

"So what made you wanna be a wedding planner?"

"Well, I used to sit at home, being all depressed because I wasn't married. The idiots that were in my life, was definitely not marriage material. So after I made the decision to get my life together, I decided to be a wedding planner. I may not have planned a wedding of my own but I found joy in helping others plan theirs. And I'm not depressed about it anymore. I've been too busy living a good life, to even think about being depressed. Things are so much better since I got my head on straight. And I want to thank you for constantly talking to me, all those times that you thought that I wasn't listening."

I gave her a hug and said, "I'm just glad to know that you are doing so well. I knew that you could do it. My love may have been tough but..."

"But that's the kind of love that I needed in order for me to get my act together. Thank you, Shawn. I know that I acted like I didn't wanna hear anything that you had to say but it was only because I wasn't in a place in my life where I wanted to receive it. But you definitely planted a seed."

To my surprise, my mom absolutely loved David. She spoiled him rotten. When she found out that I was taking care of David, she really didn't say much about it. She kinda just kept her peace about the matter.

While David and I was over at her house eating dinner, I explained to her, "Sheldon has made some great changes in his life, mama. He's stopped drinking, his marriage is back on track and his wife Lavetta is pregnant."

She smiled and asked, "Do you know why I love David so much?"

"Um...no. Not really," I answered.

"Because the love that I didn't give to Sheldon, I wanna make up for it by giving it to this young boy."

"You can still give love to Sheldon. He ain't dead."

"But it's too late for that, Shawn. He would never accept me into his life now, after all those years that I've shunned him outta my life."

"Mama, it's not too late to work things out with Sheldon."

"But what if I try and I fail?"

"Then at least you gave it a try."

A week later, I asked mama to come with me to Sheldon's house so that they could work things out. But when I called him and told him that I wanted to come to his house and that I wanted to bring mama, he didn't seem too pleased about that. But that didn't surprise me.

He asked, "Shawn, why in the world do you wanna bring mama to my house? You know that she can't stand me."

"That's not true. I think that she's finally realizing that she should've showed you the same amount of love that she showed me."

"Humph. She finally realized that after all these years? Let me guess: she's about to die and so now she wants to make peace with people?"

"No, Sheldon. It's not even like that. I just think that she wants things to be right between you and her."

"Well, I don't want to be bothered with her. She had plenty of time to make things right but she chose not to. I don't want her at my house, Shawn."

I sighed and said, "Well, I can't force you to accept her so I'll leave the matter alone. But I do hope that one day, you two will be able to put the past aside and work on having a relationship."

"You can forget that. I don't want anything to do with her."

Sheldon has always been a very stubborn person and when he makes a decision about something, he sticks to that decision whether it's right or wrong. But about a month later, I was pleasantly surprised when Sheldon came over and told me that he took a drive over to mama's house and they talked to each other for a while.

I said to him, "You don't have to give me all the details if you don't want to. I just wanna know if everything's okay between you and her."

He grinned and said, "Well, we're working on it. I'm not saying that we are close but at least we're talking to each other. But we have a lot of work to do."

"Well, at least y'all made the first step and started opening up the lines of communication. The closeness will come later."

"Humph. Maybe so. Anyway, we're supposed to be visiting your church this Sunday."

"Together?!"

"Yep. Together. She's going with me and my wife. That's never happened."

"You got that right. Man, that's awesome."

"Don't get all excited, Shawn. I'm not joining or anything. You know how I feel about joining churches; people at church are so judgmental."

"Man, I know that there are some people in the church that are so judgmental that they make a lot of people not want anything to do with God. But just remember that God is the *only* one that can judge you and if anyone is trying to judge you, they have to deal with God."

"I hear what you're saying but I'm not so sure if He's right for me."

"God is right for *everyone*. He doesn't pick and choose who He wants to love. *We* are the ones that choose whether or not we want to love *Him*. Whether you become a member of my church or not, I just want you to get to know God."

"Alright. We'll see. Anyway, I'll see you on Sunday."

When Sunday came around, I preached a sermon on faith but towards the end of my sermon, I was moved to say to the congregation, "Saints, we are in a war between good and evil. And it's present in the church. We have people in the church that are so filled with hate, that it makes us look bad in the eyes of the world because we are acting *like* the world. We have got to get our act together and start showing each other the same amount of unconditional love that God shows us. So far, we haven't been doing that and God is definitely not pleased with that. Instead of being joyful when one of our brothers or sisters are doing well, we decide to talk about them like a dog, behind their backs. We like to tear each other down with our words instead of uplifting each other. We plot and scheme towards one another and then have the nerve to say that we love God. Saints, if we don't start checking our ugly, hateful attitudes and start building up God's kingdom like we are supposed to, we are gonna be in a world of trouble. Now, I'm sure that plenty of you knew of the personal things that took place in my life. I know this as a fact because I used to walk down the halls and I could hear all the whispering that was going on. I really didn't care that quite a few people in the church knew some of my personal business because as far as I'm concerned, I don't have to explain anything to anybody. But what sadden me, was the fact that *nobody* in the church, even bothered to pray for me. Nobody called me or sent me an email or letter of encouraging words. It was just a bunch of finger-pointing, staring and whispering. But I'm not angry about it. I just want you to know that we have got to get back to demonstrating the most important thing that God wants us to demonstrate, which is love. Without love, we as a church will fail. Without love, hate will remain active. So make it your business to love because God commands us to. Love because it rebukes the plans of the enemy. Love because it will make our church stronger. Love because God *is* love."

"Amen," I heard my brother Sheldon say from his seat.